THE GAMBLER'S DAUGHTER

Very strange involved book

The lovely young Narcissa Bentham had spent her girlhood in the company of her black sheep father on his grand tour of the glittering gambling halls of Europe. But now that noble gentleman-of-ill-fortune had cashed in his final chips, leaving Narcissa alone and penniless amid the terrors and temptations of London.

Some young ladies would have bowed to fate and accepted a life of humility and humiliation, especially when forced to take a post as governess. But Narcissa was not her father's daughter for nothing. While she still had trump cards of beauty and wit to play, she would gamble all to preserve her pride and win her freedom. . . .

Despite a stuffy society that used its cruel code to try to stifle her. . . .

Despite an infuriatingly arrogant aristocrat who used his undeniable attractiveness to try to curb her will. . . .

THE WAYWARD GOVERNESS

More Regency Romances from SIGNET

THE
WAYWARD
GOVERNESS

by

Vanessa Gray

A SIGNET BOOK
NEW AMERICAN LIBRARY
TIMES MIRROR

COPYRIGHT © 1979 BY VANESSA GRAY

SIGNET TRADEMARK REG. U.S. PAT. OFF. AND FOREIGN COUNTRIES
REGISTERED TRADEMARK—MARCA REGISTRADA
HECHO EN CHICAGO, U.S.A.

SIGNET, SIGNET CLASSICS, MENTOR, PLUME, MERIDIAN AND NAL
BOOKS are published by The New American Library, Inc.,
1633 Broadway, New York, New York 10019

FIRST PRINTING, JUNE, 1979

3 4 5 6 7 8 9 10 11

PRINTED IN THE UNITED STATES OF AMERICA

1

Narcissa Bentham, after six months, was still not accustomed to living in London. She had returned to her homeland after an absence of nearly eight years and, to her surprise, found the noise of the London streets equal in earsplitting volume to those of Paris, Rome, Milan, and other Continental cities that seemed now to exist only in her dreams.

She stood at the window of her lodging house, savoring for the last time the extravagance of possessing a front room. By this afternoon such privilege would be gone, for Mrs. Yonge, the landlady, was increasingly insistent on the matter of past-due rent.

Below the window moved the morning traffic—carters and wagons bringing in the vegetables and fruit that fed all London, on their way from the rich farms south of the Thames to the market at Covent Garden.

She lingered at the window, feeling the watery April sunshine on her face, loath to move. She was not the only one leaning out a window, for it seemed to be the local custom not only to reach out to feel the spring sunshine when it could filter through the smoke, but also to exchange friendly insults with the neighbors. Some insults, as is the nature of insults, became less than friendly. The street was usually cluttered with cabbage heads and other less mentionable debris, and not all of it had fallen from the carts as they rumbled through.

The street where Narcissa now lodged was certainly not as fashionable as Mount Street, nor was it even as respectable as some of the small streets leading off Oxford. But at least it was not as low as Duck Lane, although she might make the near acquaintance of that street before the day was out.

Below her she could hear the landlady, Mrs. Yonge,

her voice rising in the chatter that flowed from her from morning until night. Mrs. Yonge was a kindly woman, when she thought of it. Narcissa suspected that Mrs. Yonge was stirred more by curiosity about her lodger's obvious gentility than by her native compassion. Yet Narcissa was grateful for the respite. For Narcissa was down to her last halfpenny. Behind her stood the trunk that her mother had given her, with her initials N. B. proudly on the lid. The trunk had accompanied her through all the cities of Europe in the past six years.

Now it was sparsely filled with a mere handful of clothes. She had corded it up, ready to move. On top of the trunk was a linen handkerchief, folded around the last of the jewels her mother had left her. It was a small pin of little value, a pearl in the center with two chip diamonds on either side. But Narcissa always considered it her Last Resource. The pin had often seen the pawnshops of Europe when the Benthams had been scraping the bottom of the barrel. Now that Narcissa was alone, there was little hope of redeeming the jewel once it was gone.

There was no place else to turn. Narcissa's father, Alfred Bentham, son of Sir Maurice Bentham, of Batley in Yorkshire, had been a singularly unlucky man. The only fortunate occurrence in his entire life, he had often said, was his marriage to Narcissa's mother, Penelope Holland, of Scarborough.

The Hollands were a great family in Yorkshire and had exerted all their considerable influence to prevent Penelope from marrying Alfred Bentham. It was possible that such organized resistance had only strengthened Penelope's desire to marry a man in whose character she soon found she had been sadly mistaken. But she had never complained. In fact, she had rarely mentioned her family. Narcissa knew only the name, for there had been no communication between Narcissa's mother and her family since the day she left home. Even when Narcissa's mother died, Alfred had not informed her family.

Instead, he had dismissed Dilly, Narcissa's governess, packed up his small daughter, and removed to the Continent, to spend the rest of his life in gambling casinos. When at last, six months ago, he decided to return to his homeland, Narcissa was twenty, a curious mixture of innocence of the ways of polite society and an unusual maturity in the expedients which she had found useful in coping with her father's unsteady existence.

When they came home to London, at last, they lodged in a street not too far from Oxford Street. Alfred, the incurable optimist, had decided that London was ready for a gambler of his stature. However, London had not been apprised of that fact, and he found many doors closed that had previously been open to him. A combination of a soggy winter, insufficient clothing for a cold climate, and growing depression finally felled Alfred Bentham. When illness struck him, Narcissa was left much on her own. She decided that the Hollands, no matter what they thought of Alfred Bentham, might at least send a sovereign or two to Penelope's daughter. She wrote them a letter, spending many anxious hours over its composition, but she never heard a word from Yorkshire. Very shortly after his illness took a turn for the worse, as did their finances, they removed to this street off Leadenhall where Narcissa now stood at the window. Alfred had died, and she had thought fit to inform his father, Sir Maurice, of the fact. But there had been no answer from him either.

Now she was down to her Last Resource. She picked up the handkerchief with the pin in it. Heavy in her hand, it was her last tie to her mother's family or to any family at all. The only person in England whom Narcissa knew was her old governess Dilly. Miss Prudence Dilworth lived in Scarborough. Narcissa had kept track of Dilly, and they had exchanged a lively correspondence for some time. But as the Bentham fortunes grew lower, Narcissa was hard put to it to keep a cheerful tone in her letters. The correspondence dwindled. Dilly, undoubtedly living in reduced circumstances, would be of no help to Narcissa.

Dilly had long wanted to operate a school of her own, but there was no money. Narcissa had hoped to help her when Alfred was in funds. But Alfred's good luck never lasted long.

Never one to shirk an unpleasant task for long, she firmly dismissed Dilly from her mind and tucked the precious pin safely in her small reticule. After taking one last glance around the empty, impersonal room, she closed the door firmly behind her and started down the stairs.

Mrs. Yonge hovered in the entry hall. With unveiled curiosity, she said, "Looks like you haven't heard from your fancy folk yet. I coulda told you no use wasting the money to send them letters. Not many folk want to hear from their poor kin."

Narcissa said with an appearance of calm, "I expect to hear at any moment. I am going out now. When I return, I shall pay you what I owe you." She hesitated a moment and then added firmly, "I should like to move to the room at the back this afternoon. I find the street much too noisy."

Mrs. Yonge nodded. "I'll see to it."

Neither woman mentioned the fact that was uppermost in both minds—that the back room was much cheaper.

She swept by Mrs. Yonge, hoping she appeared more confident than she felt. If she did not receive a good price for the jewel, she really had no idea what she would do next. Her situation was desperate. The jewel would perhaps feed her for the rest of the week, but beyond that there was nothing.

She made her way through streets filled with rotting vegetables and nameless filth to a small lane just off the Strand. There, at the third pawnbroker's shop she entered, she parted with her pin. He offered her little enough for the jewel, far less than she had got in Paris, for instance, but since it was the best price she had found along the street, she took it. She closed her eyes against seeing the pearl brooch in the dirty hands of the pawnbroker and fled, clutching a small sum of coins in her hand. There was certainly not enough money to pay the landlady or even, casting all her pride aside, to pay for a coach to Scarborough to find Dilly. At the intersection before she turned into her own street, she paused. Reflecting once again that possibly her letter had not reached the Hollands, she determined that she would make one attempt at making herself known to her mother's family.

It was a long way across town to Grosvenor Square. The day was turning warm, and she arrived hot and ruffled at the street leading into the square.

The crowds had jostled her off the walkways. Even the crossing sweeps had rightly judged that since she traveled on foot across London, without a footman or even an abigail, she could not afford the small coin they demanded for their services.

Her skirts trailed dust and mud from the streets, and her shawl was slipping from her shoulders. She paused a moment to straighten her bonnet, tuck in her ringlets, try to brush the worst of the soil off her skirt, and recover her courage. When she had done the best she could, she marched down the street into the square.

One great house stood at the corner. She regarded it with speculation. She was not at all sure which of the magnificent structures, fronting on the tiny patch of grass in the center of the square, could be Holland House.

She caught the eye of a footman, opening the door at the top of the steps. He took in her draggled appearance and cried with scorn, "Garn away! Nothing here for you!"

She stiffened, and her eyes blazed with spirited pride, almost forgotten in her weariness. She fixed the servant with an unwinking stare and said, "I hope this is not the house I am seeking, for such an uncivil remark shows a sad lack of decency."

Impressed in spite of himself, the footman paused in the act of closing the door. In an altered tone he asked, "What house?"

"Holland House."

He pointed across the square. "Yon's the Holland place. This yere is Carraford House."

Carraford? A great man indeed—or so *he* thought, she remembered. She had seen him once in Lausanne, entering an assembly, given by the Society of Young Women, a group called, pleasingly, The Spring.

Her father's luck was out at the time, she recalled, and he had stood with her on the walkway and muttered bitterly, "There, child, goes your carriage and horses that I sold yesterday—all to line the pockets of a great Marquess who has sufficient blunt to roll in it every morning!"

"I have no interest *whatever* in Carraford House," she told the footman, and turned to cross the square. Her heart pounding, she was scarcely aware of the footman staring after her. She stood directly before the Grecian portico of Holland House. Several broad steps mounted to the black-painted door. She mounted the steps briskly, before her courage ebbed, and plied the gold knocker vigorously. There was no answer. Then she noticed that the windows facing the square were boarded up. A voice from somewhere beneath her feet cried out, "What do you want?"

She went down the steps and looked over the areaway railing to discover where the voice came from. An ancient caretaker, mostly deaf and totally toothless, peered up at her.

"Where is the Holland family?" she asked. After a series of questions and answers at cross-purposes, she elicited the news that the Hollands were not in town. She could have deduced that from the boarded windows, she thought, but the caretaker, suddenly feeling that she had asked more questions than he liked, shouted at last, "Old lady be ill! They won't be in town this long time!"

Having disposed of the visitor to his total satisfaction, the caretaker slammed the door behind him and disappeared from view. There was nothing left for her to do but to trudge back to Leadenhall Street and face an irate landlady. It was nearly dark when she arrived. She mounted the steps with reluctance. But to her surprise Mrs. Yonge was watching for her, her face wreathed in smiles.

"There ye be! I feared you had fallen under a horse! Now here's a nice letter for you, at least so the man said!" Mrs. Yonge could not read.

Mrs. Yonge proffered her a missive, bulky, sealed, and franked in the corner. With trembling fingers Narcissa opened it. The envelope contained a thin sheet of paper and a small heavy packet. She looked first at the signature. "From Sir Maurice! My grandfather!" she cried. The message was short and to the point.

Granddaughter,
      You may come to Batley. Coach fare enclosed.

She counted the money enclosed. She had already inquired the fare to Yorkshire, and she realized either that Sir Maurice was as sparing of coin as of words or that he had not traveled stagecoach in some years. She thought she could just manage if she traveled the cheapest way possible.

The next few hours were a turmoil of activity. She discharged her debt to Mrs. Yonge with the pawnbroker's money, cutting short the woman's vociferous exclamations of congratulation. She ordered her trunk carried to the stagecoach office. She spent one more night, sleepless with anticipation, in her room before making her way before dawn to the Saracen's Head Inn, to board the heavy stage carriage for the north country.

The vehicle was sturdy enough, but lacking in the comfort and speed of the smart mail coaches. She could not afford luxury and had to be content with the steady, lumbering progress northward, through Islington, in the direction of Stamford and York.

They traveled all day. At Peterborough, some of the passengers got off to spend the night. Narcissa, without funds, stayed on the coach as it journeyed north. She was thankful that the coach was less crowded on the inside, but on the other hand, her two traveling companions were equally poor, and she found them less than attractive. She curled up in her corner and attempted to sleep.

Morning came, and they were still struggling up the hills of East Yorkshire. It was a desolate landscape, and Narcissa, who had spent her life in cities, began to feel unaccountably depressed. They clattered at last into the town that the coachman said was Batley.

She descended from the coach, her trunk was put on the ground beside her, and the coach rattled off. She stood alone in the middle of a dusty street which ran, so it appeared, through an entirely deserted village.

She had arrived, with empty pockets and starving, at Batley, the home of her ancestors.

2

She made serious inquiry of all she saw, from a small boy kicking his dog through the single street to the proprietor of the general store. With relief, she finally learned that there was indeed a representative of Bentham Hall in town. When he was brought to her, she saw that he was merely a farm lad.

His two-wheeled cart labored under a strong aroma of sheep, mingled with scattered handfuls of grain and bundles of straw.

The boy, whose name was Samuel, was so overwhelmed by the idea that the fashionable lady standing in front of him wished to ride to Bentham Hall in his cart that he was speechless. He nodded his head vigorously and hoisted her trunk into the cart, scraping the straw aside recklessly to make a place for it. She climbed up to the wooden seat beside Samuel, and they started on the long drive to Bentham Hall. It was late in the morning, and Narcissa had not eaten. She hoped that some of the sheep that had ridden in the cart recently, from all appearances, were now in the form of mutton, which might be served to her when she reached her destination.

Samuel clucked to the shaggy pony. Either from shyness or from lack of intellect, he was chary of conversation.

At length she ventured, "My grandfather did not tell you I was coming?"

The boy shifted a straw from one side of his mouth to the other. "Granfer? Sir *Maurice?*"

Clearly the idea that Sir Maurice Bentham had a granddaughter was beyond the ken of Samuel, the carter. Somewhat nettled, Narcissa pursued the only source of information she had.

"I suppose Bentham Hall is a grand house?"

"Aye, 'twas once. So *my* granfer said."

"But no longer? Does anyone live there but Sir Maurice?"

"Aye. Gibbs. Missus Gibbs." He had exhausted his conversation, so it seemed. The cart rattled on over the rutted roads, wending upward into the hills. There were sheep on the hillside, but Narcissa's city-trained glance merely noted them and moved on.

"Sister."

"Wh-what?" stammered Narcissa.

"My sister. Lives at the Hall." The boy turned a reproachful look upon his passenger. "You asked."

"Of course I did," reassured Narcissa.

"Name of Polly." And that was the last word that Samuel uttered.

The tops of the surrounding hills were scoured clean from the rough wind from the North Sea. Although the sea was out of sight, she knew it must be no more than fifty miles away. Its strong influence was clear in the austerity of the moors, windswept and treeless. Flocks of sheep dotted the hillsides, freed at last on the greening hills. Little lambs, their tails dragging to their heels, leaped and cavorted as though they had no care in the world.

The road wound on and on. Narcissa's attention was engrossed by hunger pangs. She entertained a mental picture of Samuel arriving at the front door of Bentham Hall, his passenger curled up into a skeleton in the cart, a victim of starvation.

When they at last turned between broken stone pillars, and she realized she was traversing the drive leading to Bentham Hall, she wished she had not been so anxious to arrive. The gravel approach had been long neglected. Samuel indicated that he was taking her up the drive in deference to her quality, and that if he had been left to his own devices, his cart would never travel the graveled road that led to Bentham Hall.

There were places where the shrubbery had not been trimmed back, as the road curved through the park, and branches scratched the side of the cart as it drove along. She could see from her high seat that tree limbs were down in the wood, some had fallen on the drive, and all the winter's litter lay undisturbed where it fell.

Evidently Sir Maurice was not overly strict with his gardeners.

The shrubs needed vigorous trimming, and the gravel drive was interrupted by patches of intruding grass. The gravel had not been raked within recent memory, but even so, it was obvious that very few carriages passed this way.

What lay at the end of the drive? She could almost imagine a decayed stone castle, connected to a ruined chapel where ghosts walked at midnight. She reminded herself bracingly that her father had certainly never mentioned such a Gothic ancestral home, and she had read too many of Verbena de Vere's novels!

When she arrived at the front door of Bentham Hall, its white columns standing proudly, the paint flaking from them and falling on the porch, she felt a surge of dismay. Clearly Sir Maurice spent no money on the up-keep of his ancestral home. Possibly the interior would be in better shape. The doors swung inward, opened by an astonished butler, and she stepped into the dark hall.

Disillusion swept over her at once. The hall was dark; there was a faint smell of uncleaned fireplaces and distressingly, a strong scent of mildew. The butler, who told her his name was Gibbs, appeared so unused to company that he hardly knew what to do with her. She told him her name and waited for him to escort her to her grandfather. He looked as though he had been presented with a problem that would haunt his dreams. "I should like to see my grandfather," she prodded gently. He turned and threw open a door at the side of the hall.

She expected to see the same signs of decay in the room into which she was ushered as she had seen so far on Bentham land. She was not disappointed. Sir Maurice, in the curtain-darkened room, sat beside an empty fireplace. She hesitated, fearing to knock over some item of furniture that lurked in the darkness. When Gibbs announced her arrival, Sir Maurice emitted a sound something between a crow of triumph and what Narcissa could only consider a moan. Finally, he wheezed, "Come near, child, and let me look at you."

She stepped closer and stood quietly. Now she could see him more clearly. His eyes were like black beads, and his great beak of a nose overhung his thin-lipped mouth. He still had many of his teeth, although they were not in good repair. His chin, as formidable as her father's own, gave him the appearance of overwhelming authority. But since Narcissa knew that chin, and knew what weakness it could conceal, she reserved judgment.

The old man was wrapped in a blanket, as well he might be against the chill of the room. Automatically Narcissa glanced at the black grate.

Sir Maurice was quick to notice the direction of her thoughts. "A cold spring. Almost the first of May, and it still isn't warm. But I won't have a fire after the middle of April. Wasteful. Shame how people indulge themselves. Hope you aren't one of them. No telling what your father got you used to, but in my house you'll learn to fit in."

Narcissa had long labored under the belief that if you had the wood and you were cold, then a fire was the logical solution. However, she kept her peace.

Sir Maurice was still looking at her. He seemed to be dissatisfied, but all he said was: "You don't look like the Benthams. I'd pass you on the street and not know that you were my granddaughter. I don't suppose there's any possibility that your mother played your father false, is there?"

Narcissa stiffened, and Sir Maurice glossed over his sharp remark with a mirthless laugh. "No, I know that she was a proud woman, and such a false action would have been against her pride."

Narcissa said with firmness, "My mother was a lady of great integrity, sir. My father, if he were here, would resent your remarks, as I do."

Sir Maurice looked at her with grudging respect. She was gratified to discover that she was correct in her assessment of his character—that she would have to stand up for herself or she would be ground to bits. He nodded, saying, "Just like the Hollands. You do take after your mother's folks. Not only in looks, for I can almost see old dowager Lady Holland looking out at me with her eyes flashing. You've also got that stiff-necked pride. But I think we'll rub along well together just the same."

"I shall do my best, sir," she said.

"Well, then, what shall I do with you?" he said more

to himself than to her. "I had not quite expected such a young lady, but it makes it easier."

"I don't understand, sir. You invited me and sent me my fare. I do not expect to become a burden."

She was puzzled at her grandfather's welcome. She should have been warned by the tepid tone of his letter to her, but she had been so cheered by the thought that at least one member of her family recognized her that she had not looked far ahead.

"Nor will you, my dear," said Sir Maurice, pulling the blanket closer around his chest. "I shall see to that. There will be ways you can work it out. But I shall have to think what is best."

Then a sudden thought seemed to strike him with force. "You're not married, are you? Or anything?"

Ignoring the temptation to demand what her grandfather might mean by "anything," she said, "No, sir."

"Good enough. I can tell you I've got your best interests at heart, girl, and you'll be thanking me before long."

"I don't understand, sir."

"Never mind. You will."

As a conversation, it lacked much in the way of exchanging information. But perhaps in the course of time she would learn more of what he had in mind. Just now she was acutely conscious of her hunger and her travel weariness.

She asked to be taken to her room. "For you must know, sir," she said, "that long ride in the cart has greatly mussed me, and I feel sadly windblown. I should like to set myself to rights before I present myself to you again."

He nodded, saying only, "No need to present yourself to me again, girl, until dinnertime."

He summoned Gibbs, the butler, by a shout, because as Narcissa surmised, the bellpull was broken, and waved her out of the room. When Mrs. Gibbs, the cook, was summoned from the lower levels, she came up puffing and blowing, brushing crumbs from her skirt. Apparently somewhere in this house someone was eating, thought Narcissa, and she vowed not to be an hour older before she, too, had eaten.

Introductions were made, and Narcissa followed Mrs. Gibbs up the broad staircase to the upper floor. The house was handsomely built, for apparently some previous Bentham had had taste and the money to accommodate it. Now the railings held a suspicion of dust, and the carpet on the stairs was obviously threadbare. Mrs. Gibbs was uneasy as she noticed Narcissa's noticing glance. At the top of the stairs she turned to the left and opened the second door. "Gibbs says as you was probably going to stay, so I had this room made ready."

It was far from ready in Narcissa's eyes. She tried to ignore the signs of decay, yet her orderly mind took note of things and stored them up for further reference. But there were signs of progress, for a maid was kneeling on the hearth, placing kindling and tinder in the grate. Narcissa suspected a fire would be welcome in the evening. The room was handsomely proportioned, but somehow vague, almost as though seen in a dream. She realized with a start that it was not a dream that blurred the colors, but a thin layer of inground dust. Mrs. Gibbs explained quickly. "The room hasn't been opened for lo these many years, and it's expecting a good deal to have it in readiness in an hour. Sir Maurice didn't tell us you was coming, else I'da had it ready."

Narcissa recognized the woman's great need to be excused and set herself to winning her over.

"I did not inform Sir Maurice of the time of my arrival," said Narcissa. "I suppose you have been here at Bentham Hall for a long time?"

"Yes, miss," said Mrs. Gibbs. "I came as maid to my lady, Lady Bentham, you know, when she was first wed. Many's the time she told me she was glad to have a little bit of home with her."

Narcissa smiled warmly. "Then you can tell me much that I wish to know about my grandmother. I never knew her, of course."

Mrs. Gibbs nodded wisely. "Nor did your father, Mr. Alfred, say much about his mother, I wager. For she died when he was but a small boy, robbing bird's nests and getting into all kinds of mischief." She gave a mountainous sigh. "Things woulda been otherwise, had she lived. She'd be pleased to see her granddaughter here at last!"

"And I'm pleased to be here," said Narcissa. "I shall

be comfortable in this room, I know." She looked dubiously about her but added stoutly, "You've done very well with such short notice."

The cook dropped a curtsy and said, "I'll have your lunch brought up, Miss Narcissa, if that's to your liking."

She turned and left the room, to give her order, and Narcissa was left alone with the frightened maid. She was surprised at the maid's uneasiness until she realized that she was standing in the middle of the room, tight-lipped, glaring about her fiercely. She softened her expression and smiled at the maid. "What is your name?"

The maid dropped a quick curtsy, and said, "Jessie, miss, if you please."

"Very good, Jessie. Do you think you could pound the dust out of that chair there so that I might sit down?"

Narcissa had no intention of descending to an empty dining room for lunch, but she was equally unwilling to sit in a chair three inches thick with dust. Mrs. Gibbs, returning with a luncheon tray, found Jessie pounding at the chair, a cloud of dust rising into the air and falling to the already-dusty carpet. Mrs. Gibbs entered the room. "The carter will bring up the trunk directly, Miss Narcissa."

Whether it was the obvious deference of Mrs. Gibbs, calling her Miss Narcissa, as befitted the daughter of the house, or whether it was something deeper in her, touching the wellsprings of her heritage, Narcissa did not know. But the change in her was marked, and Mrs. Gibbs stopped short, struck by the alteration in her new mistress. Narcissa was surveying the room with a far more critical eye than Mrs. Gibbs had seen since old Lady Bentham had died.

Narcissa thanked her absently and said, "The trunk can stand in the hall till we finish in here. Mrs. Gibbs, I realize that recently no one has used this room, but we must get it in order before I will feel comfortable, don't you agree?"

Mrs. Gibbs nodded vigorously, and Narcissa began to outline the things she wanted done—cleaning the room thoroughly, taking the curtains down and washing them before they were hung up on newly washed windows—and she had just begun. But Mrs. Gibbs, fired with sudden enthusiasm for her new mistress and the work to be done, said, "Never you mind, Miss Narcissa. I'll take care of all. You'll see."

Her words were vigorous, and her instructions resulted in an hour in a crowd of servants. Some, arriving a little later, were clearly enlisted from neighboring farms. They were fresh-cheeked, clean, and with a regrettable tendency to shy away from Narcissa like new foals, yet within a short time the room bade fair to be habitable by nightfall.

Narcissa took her luncheon tray into the adjoining room. It was a small, neglected sitting room. There was a miniature in a gilt frame on the dresser. The lady, looking out with calm, clear eyes at Narcissa, was dressed in an old-fashioned gown, her hair dressed in a fashion of nearly forty years ago.

My grandmother! thought Narcissa. She examined the sweet face carefully but could discern no resemblance to her own.

The sitting room must have been Lady Bentham's, and Narcissa believed that her grandmother would be pleased to have her use it. The afternoon wore on rapidly, and Narcissa was surprised when Mrs. Gibbs appeared in the doorway.

"We'll redd up in here, too, Miss Narcissa. But that's for another day, by your leave. We've made a good start on the bedroom, and I'll send Jessie with a warming pan after dinner. Sir Maurice is waiting for you, miss."

"For dinner? Is it that late? I must hurry!"

Mrs. Gibbs nodded. "Testy he gets if he waits for his meals."

In the dining room, the food that was served was what she only could consider pinchpenny. She ate everything that was on her plate and looked hopefully around for more. Instead, she caught Sir Maurice's eye. He was looking gravely askance. "I misdoubt that you had such a good appetite. I hope this country air doesn't increase it, else we come to a misunderstanding."

Irritated, she changed the subject. "I must say this is a handsome house. But it is too bad it has been allowed to fall away."

Sir Maurice, savoring unhappily the unpleasant sen-

sation of being put on the defensive, said, "There's been
no woman here to put it right for many the year."

Having divested himself of responsibility, he was obviously nettled at Narcissa's calm pursuit of the subject.
"Well, now you have a woman to set it right," she said.
"And I could certainly take this burden off your shoulders."

Sir Maurice was not aware that any burden sat on
his shoulders. She could follow his thoughts as they
moved along, she was sure. First there was the feeling
of being attacked. Then, as he cogitated on what he
would do with Narcissa now that she was here, he
clearly thought it could be a diversion that would keep
her busy and out of his way. At length he gave his considered opinion. "All right, if it costs nothing."

Narcissa calmly pointed out the undoubted waste of
money caused by neglect of these fine hangings and
furniture and how much it would cost to restore whatever was about to fall to pieces. "For you would not
like anyone to feel that the Benthams were out of
funds."

Grudgingly he agreed. "Haste makes waste," he said.

He said no more, and Narcissa forbore to make further comment. She had gained more than she had
hoped to, and since he had not specifically forbidden
her to spend a cent, she did not wish him to put that
prohibition into words. He had agreed that neglect was
wasteful, and she would have to be satisfied with that.

3

After breakfast the next morning Gibbs asked her to descend to the servants' hall. Since she was now the mistress of the house, she wondered whether she was going to be faced with her first crisis. Instead, Mrs. Gibbs had lined up the household staff. They were to be presented to the new mistress, in a formal fashion, as an acknowledgment of the new regime. There was Jessie, the maid, and Polly, Samuel's sister, who helped in the kitchen and ran errands, instead of a footman. There were no other servants.

Narcissa in her years abroad had had servants of her own, had dealt efficiently with hotel staff, but she had never yet managed a large house on her own.

A few remarks were clearly called for, and Narcissa did her best. "My father often spoke of his old home," she said with little regard for the truth. "I feel that already I know some of you—Gibbs and Mrs. Gibbs. Even as far away from Bentham Hall as Italy, you were still remembered."

She said a few more words in this vein and stopped, lest she become too nostalgic. Her grief was still too near the surface. Apparently her speech was satisfactory. At a nod from Mrs. Gibbs, the staff scuttled away, after curtsying to the new mistress, and found work to do in some obscure corner. Narcissa hoped it was upstairs in her own bedroom and sitting room.

Mrs. Gibbs seemed oddly embarrassed now and barely refrained from wiping her hands on her apron. Instead, she said, with blushing shyness, "Perhaps you would like a cup of tea here with us?"

The brown eyes were anxious, and Narcissa said, "Of course I will."

The steaming tea was served in an earthenware mug, far tastier than the lukewarm beverage served upstairs.

Mrs. Gibbs acknowledged the difference. "The earthenware mugs keeps the tea warm, even though they aren't as fancy."

Narcissa sipped her tea with evident enjoyment. Gibbs began a series of reminiscences. "I mind your father, Mr. Alfred, when he would come into the house with his pockets full of birds' eggs and like as not a snail or two from the brook."

Mrs. Gibbs shuddered. "Now don't bring up all those old things, Gibbs," she admonished. But Gibbs was well launched, and Narcissa encouraged him. She had been very fond of her father for all his failings. She had been so harried by his illness and subsequent death, with anxiety over what would be her own fate and the necessity of fending off landladies and finding a coin here and pawning a jewel there in order to eat, that she had had little time to consider her loss.

Here in this comfortable servants' hall, under the sympathetic eyes of people who had known her father, Narcissa began to lose the rigid chill she had erected around herself. She had time to notice that Mrs. Gibbs kept the kitchen and the servant's hall spotless, and that augured well for the future of the rest of the house when they had time to do it. But just now she was gaining a picture of the small boy who had become her father, in this gracious home on top of a rise in Yorkshire, in the midst of broad acres.

In a way it was not hard to think of her father as a child, for there had remained much of the boy in him all the years that they traveled together in Europe. She could understand, from Sir Maurice's pinchpenny ways, the reason for her father's spendthrift ways. She recognized a revolt against the meager, frostbitten life he must have led here. How gratifying it must have been to have money in his pocket! The mere fact of purchase and possession must have been balm to his spirit. Mrs. Gibbs would never have let a small boy go hungry. But even Mrs. Gibbs could not be proof against a cold grate, sparse comfort, and stinted affection.

She could wish, however, that her grandfather had been less set in his miserly ways and that her father had been more moderate in his reaction to them. It would have saved a lot of trouble in the long run, she thought with a sigh.

If she herself, were not penniless, she would be right now on the way back to town. But her naturally optimistic spirits could not stay depressed for long. Soon she was listening with apparent interest to Gibbs and his long stories of her father's childhood.

Mrs. Gibbs interrupted. "But Bentham Hall isn't as grand as some of the places you've been, Miss Narcissa."

Thus invited, Narcissa cudgeled her memory to bring forth some of the more exotic items of Europe—the boiled snails and fried frogs as ordinary items of food, for instance. In southern Italy, near Naples, there were terraces of melons, warm from the sun and juicy as peaches. The vision of gardens of fig trees and pomegranates stirred Mrs. Gibbs to exclamations of disbelief—"Well, I never!"—and Narcissa realized that the days now gone had been far happier than she had thought at the time.

Setting down her empty mug, Narcissa said, "But that's all past now, and I've come home, so to speak. But I feel such a stranger in my father's house."

Mrs. Gibbs said briskly, "I can fix that. I'll show you round, if you'll follow me."

The housekeeper was filled with apologies for the dilapidated state of the house. "Lady Bentham would never have allowed things to become so," she said. "But there, a man's never one to notice."

"We'll see what we can do," promised Narcissa recklessly.

The house itself was handsome, as she had previously remarked. The public rooms were large and well proportioned. She was shown the small salon where she had first met her grandfather, the large dining room, where once at least twenty people could have sat down in comfort. There was a front parlor, a withdrawing room, where her grandmother must have spent much of her time, and a small morning room off the dining room, a sunshiny place in winter when the sun would slant through the many windows. There was a great amount of work to do, for all the furnishings and hangings were of a past era, expensive in their day but sadly neglected. To bring the house into its former splendor, she knew, would take far more than her own efforts. If she could just have an idea of how much money to spend. . . .

There were no driving cattle in the stables. When Sir Maurice wished to drive out—"what hadn't happened in a month of moons, miss!"—a pair of farm horses were hitched up. The empty stables were one more sign that the Bentham fortunes had vanished or at least were sadly diminished.

If that were the case, she would have little enough to spend on the house. She remembered all too vividly the rise and fall, ebb and flow of her father's fortunes on the Continent. When it was high tide, she had had her own carriage, her own driving horses, of a quality that caused gentlemen to stare after her as she drove through the parkways. When her father was in funds, she lived as well as a Princess, but she also remembered as well about the lowest kinds of ebbtide. From beautiful rented houses to the seediest kind of lodging house was all too frequently the work of only a few weeks. But then, always, until the last, Alfred's luck and his spirits recovered eventually.

With an obscure feeling that fortunes brought so low must rise with the inevitability of the ocean's tides, she decided to deal with what she had at hand. Over the next few days, in her newly cleaned sitting room, she pored over lists of things to be done. Periodically she would sally forth to examine one room after another, and Mrs. Gibbs, getting into the spirit of things, began to follow her around. Together they made lists of things that must be done, this curtain to be mended, that carpet to be reversed so that the gaping hole would lie under the settee. By the end of the week a great stack of torn linen awaited her needle. She turned the small morning room into a workroom. Sir Maurice at last sent for her.

"What's this I hear about you turning the house upside down?"

"Sir, I must deny that. In fact, I have not turned anything upside down—yet—but only made lists of what needs to be done."

"I see nothing wrong here," said Sir Maurice, setting his chin firmly.

Narcissa guessed that she was proceeding too quickly. She decided to deal more adroitly. Casting aside in her mind the long list of new furniture or even of extra help to be hired to clean and paint, she fastened on the one thing she knew would appeal to Sir Maurice. "All I want to do, sir," she said, "is to mend the linen. There are such gaping holes where the mice have got at them along the fold that if I can mend them, it will save buying new ones."

Sir Maurice's thrift was clearly at war with his lurking suspicion that his granddaughter was right. He was in a dim way aware that the house had fallen upon evil times. Since he saw no reason to change his own way of living, he firmly put the derelict furnishings out of his mind. They suited him well enough. But here was this vivacious and pretty granddaughter pointing out that he had neglected his clear duty to the estate. "All right, I suppose," he said. "But don't count on me for any new sheets, if that's what you're talking about. Or tablecloths either. One working candle should be enough to do you, for there's lots of daylight now, and I won't hear of anyone else brought in to help with the linen. I expect you to work for your keep, and if mending linen is what you want to do, so be it."

She was aware of rising anger, but she knew that she must tread warily. "The house could be so beautiful again," she ventured, "as it was when you were a boy, I should imagine, for these are beautiful furnishings, and it is a shame to see them in such sad condition."

Sir Maurice surprisingly roused as though she had attacked him in a very vulnerable position. "You'll get my money when I'm gone," he explained, "and not before. You've got your eye on all my furniture and my house. It will be yours someday, I can't help that, but you won't get any money to fix it up ahead of time, I'll tell you that. When you repair the furniture, it will be your money you spend."

Narcissa lost all semblance of holding her temper. She flared out at him, "I don't want your money!"

She was too angry to say more, for she knew that she must approach her thorny grandfather with some tact and a concerted plan. She had been appalled in the past few days at the enormous amount of work that needed to be done in the house. From a lack of anything else to do she had set refurbishing the house as her task. She did expect to work for her keep, but it was a sore insult to be told that she must. Her eyes filled with scalding tears, and she turned blindly toward the door.

Sir Maurice, in a croaking voice, called her back. "Now then, lassie, don't go off in a fuddle. I meant no harm, but it is best we understand each other. It seems to me, and I've been giving it some thought, that if you were to take over the marketing now and see that the servants' hall doesn't eat up everything in sight, what you save there might be put on the furnishings."

Turning back to look at him, she saw that he had his head cocked on one side and a wicked gleam in his eye.

She said with simple dignity and a tight feeling in her throat, "I shall be glad to do the marketing."

She returned to the small morning room and began to sort out her thoughts. She looked without seeing at the pile of damaged sheets, a very fine linen tablecloth yellowed at the edges, in need of mending and a good sunning, and a pair of damask draperies with ragged lining.

She would have to take over the grocery shopping, and she had a lowering feeling he would expect her to account to him for every penny. One thing she would not do: cut down on the food in the servants' hall. Better she go herself without sufficient food than deprive the people who had served Benthams for so long.

She had found out that her grandfather's sole interest now was in reading the books that he had collected over the years, spending his days wandering among the classics, and thinking of ways to economize.

She was in no mood to sit down quietly and ply her needle. It takes a serene mind to mend carefully, Dilly had said once, and Narcissa's mind was far from serene. She resolved to find Mrs. Gibbs and see about going to town for groceries. The fresh air would do her good, and she could work off some of her irritation.

She was more in sympathy with her father than ever, now that she had a taste of what life at Bentham Hall was like. It was a miserly, penurious existence, without any of the amenities of graceful living. There was little entertainment, no new books, and no companionship. Her grandfather had, in response to the prickings of duty, given her a roof and the minimum of food. She was hard put to remember that in Mrs. Yonge's house, she was not sure of even that much, so that she was bound to feel gratitude. But gratitude, while admirable, still was not good company, and she set out for town, Mrs. Gibb's list in her reticule, in no very good humor.

Samuel was to drive her again in the farm cart, and her grandfather, when she went in to tell him where she was going, admonished her, "Now don't leave your purchases for a minute after you get them bought. They will throw in some rotten cabbages if you're not careful. See that all is safely into the cart before you come back."

There was nothing, apparently, too small for Sir Maurice to take an interest in. A pennyworth of cabbage leaves, in his mind, seemed to rank as important as a saddle of mutton. But she climbed up on the board seat beside Samuel as he clucked up the two farm horses and prepared to enjoy herself as far as she could.

The day was sunny, a welcome break from the constant lowering clouds driving in from the ocean. The air was soft as early summer, and birds were singing in the hawthorn hedges. It was a marvelous day to be alive, and after a tentative try at conversation with Samuel, she gave up and gave herself over to delight in the trip.

Batley was larger than she remembered. She made her way to the store, which smelled deliciously of coffee and spice, and placed her order. Mindful of Sir Maurice's injunctions to her, she sent Samuel around to supervise the loading of supplies into the cart, and she wandered through the store. A half dozen new books had come up from London, and she looked at the authors' names with mild interest: Fanny Burney, Mrs. Radcliffe, Kitty Cuthbertson, and Verbena de Vere.

The lady authors of what were often called "horrid novels" spun out lurid tales of romance and devilish terror as far removed from life as could be imagined. Narcissa was not addicted, but only because they were monotonously the same. The heroines lacked the elements of common sense, so she thought, and she had found that the real terrors of life—such as hunger, no prospects, no money—could not be solved by swooning away.

But of them all, she liked Verbena de Vere's novels the best, she remembered, for their plots were so ridiculous as to be amusing.

She was not much for novel reading, for she had never had sufficient time to settle down on a long afternoon with nothing to do but read. She could foresee that there would be leisure hours ahead of her, especially on rainy days, too dark to sew with one candle. She counted over the change in her hand. Not enough for a book fresh from the Minerva Press. With a regretful sigh, she thrust the coins back into her little pocketbook and went out to climb aboard the cart.

The weather was still fine. A short distance out of Batley, she begged Samuel to stop. "You go on home with the groceries, and I'll walk. It's such a lovely day, I don't want to miss any of it."

Samuel, gazing at her stolidly, shifted his straw from one side of his mouth to the other and nodded. Touching his forelock, he clucked the horses up, and soon the cart was out of sight down the road. Slowly the day grew darker, and she realized finally it was not the sun, overcast by clouds, but her own spirits. She had now had time to see what life at Bentham Hall would be like, and while it was better than starving in a gutter in London, still there was much to be said at times for the gutter. At least starvation would soon put an end to it all. Life at Bentham Hall seemed to drag on endlessly into the future, a dismal vista.

Narcissa was not one to prize luxuries overmuch, but neither was she one to live in penury if it were not required. Her life to this point had had certainly long stretches of drought, but there had been hope that something better would turn up, and it always had. Now she could see no prospects. She would not accept a destiny as an upper servant in her grandfather's house. Mistress of the house she might call herself, but it was false grandeur, for her grandfather held the reins. Without a penny in one's pocket, one was indeed a dependent. She could not now see any prospect of a change in her fortunes, but she also knew that patience was "keeping busy in the meantime," and she would have to do her best. She was so intent upon her own thoughts that her pace slowed. Returning to the present, she quickened her step and wished she knew exactly how far she was from home. The sunshine had vanished behind towering clouds hurling themselves inland, and it looked like rain again.

Making haste, she skirted the puddles in the road and hurried down the grassy center of the track. She paid no attention to her surroundings till almost too late. Suddenly she became aware of the sound of hooves and wheels drawing closer, and she looked up in alarm. The curricle was almost upon her.

She caught a glimpse of a ruddy face and sandy, coarse hair visible beneath his round hat. He was of portly build, a man whose prosperity was obvious. His eyes were fixed down the road, and she was positive he did not even see her.

He drove like a madman or like a man unaccustomed to consider any obstacle in his path.

He made no effort to slacken pace, and she leaped to the side of the road out of the way. The vehicle hit the puddle full tilt. Mud and water sprayed out on her, and she looked down at her spattered skirt. With a cry of dismay she took a handkerchief and began rubbing off the soil, but it was clear to be seen that the skirt was almost beyond repair. Perhaps if she hurried home and got it cleaned before the mud dried in, it would be all right. But she was in a furious temper when she resumed her hasty walk toward Bentham Hall!

4

That day she had come home raging against the boorish driver who had spattered her gown and thought, of all the places in the world she wanted to be, Bentham Hall ranked lowest on the list.

In a few days her irritation spread to Sir Maurice, who had developed the vexing habit of appearing, when she was deep in the trying task of mending linen, with an unlimited store of niggling criticism.

"One thing your mother never taught you," he pointed out unjustly, "was fine needlework. I should think you would be ashamed to do such slipshod work."

She looked critically at the stitches she had just taken. They would have passed even Dilly's stringent standards, she thought, but she stifled the retort that rose to her lips. Instead, she said simply, "But any stitches, sir, are better than none at all. I can hardly credit the neglect that results from a strictly masculine establishment."

He was routed for the moment.

And then, one week after she had returned from shopping in town, all seemed miraculously changed. Sir Maurice, in fact, approved the new aspect of the small sitting room where Narcissa spent much time and even approved the disappearance of much of the procelain that cluttered the buffet in the dining room. The good silver and the serving pieces she left. There were a number of small vases, odd cups, some chipped porcelain, some old Wedgwood, from the first output of Josiah Wedgwood's factory, and those she instructed Gibbs to put on shelves in the kitchen.

She was amazed by the number of pieces in her grandfather's china cupboards. The bewildering variety of artichoke cups, broth bowls, butter tubs and stands, chestnut vases, custard cups, radish trays, root dishes, turtle pans, and violet baskets reflected a past generation of ample hospitality.

She marveled at the punch bowls capable of holding at least two gallons, made with a tall foot rim to protect the table surface from the hot liquid.

She held in her hands a Sèvres figurine. "This is immensely valuable," she mused. "It must be very old." She traced with her forefinger the curls of the two innocent nymphs, frozen in biscuit porcelain.

Mrs. Gibbs nodded. "Aye, it was here when my lady came. It *is* a pretty thing, although a mite heathenish, but not of much use, you might say. What makes it so valuable, if you please, miss?"

"Only that it is so rare, Mrs. Gibbs. I was told in Paris last year that the Prince Regent had bought up everything he could find from the Sèvres potteries— made before the war, of course. I doubt the potteries are still in existence."

"Them Revolutionaries." The housekeeper nodded wisely. "They ruin everything. And that Bonyparte wasn't much better, from what *I* hear. But then, miss, you want this all put away?"

Narcissa nodded. "Far away, as safely as possible."

Within a few days the dining room smelled of beeswax, and nearly every surface reflected polished silver. The twinkling crystal chandelier had emerged from its grimy disguise, and even Sir Maurice was pleased.

"Looks better already," he crowed. "I knew you could do it with a little ingenuity, didn't cost a cent either."

Narcissa bit her tongue. Sir Maurice said, "Sly little puss, you've changed my ways altogether. I didn't realize how much I was missing until you came along, child."

He reached out and playfully pinched her cheek. He evidently considered himself a gay old dog, and since he was not the first of that ilk she had encountered, she merely smiled slightly and said nothing. But Sir Maurice had more on his mind. "I've decided that what this house needs is a little liveliness. I certainly don't want my granddaughter to long for foreign capitals when we have a spirited group of people in our own neighborhood. It's time you got acquainted with them."

Narcissa's eyes widened, and she smiled enchantingly. "Of all things I should like that! Tell me what you wish me to do."

He rubbed his hands gleefully. "First off, we will have a small dinner," he said. "I think a big ball is out of the question to start with. The staff isn't up to it, for one thing, and it would be too much work for you."

So it was decided. Narcissa was entranced by the vista opening up. She consulted with Cook, to plan an elaborate dinner. Mrs. Gibbs was somewhat reluctant at first, but she went along willingly enough when Narcissa led the way. There was to be a saddle of mutton, a trifle, an apricot tart, a variety of biscuits and cakes, and two kinds of fowl. At length Mrs. Gibbs nodded her head, saying, "I can handle it all, Miss Narcissa." She looked at the notes in her hand. "I must say, it will be like old times. I do hope I haven't lost my touch with the pastry. It would be just like me, seeing as I haven't had the chance to keep it up. But they do say, miss, that it's a gift, like."

"It will be a lot of work," said Narcissa doubtfully.

Mrs. Gibbs consoled her. "Never you mind, miss. None can say that this kitchen isn't a credit to you." She thought a moment and then asked, "How many shall I plan for?"

Narcissa stared at her and cried out, "How strange! I never asked. But I will find out, for I should guess at least half a dozen guests. He did say we would start off in a small way, but one can't have a decent sit-down dinner for fewer than six."

The look in Mrs. Gibb's eyes put the lie to that remark, but since Narcissa did not see it, she was not required to answer. But when she broached the subject to Sir Maurice, she was shocked to find that her grandfather considered six guests to dinner riotous, extravagant entertainment. "No, there'll be just friend Appercott. One is enough to start with."

She opened her lips to protest vigorously, but since he had delved back into Homer's *Odyssey*, she knew she could not compete with the wiles of Circe. She turned on her heel and left, restraining a regrettable impulse to flounce as she went out the door.

The date for the dinner was set for that week. The only information her grandfather had given her about their dinner guest was that his name was Lucius Appercott, he lived on a neighboring farm, and he had plenty of brass. She wished, considering Mr. Appercott's prosperity, that her grandfather had not scratched off one of the removes and both fowl from the dinner menu. It looked a shabby setout to her, but his instructions were not to be defied. Since Sir Maurice had coupled his restrictions on the menu with his intention to take over her small sitting room as his own study, she felt she could not fight a war on two fronts. She retreated on the menu.

"I daresay you will find this more to your liking," she said artfully, glancing around her at the sunny room. Lady Bentham's small desk stood in the corner near a window, giving onto the broad lawn to the rose garden at the far edge—another task she must see to, she thought, to get the roses trimmed—and Narcissa loved the cheerfulness of the room. "Too bad I'll have to be in and out all the time, but I daresay I shall not disturb your reading."

"In and out?" said Sir Maurice suspiciously. "I expect that you'll move your business to another room."

"I hardly see how, sir," she said with an appearance of innocence. "This room is right next to the kitchens. It is handy for me. But then, the noise of the servants and the cooking will not bother you after a time, I'm sure."

He favored her with a sour glance but, looking around him, said gruffly, "It's too bright anyway. I prefer not to sit in the boiling sun all morning."

She smiled sunnily and said, "I shall tell Mrs. Gibbs your wishes on the menu."

When the day arrived, all was in readiness. She walked through the rooms, exulting at the transformation. The maids had done much of the hard work, but most of it was due to her own moving spirit.

The dinner guest arrived. She felt her heart thudding within her breast, for this was the first of her grandfather's friends she would meet. Her grandfather, dressed in old-fashioned knee breeches, ushered the guest into the small parlor where she waited. She rose to her feet, hardly believing her eyes.

The newcomer was sanguine of cheek, and his coarse sandy hair stuck out stiffly, rebelling against the brush.

His stoutness strained against the seams of his coat, and his pale blue eyes bulged.

It was the driver of the rig that had splashed her so severely, the boorish driver who had ruined her clothing and then passed on without ever looking back! She was ready to sink into the floor from dismay. If this were the caliber of the best of her grandfather's friends, she did not look forward to the rest of her life here.

Mr. Appercott did not recognize her. When at last they were ushered by old Gibbs into the dining room, she could not help being proud of the staff. The linen was snowy white; a day or two of hanging in the bright sunlight had taken away the yellow of the Irish linen. The silver was polished, and the meal was well dressed. She could wish the menu had been more abundant; but such as it was, it was very well cooked, and she realized that Mrs. Gibbs had at one time served in a household more exacting than her grandfather's.

It had been a long time since Gibbs had served guests. She could see the puzzled frown on his face as he looked at the dishes, deciding what to do next. Sometimes his lips moved, clearly reciting rules he had learned long ago. At first she had tried to keep some charge of the conversation, but it was clear that her grandfather and Mr. Appercott had much they wished to talk about. She might as well not be sitting at the table at all, she reflected.

Halfway through the meal she realized something else. Mr. Appercott was a "sheep man."

There was very little else on his mind, to judge from his conversation. Between huge mouthfuls of mutton, he extolled the virtues of his sheep, many of whom had individual names. She was hard put to understand that he was not speaking of his family. How any man could have a niece, for instance, named Bluebell was more than she could fathom at first. Then when she readjusted her mind to realize that these names applied to various ewes of his personal acquaintance, all fell into line.

"Aye, my Cheviot ewes are fine sheep; but the new lambs now are half Border Leicester, and I expect to get twice the value with the wool. They'll mature faster, so I deem, than the regular Cheviot strain. Now there are some who'll tell you that the Rambouillet is best, but I hold by the English sheep, purebred English, I say. Cheviots raised on these hills since olden times, and the Borderers, too." He winked broadly. "Can't tell me much I don't know about sheep, Miss Bentham."

She longed for the end of the meal, when she could leave the men to their wine, but such was not the custom in Sir Maurice's house. They all moved to the drawing room, and the wine was served there. Whatever other faults Sir Maurice had, stinting on wine was not one of them. By the time that Narcissa had settled down with her embroidery, using the light of the candles with gratefulness, for they were far brighter than the one working candle that Sir Maurice considered adequate, Mr. Appercott had remembered that she was in the room. He moved to sit beside her and eyed her work, slapping his fat hand on his knee.

"What kind of work is that?" She realized it was only a polite question, and she gave him a brief answer. He was already moving on to the next question. "I'd like to see that bit of work in my house. I've got a fine house down the valley, all made of stone and snug as a rug," he said, winking conspiratorily at her. "Snug as a rug," he repeated and added, "Only needs a woman!"

Sir Maurice moved in with another glass of port. Mr. Appercott's already red face took another step toward scarlet. She thought he had already had more wine than he needed.

With this last glass, Mr. Appercott lapsed into blessed silence. But since he sat on the edge of his chair, regarding his hostess with an unwinking stare, she was still not at ease.

Narcissa reflected upon the many men she had entertained at her father's table. Those guests had fallen mainly into two categories—rogues and bores. Of the two, Mr. Appercott was clearly a bore. She had always found rogues more entertaining. She could only hope that future guests invited by her grandfather would be more congenial than this thigh-slapping, winking Mr. Appercott. She had a lowering feeling that her wish would not be granted.

At long last, and with unbounded relief, she saw that Mr. Appercott was preparing to take his leave. He bowed over her hand and finally said, "I do drive well. You need not be afraid with me. I should like to take you on a drive. I believe there is a wishing well that the ladies always like to see."

Heaven deliver her from a driver such as Mr. Appercott! But heaven did not intervene, and she was forced to stammer something that she hoped was civil, if not enthusiastic.

Sir Maurice escorted Mr. Appercott to his carriage and stood talking to him for a long time. Probably, thought Narcissa with a touch of exasperation, something more about those idiotic sheep!

5

A week slid by before Narcissa realized that the season had moved into May. Spring came much later in the north country than it did in, for example, the south of France or even the north of Italy.

Along the Mediterranean, the peach trees and the apple trees would be in full blossom by now, already with tiny fruit set. Songbirds would now be filling orchards with brilliant, liquid music, and the sun would be almost hot on the shoulders. Everywhere there would be strong, vigorous colors.

But here, on the highlands of Yorkshire, winter still held a firm grip on the land.

Even in the middle of May the sunshine was pale and watery, like the primroses that bloomed under the hedges, almost afraid to thrust their clear colors to the fierce winds.

Mending, predictably, became too confining, and Narcissa sought relief in long, leg-stretching walks across Bentham land. Each day she chose a different way and learned to know the rise and fall of the fields.

The Bentham land stretched west to the south Pennine moors. From the far limit of Bentham fields one could look north toward the Aire Gap. It was a picturesque scene, wild as any novel reader could wish for and almost deserted. Narcissa was not a countrywoman, and the import of the untilled fields came very slowly to her.

Surely there should be farming going on. Where were the livestock and the corn to feed them? There ought to be sheep, she suspected, remembering the beasts she had seen on the slopes on her way from Batley.

There were surely sheep in the region, she remembered, for Lucius Appercott had talked of nothing else!

She was not informed about agriculture, and she was

aware of no great want in her education. Leave agriculture to those who knew, she decided, and she would content herself with enjoying the desolate scene.

She had, in most cases, a satisfactory life, but she knew she would never be totally happy here.

But one day she came back to the house with a new determination. There was a way to mitigate the long, lonely evenings, the total solitude, for she could not count Sir Maurice as an entertaining companion. Seeking him out in his study, she broached the subject. "Sir, when are we going to entertain again? You spoke of entertaining the neighborhood."

Her grandfather, finger still in his book to hold his place, indicating that he hoped the interruption would be a short one, replied, "First, we have to be repaid for the expense of entertaining Appercott." Seeing her raised eyebrow, he continued, "You think I'm entertaining for the fun of it? Not me. When Appercott pays us back, and he will, then it is time to look farther afield. You were pretty rude to him the other night, you mind that?"

Stung, Narcissa retorted, "I hardly had a chance to be anything to him. He had no interest except sheep, and he found your conversation along that line far better than mine."

Sir Maurice laughed, a malicious chuckle. "Now then, lass, don't get on your high horse. You'll have your chance at Appercott soon enough."

Narcissa stared at him. Clearly he had something in his mind. "What is it, sir? What do you mean?"

He told her. "We're invited to Appercott's for dinner today. That's what I've been waiting for, and the invitation came this morning. Now there's a lot riding on this, and I want you to mind your manners, girl. Understand me?"

Narcissa, not having been chidden about her manners since she was thirteen, was too mortified to reply. She thought with an inward sigh, I will never understand my grandfather, never! He was as changeable as a weather vane, and she could never know whether his mood presaged a storm or fair weather.

This moment a spell of stormy weather buffeted her. "I expect a little decorum from you, girl, and none of your long-faced moping. You were glad enough to come here when you didn't have any place else to go, hey? And what do I get out of it?"

Narcissa cast her mind back over the refurbishing of the few rooms downstairs, the endless mending of linen, the shopping in Batley, her plans for a kitchen garden to grow their own vegetables, and kept silent. Not from modesty, she thought, but from a certain conviction that were she to open her lips she could not control what came forth.

He stared at her, a small blaze in his eyes, as he continued. "Did you hear me? Are you going to wear that dress? Looks like you've been out tramping along the hedgerows like a Gypsy!"

Narcissa cried out, "This day?"

Sir Maurice said, "I said so, didn't I?"

He returned to his book, and she was clearly dismissed. She hurried up the stairs, turning over in her mind the few garments that she owned, trying to decide which would be most suitable to visit a sheep farmer. She was not at heart a snob, and it was not the fact that he was a sheep farmer which concerned her. It was the prospect of a long afternoon of the most boring conversation she had ever been privileged to hear.

The afternoon stretched out before her like a life sentence, and she was forced to remember that Sir Maurice was giving her a home when she had no place else to go and, according to his lights, was generous.

She dressed very carefully in a dark green dress, tied a bright scarf around her curls, and professed herself ready. She eyed the coach in which she was to travel with misgiving, for it looked as though it had not been out of the stables for a decade. Newly applied grease at the wheel hubs still dripped down the spokes, and she hoped that the frame had not dried out so much during its enforced rest that it would fall apart before they got home.

The coachman, appearing as uneasy as she felt, was Jenkins, who tilled the Home Farm in a halfhearted fashion. His daughter, Polly, and his son, Samuel, brought home their small wages to him, and he lived, to his notion, quite well. He resented being called upon to exert himself, as he now must, but he grudgingly touched his cap as Sir Maurice and Narcissa mounted into the ancient vehicle.

She was agreeably surprised by Appercott's house. They topped the last rise and looked down into the valley to see a large stone building nestled among trees. As they pulled up to the front door, their host himself came out to open the carriage door. After he helped her down, she stood on the gravel for a moment, looking about her. The house was long and low and gave out an indefinable air of comfort and prosperity. It lacked the handsome proportions of many houses she knew, but there was a warmth of generosity that exuded even from the walls. It was clear that Mr. Appercott did himself well.

The meal was bountiful to a fault. The board was set with enormous tureens of soup, great bowls of vegetables, puddings, and several platters of meat. It was served farmhand style, and they required very little service.

She had to give him good marks for his lack of pretentiousness. Yet after dinner, when they moved into the next room, she discovered his generosity extended only to creature comforts, not to the nourishing of minds. There were no paintings on the walls, for example, and not a book in sight. She put herself out to be civil and was rewarded by seeing Sir Maurice's approving eye on her.

She judged that Mr. Appercott must be nearly fifty, and she smiled at him in a filial manner. Encouraged by this, Mr. Appercott launched into a series of anecdotes about himself and a good friend when they were boys. The good friend's name was an odd one like "Stupp," and it came with something of a shock to her to find out that he was, in fact, speaking of his childhood friend Alfred Bentham. Her father and Lucius Appercott, boys together! She managed a smile. Appercott moved his chair closer and said, "You know what your father called me?" She shook her head. He insisted, "Now hazard a guess!" His little eyes were bright with boyish expectancy, and she forced herself to make some kind of odd guess.

But she was wide off the mark. "Foxy!" he crowed in triumph. "He called me Foxy, and I called him Stupp. What do you think of that?"

Narcissa's wits scampered about, trying to find an escape from this intolerable position. "It's like nothing

I've ever read in books," she said desperately, "but I see you have very few books. Perhaps there is a library beyond?" She gestured toward a closed door.

Lucius Appercott shook his head decisively. "No books in my house. They just fill a wife's head with nonsense and send her into a decline. A good wife has no time for nonsense like books. She's out taking care of chickens, the new lambs, making sure that the maids do their work, churning, setting food on the table, and taking care of the children. That's work enough for any woman, without filling her head full of nonsense like books."

Narcissa was aware of a sick feeling. She did not recognize the source of her disquiet, but she stored up a question or two for her grandfather.

Appercott was still talking. He said, slapping his knee with his great ham of a hand, "I'm just as good a man as I ever was!" He accompanied this with a broad wink that sent Narcissa's spirits to her toes. Somehow they got through the afternoon and started on their way home. They were barely out of earshot of the house when Narcissa turned to her grandfather and said, "Well, we now have been paid back, sir. I trust that our next guests will be more congenial."

Sir Maurice glanced at her from the corner of his eye. He seemed self-conscious. It was so unlike him that her spirits began to sink in apprehension. He did not reply directly but said, "Appercott's rushing it a bit. I told him not to push too much, but perhaps it's the best thing in the long run."

Narcissa echoed, "Rushing it? I don't know what you mean, sir."

He said obliquely, "What do you think of him? Appercott, I mean, of course."

Narcissa was about to launch upon a tirade of invective against this man whom she found common, to say the least. He was boorish, nearly indecent in his winks and his broad hints, and she longed heartily to see no more of him. But caution held her back; she knew her grandfather well enough now to know that he was capable of strong deceit and devious methods.

"He sets a generous table." It was all she could manage.

Sir Maurice said, "Well, that's a beginning. You keep

remembering that that man has plenty of money, and you'll find it works out well in the long run."

She drew back against the squabs and demanded, glaring at him, "What do you mean? Why should I get used to it? What's going on?"

Impatiently Sir Maurice explained. "I mean that any man worth a rush has to give himself over to a little courtship, a little pandering to the vanity of a foolish woman, that's what I mean."

After a moment she said, "I cannot understand what you mean, sir. Surely Mr. Appercott is not hanging out for a wife?"

"You think not?"

She glanced at Sir Maurice's grim expression and felt her heart begin to hammer uncomfortably. "He surely cannot aspire to a baronet's granddaughter?"

"No matter what he aspires to," said Sir Maurice. "I have my say in this, girl, and I say you're going to marry him."

It was as though he were relieved to have it out in the open. He watched her through narrowed lids and said, "Now don't turn missish on me, for you know that I'm making you a good match."

Besides his relief at having it out in the open, she thought she could read his pleasure in having surprised her. But she saw him through a red haze of indignation and fury. She said, "I shall not do it. Every feeling must rebel against such a match. We have nothing in common, all he expects of me is a housekeeper. . . ."

Her voice fell away lamely, as she realized that was all Sir Maurice expected of her, and she was already doing his housekeeper's work for him. She contented herself with muttering once more, "Every feeling must rebel!"

Sir Maurice said silkily, "Even hunger? You were not in such high fettle when you wrote to me asking for help."

She said, stung, "Help for my father."

Sir Maurice said as they turned in the gates to Bentham Hall, "You think your father wouldn't be happy to see you settled, hey?"

She didn't answer, and Sir Maurice added as his final word on the subject, "Appercott's well padded, and you'll do fine."

6

She smoldered in silence all the way home. She alit from the carriage without waiting for Gibbs and stalked into the house, intent upon reaching the haven of her room before giving way to the furious tears that smarted behind her eyelids.

Pausing halfway up the stairs, she turned and looked down at her grandfather, who was watching her with an odd expression in his eyes. "I truly do not wish any supper," she told him. "Your ill-timed jest has quite taken away any desire for food."

He nodded. "It takes some getting accustomed to, I agree. It's not every girl has such a chance as this."

"Chance!" She gathered up her skirt and descended a few steps. "A betrothal to a farmer?"

His eyes narrowed. "I had not thought that you were a snob, miss." His voice was dangerously low.

"No, not a snob! How could you think so? But surely a baronet's granddaughter could expect a husband of some education, some standing in the world."

Sir Maurice gave the abrupt sound that passed for a laugh. "Who would want to marry the daughter of a spendthrift, a gambler, and who knows what else? Your father had so little sense of family that he never spoke to me once after his marriage. He could have been dead a hundred times, and I would not have had any word."

It was a window opening into Sir Maurice's soul, she recognized, and her feeling toward him softened. A father bereft of his only child, his son and heir, and bitterness had taken over the void left by her father's actions.

But abruptly Sir Maurice drew the shutters, so to speak, and his gaze chilled. "So talk no more to me of family! I have long since forgotten I had one!" He turned abruptly and entered his library, slamming the door behind him.

She was shocked, angry, and conscious of a small flicker of fear at bottom. Once in her room, the door latched behind her, she took off her bonnet and dropped it onto her bed. She crossed to the window and laid her head against the frame. It was cool against her fevered forehead, and she was swept by her chaotic thoughts.

She could not at first believe that her grandfather was serious, betrothing her to a man of such clear inferiority in the social scale. His character might be fine, but she was the granddaughter of a baronet, and her grandfather must have known that she would not consider such a lowering marriage. He should have himself had more pride than to betroth her to a sheep farmer.

Appercott was well padded, she had to agree. A long forgotten verse from the Bible came back to her—"Better is a dinner of herbs where love is," but she forgot how the rest of it went. A dinner of herbs, while not necessarily appealing, was yet more acceptable than marriage to a man old enough to be her father, with fat, sausagelike fingers that clearly itched to make a closer acquaintance with her. She had no illusions about Appercott's meaning when he said he was as good a man as he ever was.

At the end of a sleepless night she had come to one conclusion. There was a choice for her, and she must explore it. Perhaps her grandfather was jesting—and she could remember his look of pleasure at her surprise—and it was merely a simple practical joke.

The alternative, that he was serious, was much less palatable. But she thought she might possibly be able to deal with that. If her objections were strong enough, even her grandfather could not force her into a marriage that she rebelled against. Her best action was to pretend not to take the jest seriously.

At breakfast that morning Sir Maurice greeted her with a rare smile and said, "My dear, I hope you slept well. The long ride in the air must have been tiring."

It was as close to an apology for the scene on the stairs as she would hear, she knew, and she accepted the unspoken amends with a sunny smile. But he added, with an arch expression, "Got your trousseau planned? I know you girls like to think of your bride clothes."

Narcissa said with a deceptive appearance of calm, "The question does not arise."

Sir Maurice, nettled, said, "You have not much time to get them ready."

Narcissa said serenely, "There is no acceptable bridegroom in sight. I think I have sufficient time."

He pounded a fist on the table and shouted, "You heard me yesterday, didn't you?"

"Of course I heard you, sir. But I cannot think you are so anxious to get rid of me. The rooms are not finished yet, I have still a huge stack of mending to get through, and soon it will be time to have the garden set out so that we will have food next winter. You won't want to get rid of me before that is done, I vow."

She watched from under half-closed lids. She could see the uneasy speculation riding across his thoughts, and finally, he said, not as sure of himself as he had been, "Artful puss. Don't want to leave your old grandfather, hey?"

She borrowed a phrase that he had used once and said, "I think we rub along together fine."

It was, in its way, a statement of truth. When she considered the contrast of rubbing along with Lucius Appercott, she did better at Bentham Hall!

Her grandfather did not mention the subject again for two days, and she thought she had gained a reprieve. She then broached the subject of other neighbors to dinner, and Sir Maurice, while he did not refuse, postponed the entertainment to yet another time. He had no reason to give, and she realized at last that her respite was brief.

There was truly no place for her to go. Either she stayed at Bentham Hall, or she married Lucius Appercott. It was a clear-cut decision, and she feared that it was not even her decision to make. If her grandfather had made up his mind, it would take all her ingenuity, of which she had a great deal, to avoid his plans for her.

The further thought came to her that if he was willing to accept Lucius Appercott as a grandson-in-law, then this was an indication of his social ineptitude. If Appercott were refused and that marriage was broken off, then his next choice might be even worse. She shuddered, thinking that there could be little worse.

Bentham Hall had become a dead end. There was no place to go, but she could no longer stay. She cast her mind over other possibilities. She had some experience as a housekeeper, but she was aware that to find a suitable position would take months. And she had no illusions as to the amount of time left to her. If Sir Maurice had become convinced that she would actually refuse Appercott, then it would doubtless be only a short time until some other match was proposed.

She still possessed the Holland connection. Her mother's family had ignored her letter. But it was possible that they had not received the missive written with such brow-wrinkling care. The mails were notoriously wayward—she must hold to that thought.

The London house had been closed. But if they were in residence in Scarborough, then she had a family living only a day's journey across the Yorkshire moors. They had cast her mother out, though, and never tried to communicate with her after her marriage. Narcissa dreaded to pursue her one last chance—if the Hollands were to turn her out, then there was literally no place in the world for her to go.

Dilly, too, lived in Scarborough. Narcissa could not force herself on Dilly, for Dilly had only her savings to live on. No, there was no help but to try the Hollands again. She counted her money, to see whether it would be enough for coach fare. She looked at the coins in her palm. She missed her father greatly, and never more acutely than at this moment. Alfred Bentham would have taken those small coins and, if his luck were in, made a fortune of it. They could have hired coaches and gone wherever they wanted to, to Scarborough, Harrogate, or abroad. But Alfred's luck, good or bad, had deserted her. There was no way she could miraculously make these coins into a washleather bag of jingly gold.

A day passed while she tried to make up her mind what to do. She went out for a walk. There wasn't a cobweb in sight in Bentham Hall now, thanks to her vigorous housekeeping. They all seemed to have concentrated in her brain!

She had reached the end of the lane, out of sight of

the house, when the wind began to rise. The little dead leaves, left over from winter, scampered around her skirts like children around a Maypole. She watched them idly, and then, as the gust came and blew them all across the hedge into the next field, she became aware that there were storm clouds on the horizon.

The black bank of clouds lying to the west was ominous and rising rapidly. She began to hurry home. She watched the clouds uneasily and had serious doubts about getting to the house before the storm broke.

Her luck was against her. The first tentative drops began to fall as she rounded the bend by the stables, and she picked up her skirts and ran toward the back of the house. Polly was watching and opened the door for her. She took off her bonnet and shook off the raindrops. Mrs. Gibbs rushed in and clucked, "Hurry upstairs, and I'll send Jessie up. This looks like a bad storm, and I don't want to leave the fire in the kitchen. The gusts are coming down the chimney, never seen the like!"

Gaining her room, Narcissa looked longingly at the black hearth and decided against kindling the fire in such a wind. After quickly changing her clothes and rubbing her wet skin with a thick towel, she dressed again. She could hear the storm's roar as the gale lifted tiles from the roof of the house and sent them out across the lawn.

She watched from the window as the wind took hold of the trees. Turning the leaves wrong way out, the gale bent the trees halfway to the ground before relenting and releasing them. The tops of the great beeches swayed back and forth in powerful gusts, and it seemed as though the whole world had lost its footing and streamed past in the wind.

The moaning of the gale in the chimney was distressingly human. She could almost believe that all the woes of Bentham Hall—the suffering of Lady Bentham, her grandfather's grief, her own father's unhappiness—had somehow been given voice and come alive in the storm.

And then the rains came, a river of water down the glass, a silver curtain that isolated the house from the world. When at last the storm died down, she sallied forth to see the damage. The worst harm was done to the roof, where black splotches marked the places where the slates had been torn away. Another storm would do incalculable damage unless the roof was speedily repaired. She insisted that Sir Maurice come out and survey the damage himself.

"We've got to get the slates replaced," she said impatiently when he made no comment.

He exploded. "You're trying to spend all my money! If it isn't one thing it's another—a new rug, new curtains, new roof! Bentham Hall will be yours, but not my money."

She retorted, "I never asked for a new rug or furnishings!"

Sir Maurice growled, "You want them, that's enough."

He stalked back to the house. Watching the bent old man walking toward the house, she was conscious of his great loneliness. But he was also worried, she guessed.

The answer came to her with a great rush. He was not merely miserly—he was simply bankrupt! He had no money at all, beyond the barest necessities! She should have known. . . .

This would explain the lack of good cattle in the stables. It would explain the meager fare on the table. It would also explain why he was anxious to get her out of his household, letting Mr. Appercott take the task of feeding her.

She hurried after her grandfather. Catching him in the study, she cried out, "Sir, if we are down on funds, I wish you had told me. We could do something; we can work together to recoup our situation. We can work together without marrying me off."

The look on his face, full of resentment, was forbidding enough to daunt almost anyone, but Narcissa dared not stop. She forged ahead.

"Suppose I found a position as a governess—"

Sir Maurice's stony look stopped her. "I have already made plans."

"If you mean marrying Mr. Appercott," she said, more stoutly than she felt, "that is not a solution."

"You want to take care of children?" said Sir Maurice surprisingly.

"I should like to try," she said. Perhaps he was coming around to her way of thinking. "I have been well trained. My own governess was exceedingly competent, you know."

A smile touched Sir Maurice's thin lips. "If you want to help, you can."

"Oh, sir, I should like it of all things!" cried Narcissa. "I shall do my best in any household you can contrive. Do you know of any family needing a governess?"

"I might just be able to think of one," he said. "Close the door when you leave."

How strange he is! she thought, closing the study door as she had been bidden. I had not expected such an easy victory!

7

Since there was no money for hiring a slater from the village, it was left to the farmhands to restore the roof. The patchwork looked uneven to Narcissa, but at least it bade fair not to leak, so she accepted what she could get.

She had been here a month, and already there were signs of her industry. She could take credit for a great deal, for without someone to make plans and give orders, the servants would have done little. The third day after the storm she was in the garden, reflecting on how much to allow for a new herb garden.

"If we could just have a bit of savory, Miss Narcissa," said the cook, "and a little rosemary for the fowl. I didn't wish to make a garden by myself, you know, without knowing where to put it."

"We'll have it!" promised Narcissa impulsively. "And thyme and marjoram. Do you use basil? I have known it in Italy a great deal. And perhaps a few cucumbers, for I have tasted duck stewed in cucumber, and the taste is quite ravishing!"

Mrs. Gibbs's eyes lit in anticipation, but she said repressively, "English food is good enough for anyone. But I wonder—"

She would try it at the first opportunity, she vowed, returning to her kitchen, no matter whether it was Frenchy or not. Narcissa's thoughts moved on another path. For if her grandfather kept his promise to find her a place as governess, then she might have to leave Bentham Hall quite soon. She promised herself that she would at least get the herb garden laid out first.

She lingered in the pleasant sunshine, remembering the spectacular gardens belonging to the town palaces of Genoa. She had been taken to visit one while she and her father waited for a ship to Marseilles. She

could not manage to reproduce the four box-edged par-
terres, but perhaps she could copy the old-fashioned
rose pergola of that garden. . . .

She heard footsteps approaching. Her heart sank
when she saw Lucius Appercott crossing the lawn
toward her. She looked wildly around for a means of
escape; but he had seen her, and she must wait for him.
He came toward her with a friendly smile.

"You shouldn't be out here in the sun!" he said, an
anxious frown creasing his forehead.

Cautiously she replied, "Oh, I'm healthy enough. I
won't mind the sun."

"I'm glad to hear that," he said seriously. "I should
not like to have you ill."

"That's very kind of you, Mr. Appercott," she said,
allowing a daunting coolness to appear in her voice.
Mr. Appercott's concern about her health, she thought,
was not an attitude she wanted to encourage.

He continued, unmoved. "A man in my position cannot afford an ailing wife. It's not the doctors so much
as the house goes to pieces when the wife is not up to
snuff. And then there's always the question of a sickly
heir when I need sons to come out and tend the sheep
with me."

Faintly she said, "I quite agree."

His eyes lit up, and he gave her the impression he
was going to dig his elbow into her ribs. Automatically
she stepped back.

He looked at her speculatively, and she felt her heart
sink. She had not expected such a confrontation, for
she believed Sir Maurice would have told Mr. Appercott at once that she had refused the match. But the
farmer gave no sign of being rejected. Sir Maurice—and
she should have suspected him of procrastination at
best—had not told Appercott her decision!

She said gently, "Mr. Appercott, the question does
not arise. You need have no fear that I would fall ill,
for it does not concern you."

Appercott hurried on, as though she had not spoken.
"I'm giving you a free hand with the house. We'll send
our sons to school, but you can have a free hand with
the girls. They don't need book learning. It's enough
that they can sign their name on the marriage contract."

She was shocked. His crude and excessively vulgar planning repelled her strongly. He ignored her feelings, as though she were a mere statue to receive his devotion—or, she considered with an ominous tightening of her lips, as though she were a nubile ewe!

He said, "Mind, we'll be comfortable enough as it is, no need to redo the whole house. Besides, it won't be long before you'll have your hands full!" He laughed wickedly.

She grasped the reins of her temper in both hands and said quite firmly, "Mr. Appercott, you are laboring under a misapprehension. I fear my grandfather has not told you, and I am sorry for it, that I will not wed you. I have absolutely no plans to marry you or to have a free hand with your house."

Her voice was rising, and she heard as though from a distance the note of hysteria that invaded it. She could not lose her head now, she told herself. She shut her lips desperately on what she feared might become a rising scream.

To her utter amazement, Mr. Appercott laughed loudly. With genuine mirth, he slapped his thigh. "I like my women shy! Although, I should say, you'll have no complaint about other women. But I do like a shy woman, I do!"

She stretched her hand out to him. "Mr. Appercott—"

Interrupting her, he reached for her outstretched hand. "Aye, I'll teach you better. I'll make you lose your shyness after we're wed, for I'm still a lively one, have no fear of that!"

She withdrew her hand, as though his touch had scorched her, and at last got his attention. With blazing eyes, she said to him, "I will not wed you. You are wasting your time, Mr. Appercott. I regret the necessity for this interview, and believe me, I do not wish to wound your feelings; but I will not marry you. Please go away!"

At last she had reached him. His eyes took on a bewildered look, something like a sheep that did not know which way to go. She felt a pang of pity, but she stood adamant. At length, to her great relief, he turned and left. He said nothing and looked—strange how livestock similes occurred to her!—rather like a bullock going to the slaughter.

She was sorry for him in a remote way, but she was also furious with her grandfather for not having protected her against Mr. Appercott's vulgar importunities. She went into the house, waiting long enough to be sure that Appercott had gone.

The house felt warm, after exposure to the strong wind blowing in from the sea. The weather was going to set in cold, she thought with a part of her mind, but just now the immediate future promised a hot interview.

She burst into her grandfather's study. Without ceremony, she said, "I have just come from a very unpleasant interview with Mr. Appercott."

Sir Maurice said coolly, "I'm glad you came in. There are some papers for you to sign here."

Automatically, in response to the authoritative tone in his voice, she advanced to the table. "What papers are these?" she asked.

He didn't answer, and she picked up the top one. After scanning it at first, she went back to the beginning and read it carefully. When she was done, she felt drained of all feeling except a white hot anger. "These are marriage contracts! To Lucius Appercott!"

Sir Maurice said, "Sign them."

"We agreed that I wouldn't have to marry him! We agreed that I would go as a governess if you were to find a position for me. I had thought that we could work together—"

"I don't remember that we agreed, as you say, on any such project."

She stared blankly at him. "Oh, sir, you *must* remember. You asked me if I enjoyed working with children—"

The wicked gleam in his eye told her how completely he had betrayed her. She stiffened and said quiveringly, "You could not be so crude, so heartless."

"Don't be missish, girl," he said harshly.

"You betrayed me," she said, feeling turned to ice. "I should never have trusted you."

"Quite right," agreed her grandfather, "but I know what is best. Sign the contracts."

She picked them up again and pretended to read

them all, to gain time, to send her wits scampering to find an escape. She would not marry Appercott, not if her life depended on it.

"No need to read them," he said sharply. "Here, just sign there."

His finger pointed to the line at the bottom of the sheet, his hand covering the text of the contract. Suddenly suspicious, even though belatedly, she jerked away.

"I should like to read the contract myself," she said pleasantly, "for you must know I have seen many occasions when there were some unexpected results from an unread contract."

"It is hardly feminine to be so knowledgeable," objected her grandfather.

"But necessary," she said sweetly, "when dealing with a man like my father." And like my treacherous grandfather, she thought but did not say.

Her persistence was rewarded. She read the third paragraph, and immediately she understood the whole. "Here," she said, "is the point." She saw the embarrassed expression on her grandfather's face, and she burst out, "You are *selling* me!"

"Mind your tongue!"

"I shall not! You have got yourself saddled with a monstrous debt to Appercott, and he will forgive the sum if I marry him? Can it be that this is *true?*" She dropped the contracts as though they had burned her fingers. "How could you?"

Sir Maurice snorted. "You could earn your living on the boards, for I have never seen such high tragedy. You would think I were not arranging a fine, generous husband for you, prosperous beyond anything you've had before. What difference does it make to you what I get out of it?"

She looked at him with loathing, unable to speak. But even Sir Maurice recognized that the time was badly chosen to insist that she sign the contracts. In fact, it would not have been possible, for almost as in a dream she picked up the legal papers and tore them across once and then twice.

"Here! Those cost money!"

She paid no heed, turning and walking with stiff dignity to the door, thankful that he made no move to stop her.

The weather set in cold that afternoon, and by evening it was damp and raw. The wind moaned around the shutters, crying like a desolate child, and the sound lacerated her already frayed nerves. The cold seeped in around the window sash, and at length she rang for the maid. Jessie should long ago been up to light the fire, for it was nearly dark. When Jessie came, Narcissa asked her to light the fire. "And you might bring up extra wood, for it looks like a cold night."

Jessie stood in the middle of the floor, looking distressed and wringing her hands. "Begging your pardon, Miss Narcissa."

"Yes, what is it, Jessie?"

"Master said, no fire."

"You mean no fire upstairs," suggested Narcissa.

"No, ma'am. Fires downstairs, but no fire here."

Jessie was a girl of few words, but those words were to the point. Sir Maurice had given instructions that his granddaughter be denied a fire. Ordinarily it would not have bothered her too much, and she could talk to him; but it was clear that this was a deliberate denial. Under the circumstances she felt that any argument with her grandfather could lead only to worse trouble. He needed time to cool, and so did she. A part of her mind told her, with a night like this, you will cool soon enough!

It was a frivolous thought, but based on truth. Jessie, more unhappy over Sir Maurice's orders than she could show, produced a small candle stub from her apron pocket. "Let me just light this for you, Miss Narcissa." Looking around her, Narcissa realized that all her candles were gone, and the tinder, kept next to the candles ready to light them, was gone also. The reason was clear enough—Sir Maurice had also given orders about the candles. Jessie's small stub was a measure of the girl's devotion to Narcissa, and Narcissa took it with thanks.

It was a cold night, and morning was no better. The weather had changed in earnest, and there was to be no respite from it for that day at least. The wind blew steadily from the North Sea, and the clouds rolled in like an invading force.

Narcissa arose, finally, when daylight reached into
the room and she realized that there would be no
early-morning tea. With chattering teeth and blue fingers, she dressed hurriedly, wrapped a warm shawl
around her, and went downstairs. She had the intention
of bearding her grandfather and demanding at least civ-
ilized treatment until they had argued out the point of
the marriage. But Sir Maurice had forestalled her.
Gibbs told her that her grandfather had gone out on
the farms, a rare occurrence, and would not be back
before nightfall. She stayed near the fire downstairs until late in the day. She went to her room and found it,
to her mild surprise, just as she had left it. Apparently
even Sir Maurice's absence did not dispel the fear that
he had instilled in his staff. Not one of them, it was
clear, would dare disobey his explicit instructions. The
bed was not made, nor the room set in order. It was a
gratuitous insult.

Narcissa, her anger held in check far too long, decided that she would take steps of her own. Two could
play at the game that he had initiated. He expected to
break her spirit, she thought. He didn't know her very
well, she thought, for her spirit had sustained far
greater blows than an unmade bed!

But it was clear now that a further stay at Bentham
Hall was out of the question. There was only one way
of escape, for flight into the twitchy hands of Lucius
Appercott was not to be considered. She suspected her
grandfather even of stealing her few small coins. She
rushed to look in the drawer where the hoard had been
hidden. It was still there! Even Sir Maurice could not
stoop so low. She needed to escape, but there was almost no money. She sat huddled long that evening, by
the flickering light of her little work candle. On a sudden thought, she extinguished the flame, for if Sir Maurice learned that Jessie had disobeyed him, it would go
hard with the maid. Narcissa sat in the dark, hearing
the wind, listening to the branches of the great trees
rubbing against each other with an eerie creaking
sound, and plotted.

She must leave Bentham Hall, but there was no
money. Even a servant girl would have a few coppers
in her pocket, from the most miserly of employers.
Without money there was no way of escape except to

trudge like a Gypsy down the highroad, and she dismissed that idea out of hand.

Her remaining hope was to go to Dilly in Scarborough. But she must be able to contribute something to Dilly's expenses, and she had only the small coin left from her trip from London.

There was no way she had of getting money on such short notice, unless—

If her grandfather were without honor, then she, a Bentham born, could match his deviousness. A scheme burst into bloom, and she smiled. His money was as good as in her pocket, for after all, the laborer was worthy of her hire, no matter how she got it!

8

Sir Maurice was agreeably surprised the next morning. His granddaughter proved to be a radiantly sunny companion at breakfast. Although the weather outside was still gloomy, yet her smile lit up the room.

"Couldn't take it, could you?" he chortled. "I knew that's the way to bring you around."

If he had been observant, he would have seen the knuckles on her hand turn white, but there was no trace of any emotion in her voice as she said, "I find I have grown used to comfort here."

It was a measure of Sir Maurice's self-satisfaction that he heard no sign of sarcasm in her voice. "You women are all like cats," he said. He didn't try to hide the amused contempt in his voice as he added, "Nothing better than curling up in front of a good fire and relaxing, you and the cat both."

Her temper was beginning to lift its head, and she knew that she must make her play, as her father would have said, before she was baited into losing her temper. "Upon reflection, sir, it seems to me that I could work no harder for Mr. Appercott than I have worked for you." Her sweet smile seemed to take the sting out of her words, and Sir Maurice's sudden suspicions were stilled.

He was still chuckling over his superior cunning and said in triumph, "I knew you'd come around, so I have called for the lawyer. Eads will be here in an hour with a new set of papers."

Feeling like an unusually rebellious leaf floating on the surface of a stream, she was ushered later into the study where not only her grandfather but also Lucius Appercott and the attorney, Mr. Eads, were present. The desk was covered with legal documents, and at the sight of the formidable and binding contracts, her heart quailed. Suppose something went wrong with her plans and she was caught here with no way of escape? If she set her hand to those documents, she pronounced her own sentence. She made a pretense of looking at the contracts, only to postpone the fatal moment when she must sign. She had thought there would be a few days between the time she agreed to the marriage and the time that the contracts could be ready. How wrong she had been!

She held the foolscap sheets in her hands, seeing with gratification that her hands did not shake. Her eye fell upon the provisions of the document. One word caught her eye, and she turned in abrupt astonishment to her grandfather. "A week only?"

Mr. Appercott interceded, saying, "An anxious bridegroom, you know! I want you as soon as possible."

After sweeping him with her glance, she looked at the lawyer. He seemed discomfited and shrugged his shoulders almost imperceptibly. "But I can't get ready in a week!" she protested.

She had not expected to be so pressed for time. There would be no leisure for working out of her plan; instead, she must put it into action at once.

"Bride clothes," said Sir Maurice grudgingly. "Well, I don't think you'll need a great deal—"

"Oh, but I will! I came with so little extra baggage. I could not be a credit to you. I must have new bride clothes, and I must get to work at them at once!"

She was nearly frantic with the sudden shearing away of the comfortable time cushion she had allowed herself. Her wits scampered about and fastened upon the one thing she needed—money. "I should need a hundred pounds to get ready for this wedding, especially when it must take place in such a short time. For you must know, sir, that a seamstress will not hurry herself unless the price is worth it."

Mr. Appercott, alarmed at the scope of his prospective bride's ideas of proper expense, said, "Now it's not in reason that you must set all the seamstresses in Yorkshire to work!"

She paid him no heed. "You would not wish me to put Mr. Appercott to the painful task of providing me with my necessary garments, sir? I am persuaded you agree it is not proper."

Her anxious bridegroom said, "Most improper!"

Mr. Eads, a man of compromise, said, "Perhaps not as much as that, Sir Maurice. But the ladies do set store by their fripperies!"

"She looks all right to me," said Sir Maurice.

She had thought that in front of the other men her grandfather would be shamed into capitulating. But remembering the night before, she could believe him capable of any degree of base behavior.

She looked at the men with appeal in her eyes, her hands raised in a gesture of helplessness. "A hundred pounds, out of the question!" said Sir Maurice abruptly. His face closed in with the familiar grim look she knew so well, and she realized that she must temper her demands to the state of his purse. She argued a little more, but only halfheartedly, for she knew she could not get money where there was none.

Mr. Appercott, with a sly look in his eye, making him look more than ever like a ruddy fox, said, "You won't need much in the way of bride clothes! You'll be content to stay at home in the valley, and we're not particular to see fancy clothes. I imagine I'll be able to see that you are suitably occupied!" He dug the lawyer playfully in the ribs, leaving no doubt of his meaning.

Everything was going awry, and her well-laid plan was shattered. She still had one last line of defense. When the pen was handed to her, she held it and pondered for a long time. Upon the gentlemen's urging, she looked up naïvely, "I'm sorry, gentlemen, I wasn't thinking about the contract," she lied. "I was thinking about going to town and getting a few ribbons to refresh some of my own garments. I am sure your *credit*, sir, is excellent in town, and I was thinking just how I would go on, you know."

"Credit, is it?" said Sir Maurice harshly. "Very well, miss." He rummaged in a desk drawer and found a couple of gold coins. "There you are. And that's the last of it."

Without bothering to count the money, knowing she had got all that she could possibly obtain, she wrote her name on the contracts where Mr. Eads told her to.

She excused herself and ran up the stairs. She had no time to lose. She had wanted to take her trunk with her, but the time was so short that she could not. The trunk, with its initials, stood in the attic, where she would have to leave it as a memento to her grandfather, and future generations, that Narcissa Bentham had stayed, if for only a short time, at Bentham Hall. She dragged her bandbox from the bottom of the wardrobe and opened it on the bed. She emptied the drawers of the big chest, one after another, scarcely heeding how she packed the contents into the bandbox. She was in such turmoil that she completely failed to take into account that the items she tried to cram into the small box, meant for only a few ruffles or perhaps a hat, had originally been packed in the trunk.

"Oh!" she cried aloud in disgust and then added, "It really is not the thing to lose my head—not at this juncture! I must *think!*"

Her cogitation resulted in choosing the barest of necessities: comb, brush, nightgown, two morning gowns, and an extra pair of slippers. She surveyed the box, frowning, and then took her night robe out of the wardrobe. She repacked the box twice before the robe could be accommodated, but at last she was, if not satisfied, at least sure she had done the best she could. It now remained to remove the luggage from the house, in secret. The solution came from an unexpected source.

Apparently the ban on service for Narcissa had been lifted, for Jessie appeared in the doorway, armed with an armload of wood for the fire and her pockets full of candles. She stopped abruptly at the sight of Narcissa packing her bag. Narcissa was forced to explain. Once caught up in the excitement of what she considered to be almost as romantic as an elopement, Jessie offered her unswerving assistance. Having fastened the full bandbox, leaving out only her warmest cloak, and a bonnet, Narcissa sent Jessie downstairs to hide the bag in a place where she could pick it up later. Jessie knew exactly the spot. "In the shrubbery, beyond the gate, there's a place I know. Pick it up there, if you will, miss."

Narcissa spared a thought to wondering how Jessie came up so quickly with an appropriate hiding place and then decided she did not want to know. She watched Jessie cross the lawn and disappear down the drive, looking behind her in a way that shrieked aloud of criminal intent.

Mr. Eads and Mr. Appercott stayed for lunch, and fortunately for Narcissa, the conversation was entirely masculine.

The subject of sheep was mercifully forgotten. Narcissa found she had a marked aversion to hearing about creatures named Flora and Daisy while masticating one of their sisters-under-the-wool.

Mr. Eads had a dry tale or two about the Assizes, which had met the previous month in Bleak Barnsley, and his convoluted legalities occupied the conversation for some time.

She had still not considered how much money she had. But it was more thrifty—perhaps she was more Bentham than she thought!—to tuck away as much food as she could before venturing into the unknown. She bent over her plate with single-minded purpose.

After the guests had gone, Sir Maurice, full of satisfaction at his day's work, pinched her cheek playfully and told her, "Sly puss, you got some coins from me, and I suppose you're in a hurry to spend them. I'll be in the study, so don't worry about me if you want to trot off to town."

He disappeared into his study, and before long, sounds issuing from the room told her that his book lay forgotten on his lap, his head no doubt dropped on his chest, and he was sound asleep. Now was the chance she had been waiting for!

She hurried toward the back of the house, pausing only when she saw Mrs. Gibbs alone in the kitchen. She stood in the doorway, not knowing quite what to say. But Mrs. Gibbs understood, and Narcissa was sure Jessie had explained everything to her. Mrs. Gibbs came over, dropped a curtsy, and said, "We'll miss you, miss."

It was all that she could say, but it was satisfactorily vague, for she would not put Mrs. Gibbs in the position of knowing her plans, in case Sir Maurice questioned her, as she was sure he would. Mrs. Gibbs's remark could apply equally to Mr. Appercott carrying Narcissa off as his bride or, as the case might be, Narcissa's escape from the house.

Suddenly, feeling that Mrs. Gibbs was the only friend she had here, she threw her arms around that startled lady and hugged her. Mrs. Gibbs, straightening her cap, could only say, "Bless you, miss. Now best hurry!"

Narcissa took her advice and hastened across the yard, to reach the drive. She hurried down the drive, the first bend taking her out of sight of the house, and she made her way to the crumbling gates. Retrieving her bandbox, exactly where Jessie had said she would find it, she swung it by its strap as she stepped out smartly on the road to town, to take the coach to Scarborough.

9

The Batley agent for the stagecoach company frowned at her small store of shillings and then without comment gave her a ticket. At that moment the horn sounded, heralding the approach of the coach, and hurriedly she tucked the scrap of paper carefully inside her reticule and, with her last penny, bought a plain bun for her supper.

She was penniless, yet she felt exhilarated. She was free, free of that deteriorating house, rid of the demands of her grandfather, and delivered from the vulgar winkings and playful manner of dreadful Lucius Appercott.

The coach was crowded, and she was squeezed into one corner. Holding her bandbox on her lap, she made herself small. However, her companions, after one look at her, decided to ignore her. She was clearly of a quality that did not usually ride on coaches, and they did not know quite what to make of her. She herself, thinking only of how she made her escape, wore a serene smile on her face and was almost unaware of the jostling discomfort.

Every turn of the wheel took her mercifully farther away from the home of her ancestors. Her success in escaping gave breath to unremitting optimism for the future. Her rising spirits sustained her as she planned her approach to the Hollands. There was no real reason why the Holland family should ignore her, for her mother's fault was not hers. She comforted herself with the idea that her letter to them must have gone astray. At any rate, they could in all decency at least give her lodging for the night. They might even, if only to be rid of her, manage some form of employment for her, as a governess, a companion, or whatever.

Even her experience with Sir Maurice, who had expected to get more than he gave, did not dampen her mood. She had not realized how much she loathed the idea of marrying Mr. Appercott until the real danger was over. Now she felt as free as a bird, and if she had been able to fly, she felt buoyant enough to lift off the ground.

But one does not travel far in the company of others, so close that their luggage spills over to one's own lap, without paying attention to them. Especially startling to her was the talk that developed soon of highwaymen.

The man opposite her, riding backward, was a thin wisp of a man, with a clerical collar. It developed that he was curate of some obscure parish on the moors, and it spoke well for his faith in his Creator that he trusted himself to this stagecoach. The vehicle was badly sprung; the roads were increasingly worse; the weather was getting worse by the mile. The poor horses were struggling through the mire that the rains of the last week had produced in the ruts. It had just begun to rain again, with abandon, hurling waves of water against the coach. A farmer and his wife, beside Narcissa, were both well fed and comfortably expansive, but they sadly crowded her. Opposite, next to the curate, sat a sinister-looking man, with thin lips and a cold look in his eye. Narcissa fancied that when the word "highwayman" was mentioned, he looked knowing, and she remembered that sometimes highwaymen rode on the coaches to find out who had enough money to make a robbery worthwhile.

There was little enough money apparent in this coach, so Narcissa silently rebuked her overactive imagination and settled down. Nonetheless, she was greatly relieved when the silent man with the threatening—so she thought—expression jumped down at a small wayside inn and vanished into the darkening storm.

The sixth inside passenger was a gangly youth, still in the pimply age. He fixed his eyes owlishly on her and regarded her with an unwinking stare.

The route for this secondary coach line ran almost due east from Batley, through Selby, on to Beverley and Great Driffield, where she believed she must change coaches for Scarborough. It seemed a roundabout way, but the fare was cheaper than on the mail coach line, and besides, this coach left Batley in the afternoon. Had she waited for the mail coach, she would have run a real danger of being overtaken by Sir Maurice. The appeal of this coach was quite simply the fact that it had been the first means of getting out of town.

An especially severe rut threw the coach sideways, and she fell against her neighbor, the farmer's wife. She murmured apology, but the goodwife said with a comfortable chuckle, "Aye, no harm done. A good thing I'm better padded than the seat, hey?"

Her husband, now that the ice had been broken, joined the conversation. "Weather's getting worse, and this isn't the end of the mud, I'll be bound. Wouldn't be surprised a-tall if we didn't get mired afore we got there."

"Mired?" echoed Narcissa. "Oh, no!"

"Hear the rain?" said the curate, clearing his throat as for an impressive pronouncement. "I judge that the roads may become impassable. The rain, you see, is heavy."

It was indeed. The heavy rain drummed deafeningly against the wooden panels of the coach. The leather curtains were not proof against the weather, for a trickle of water descended from the corner of the window, and Narcissa felt the icy wetness against her knee.

The curate frowned. "It was my understanding that the farmers of the area were to work on the roads, keep them passable, but surely not a shovel of dirt has been turned—at least this year."

He eyed the farmer opposite him with disfavor. The farmer returned the cleric's glare with interest. "Think all we got to do is run out every time it rains and put in a day's work on the road? It's something different, I can tell you, to get in the crops and see to the lambing—"

Narcissa thought for a hysterical moment that she had fallen asleep and begun to dream about Mr. Appercott's precious ewes. But the farmer's wife nudged her helpmate fiercely, and quiet, except for the thunderous rain, ruled once more.

"Besides," chortled the farmer, intent upon one last word to show he was not under the cat's foot, "such bad roads keep the highwaymen at home, right?"

The afternoon wore on, and Narcissa was not even conscious of being hungry. The weather was worsening.

The farmer and his wife, when the coach stopped at a crossroads, piled out with their baskets and their rugs and were met by a farm cart. Eventually, down the road a few miles, the timid curate got off, visibly thanking Providence for having delivered him thus far, and she was left alone with the gangly youth, who immediately moved to ride forward, next to her. He tried to make conversation; but her replies were short, and disappointed, he got out at the next crossroads.

In the early evening, when it was nearly dark, the coach topped a rise and came to a halt. She pulled the leather curtain aside, and thrust her head out of the window. She called up to the coachman. "What's the trouble?"

He said, "This is as far as you go."

"But I'm going to Scarborough! Surely we're not there yet."

The coachman growled, "Look at your ticket, miss. Only to Penton Crossroads."

The scrap of paper in her reticule clearly read "PENTON CROSSROADS." The coach had come in, she recollected, just as she had received the ticket, and she had foolishly forgotten to look at it as she turned away from the ticket agent.

"How much did you pay?" demanded the coachman. She told him, and he nodded wisely. "That's the mixup, miss. That is the fare from Batley to Penton. I'll take you to Scarborough for another seven shillings."

Seven shillings! He might as well have asked her for as many guineas. "I don't have it!" she said, panic sounding along the edge of her voice. "What will I ever do?" she cried out.

The coachman was sympathetic, but adamant. "Isn't there anybody you know?" he demanded.

"In Scarborough," she answered. "If you would carry me there, I could ask my—my family to pay you."

"Company'd kill me," he said briefly.

"This is a lonely crossroads, and who knows what may happen to me?"

He took off his cap and scratched his head. "Aye, it *is* lonely, but what happens to you won't be a patch of what happens to me if the company finds out I let you ride free."

Hope lit her eyes, and she promised, "I wouldn't tell anyone!"

The coachman considered further but finally decided. "But you could be a spotter for the company, and then I'd be in for it. No, miss, down you get!"

Her sense of fairness admitted that the driver was justified in his fears. But she found it hard to be impartial as she watched the red lights at the rear of the coach dwindle into nothingness in the direction of Scarborough. Her eyes streamed with rain or tears—she was not sure which—and she repressed a strong impulse to sit down by the side of the road and howl like a deserted puppy.

The thought came to her that just now she could be sitting in her grandfather's parlor, opposite her robust suitor, sipping hot tea. "I don't regret it for a moment!" she said aloud, and somehow the sound of her own voice brought a return of her resolution.

She bent to shake out her sodden skirts. If she rucked them up so that they would not slap against her boots, she could walk more easily. It was imperative that she move away from the storm-scoured rise where the two roads met.

The clouds had come down, relieved of their rain, and became swirling, writhing fog. The wind from the east, directly from the North Sea, was brisk and heavily salt-laden, briny to the tongue.

The fog struggled valiantly against the constantly blowing wind, and if there ever was a place that deserved the description "bleak," this was it!

She began to fear that she must spend the night on the road, on foot. Any place would be better than where she stood, her skirts whipping wetly around her ankles. She picked up her bandbox, thankfully remembering she did not have the trunk. She might have to walk all the way to Scarborough!

Tears rolled down her cheeks, unbidden, mingling with the rain. Her situation was unpleasant at the very least and perilous in all likelihood. Even her cold room at Bentham Hall, with no fire in the grate and the impossible prospect of Mr. Appercott, was not so bad as this, she reflected, but only for a moment. *Nothing* was worse than Mr. Appercott and his eagerly twitching fingers and his lickerish eyes!

Luck had deserted her—for the present. But hope stayed with her, and she believed it was quite possible that something would turn up. Just now she would look with heartfelt gratitude upon a haystack—dry on the inside!

Suddenly she became aware of the sound of wheels and horses' hooves, galloping from the west, at speed. She hesitated, fearing the arrival of someone with criminal intent. Then she concluded that no felon ever approached his victim in such an overt, noisy fashion.

Perhaps she could beg a ride if the driver was going to Scarborough. Upon reflection, she would accept a ride to any destination—any at all.

The vehicle drew nearer and finally came into view. The driver, peering through the gloom, drove up to her and leaped to the ground. By the lantern he held, she could see that he was in livery. He touched his cap deferentially and said, "I'm Dawson, miss."

"D-awson," she repeated idiotically.

"Sorry, miss, the weather got bad suddenly, and I was delayed."

"The storm was certainly severe," she murmured, hoping that some sense would soon emerge from his odd encounter.

To her great surprise he swung her bandbox into the boot of the pony cart. Paralyzed with surprise, she watched him deftly rope the small box securely into place, and then he turned to her.

"If you are ready, miss?" he suggested. "We have a long way to go, and we had best start."

Clearly he thought she was someone else, she decided, but if that someone whom he expected was supposed to arrive on the stage, she hadn't come. It took only a moment for her to realize that if the expected person had not come, and there was no other coach along tonight, somewhere there waited a warm, dry bed and possibly something to eat. She had hopes even of a hot cup of tea. It would be a great shame to let a dry bed and hot tea go to waste!

Without further ado, Narcissa climbed up into the cart next to the groom.

10

They turned back toward the way he had come and left the crossroads behind them. She was clearly an expected guest and—she deduced from Dawson's puzzled stare when he saw she had only a small piece of hand luggage—had been invited for a protracted stay.

But if she were expected, then she would arrive, and at that time her hostess would see the mistake. But perhaps she would not be thrown out into the stormy night, and any decent householder would give her at least a cup of tea and a morsel of food.

It would all be straightened out. She surely could not fault Providence for its arrangements for the night!

She longed for arrival at their destination. Her skirts were soaking wet and were clammy around her legs; but the groom had tucked a fur rug around her knees, and the warmth was more than welcome.

Dawson whipped up his horse, and they fairly flew over the ground. He explained briefly, "I want to get home before dark."

Narcissa thought it was already dark enough. The man must have eyes like a cat to see ahead of him. But apparently the road was well known to him, for he never slackened pace.

Narcissa, finding that the groom was not talkative and indeed not wishing to distract his attention from his driving, sank into reflection. It had been a long day. She had signed legal contracts, and made her desperate escape, and suffered the uncomfortable coach ride which had done little to add to her comfort. But she could not help marveling at the ways of Providence, which had plucked her out of an impossible situation, removing her deftly from the dark and the storm and setting her in motion in a pony cart. While the pony cart was regrettably open, and she spared a thought

66

that Providence could have managed a closed traveling coach, yet she was more than grateful. Anything, even an open pony cart in the wind and rain, was better than standing at the crossroads or, even worse, walking along the road to Scarborough.

Her spirits began to rise. They traveled for a long time before the groom offered another comment. Instead of clarifying the situation, his words only served to deepen the mystery. "Her Ladyship will be anxious."

"Anxious?" It was all Narcissa could manage.

The groom said, "The Countess."

When Narcissa said nothing, the groom added, "The dowager. Countess of Hapworth."

Narcissa asked, "The dowager Countess?"

But it was the wrong question. The groom eyed her suspiciously. She could feel his glance in the dark. She must not give herself away. If she was supposed to know who the Countess was, so be it. She would have to wait until she arrived to discover more. But if she did know to whose house she was going, there was still one more question in her mind. Who was she herself supposed to be? No doubt Lady Hapworth would inform her!

Her father's training stood her in good stead. His motto was: Bad luck always turns better. And it always had, until the last. But he seemed to ignore all his life the other side of the coin—that good luck could turn bad. Apparently he had taken his luck with him when he died, and she had none of her own.

The constant motion of the cart and the warmth, damp though it was, stealing up from the fur rug made her drowsy. Snatches of her life with her father in Europe flitted before her eyes, so quickly gone that she could not grasp them. She was half asleep, feeling that she had been riding in a moving vehicle for most of her life.

But eventually, as all things do, the drive came to an end. The cart slowed and turned between mammoth gates onto a gravel drive. They traveled quite a distance before the lights of the house appeared.

She hoped the house was better kept than the one she had quitted that morning, but at this point four walls and a roof would be sufficient. At last they left the wooded part of the park and emerged onto the broad sweep before the house. Broad steps led up to the entrance. The door was thrown open, and light streamed out across the steps. The house must be large, for she could discern two sets of windows on each side of the big double doors.

A footman stood smartly beside the door, demeanor of the well trained, and the butler, waiting for her to enter the foyer, suggested to her that this was the residence of a person of some consequence.

The sudden light from the many wax tapers blinded her—how Sir Maurice would have sputtered at the prodigality of candles! The butler showed her through a door along the sidewall of the entry and closed it firmly behind her.

In moments she would be unmasked as an unbidden guest. But surely it was too late to be returned to the crossroads whence she had come!

The room into which Narcissa was ushered was curiously furnished. It always took several years for the latest fashion, in furniture or in dress, to reach the farthest shires, and once arrived, it lingered inordinately long. This small salon had been caught up in the wave of Egyptian influence following Napoleon's conquest of Egypt and his sponsorship of a book, by his aide Denon, called *Voyage into Upper and Lower Egypt*.

Everywhere her glance traveled it fell upon lotuses and tables supported by sphinxes. Apparently Lady Hapworth did nothing by halves.

Her hostess sat in a chair in the far corner of the room. Her voice was sharp as she ordered, "Come here to me."

"Yes, Lady Hapworth," Narcissa murmured demurely, and obediently advanced to stand before the Countess.

The Countess, far from being an antique dowager, was a woman of no more than middle years. Her hair was jet black, owing much to artifice, and arranged with curls in front and over her ears. Her nose was a great beak, and her eyes, black as raisins, were lively. Her mouth was firm, indicating a woman of decision and resolution. Narcissa felt her spirits slipping into her shoes. For she was not the person that the dowager Countess expected, nor did she know exactly who she was supposed to be.

The Countess said, with a short laugh, "You don't look like Hester Adams!"

Well, at least, Narcissa thought, now she knew her name. She began to offer an apology, but the Countess paid no heed. "I like to have names match people, don't you?"

Narcissa could think of nothing to say. The Countess continued. "Sorry if I hurt your feelings, but you don't look like a Hester. But I suppose that will have to do, if your mother thought it appropriate."

Narcissa wished she knew more about Hester Adams. The Countess said, "Did you have a long trip?"

Narcissa answered cagily, "The weather was very bad, but otherwise, it didn't seem long."

The Countess nodded sharply and said, "It's so unsatisfactory to interview by mail. I must say you're better than I thought from your letter."

At least the Countess had never laid eyes on Hester Adams, Narcissa thought with thankfulness. She was once again glad that her trunk, with the initials N. B. still reposed at Bentham Hall. She would be hard put to explain N. B. on a trunk that was supposed to belong to Hester Adams!

The Countess scrutinized Narcissa, unnervingly, through half-closed lids. Suddenly she said, "You have a strong resemblance to somebody I know. But I can't think who. You said in your letter that you had no relatives. Is that true?"

Narcissa lied, "Yes." But it was not quite an untruth, for practically speaking, both the Benthams and the Hollands were no part of her life.

"Are you sure? Are you a long-lost heiress?"

Narcissa shook her head. The Countess pursued. "You are obviously gently born. Are you in any trouble? Perhaps somebody is pursuing you? Are we to expect someone hammering at the door in the night, demanding your return?"

Narcissa forced a laugh. "No, Lady Hapworth, no one is chasing me." She laughed. "I'm not the heroine of a Gothic novel."

The Countess smiled slightly. Dismissing that subject, she said, "You will meet your charge in the morning. We keep early hours here in the country, and I'll bid you a good-night. If you will ring, Mrs. Roy will take you upstairs."

The interview was over. Narcissa had not been thrown out into the storm. A comfortable-looking housekeeper appeared in the hall and introduced herself as Mrs. Roy. Narcissa smiled inwardly at the thought of her grandfather as she followed Mrs. Roy up the broad, carpeted stairs to the upper floor. Sir Maurice would hardly believe that she could have fallen upon such a happy event. By no stretch of the imagination could he imagine her in a house of such elegance. She did not know precisely where she was, but she did know that she had spoken only the truth to the Countess when she said that no one was pursuing her. Sir Maurice would not be apt to spend money to send someone to track her down. She was safe from him.

Narcissa gave little thought to the details of the room to which she was shown. It was enough that it was warm, the bed appeared soft and clean, and a servant girl was passing a warming pan between the sheets. A fire crackled in the grate, and a scuttle full of wood stood on the hearth.

Her bandbox had been unpacked, her brushes laid out on the dresser, and the pale green velvet chair had been drawn invitingly close to the fire.

"Here's Kitty, you are to ask her for anything you wish, Miss Adams. Perhaps after your drive you would be glad of a glass of milk and a macaroon?"

Narcissa would. "I have had little since noon," she confided, "and a glass of milk sounds most welcome."

Mrs. Roy clucked. "Not since noon? Those coach people are regular slavers, ain't they? I'll send you up a tray directly. What a shame! Nothing to eat all day! Well, in this house no one ever goes hungry, I promise you!"

She trotted briskly to the door, but stopped short. "Those clothes are wet, miss. Best take them off, and Kitty will lay out your robe. You won't want to catch your death!"

She was gone, and Kitty set the warming pan aside. Narcissa's robe and slippers were already spread before the fire to warm. Kitty brought a thick towel. Narcissa divested herself of her wet clinging garments as in a dream. She wondered whether she had unknowingly found a haystack on the road to Scarborough and fallen asleep into a marvelous fantasy world. If so, it was remarkably real. She could feel the heat of the fire, she could welcome the comforting feel of the soft flannel robe, and just as she sank into the deeply cushioned chair, she became aware of tantalizing aromas from the tray that Mrs. Roy brought.

Haystack or no—this moment was pure heaven!

After she had placed the empty tray on a table in the hall, she returned to the fire and sat looking into the flames for a long time. The events of the day seemed to have taken a week, and she was wakeful.

She could almost hear her father's voice saying to her, "The golden lady has come around, as I knew she would." He spoke of luck as the golden lady when he was pleased with her. Perhaps, for once, he was right. She could not help wondering about the real Hester Adams. Who was she, and what was to be her position in this household? The Countess had spoken of her charge, so it seemed clear that Narcissa was to be a governess.

But the morrow would take care of itself, she reflected. She had been miraculously rescued from a situation that was fraught with dire possibilities, and Lucius Appercott would not trouble her dreams tonight.

She rose and stretched, suddenly exceedingly weary. The rain whispered against the window, a soft lullaby, and Narcissa, with an unspoken prayer of gratitude on her lips, climbed into bed and was instantly asleep.

When she opened her eyes, she was looking into a pair of dark eyes, almost as dark as the Countess's, in a pleasant face. For one wild moment Narcissa could not think where she was.

"You're awake! Oh, good! I couldn't wait to see you!" The vision had a sweet voice and a mischievous dimple high on one cheek. But her manners, so Narcissa thought, were sadly lacking. She struggled to set up. "Who are you?"

"Dear Hester, may I call you Hester? It seems so strict to say Miss Adams. If I didn't like you, I would call you Miss Adams. I think you're going to be the greatest friend I ever had. I want to call you Hester."

Chattering artlessly, she soon told Narcissa all that she needed to know. Isabella Gaines was the daughter of the Countess. She was sixteen, going on seventeen, and dear Hester's job was not so much governess as chaperone.

Narcissa wondered wildly what kinds of standards existed in the wilds of Yorkshire that a girl of twenty was considered a proper chaperone to one of sixteen. She might not be a governess, but she could see easily that her first task was to establish some kind of control.

"I do wonder at you," said Narcissa pleasantly, "not to knock at a door before you enter."

Bella was not dismayed. "Oh, I did, but you didn't answer. And I was so anxious to see you. My name is Isabella Gaines. My friends call me Bella. Do say you'll be my friend, for I truly need one. Only for just a little while, you know."

Narcissa could echo that, but her reasons were not Bella's. She inquired further, "Do you think I will not stay?"

Bella said with great good humor, "Of course you won't."

Narcissa took a deep breath and probed. "I presume you mean to rout me from what you say. Is this your usual habit with companions?"

Bella confided artlessly, "I never had a companion before. But I was never one to send governesses away. I had one governess all my life. But she's gone now, of course. For I am much too old, you must know, for the schoolroom. But you will not stay long, for a married lady does not need a companion."

"Married? At sixteen?"

"I'm almost eighteen. Or at least, my birthday was last month and I was seventeen. Truly grown up, you know, and—Hester, you don't look a *bit* like what I expected."

Narcissa could easily believe her. "What did you expect?"

"That letter. Did you have someone else write it? The letter was so—so *commonplace*! There, I'm sorry if I've hurt your feelings, for I wouldn't mean to do so for the world. But it is true, just the same."

Narcissa was amused. "Then why did your mother send for—Hester Adams?"

"Because," said Bella with devastating frankness, "no one else answered her advertisement. And she said, *anyone* is better than nobody, for I must have someone to go with me when I shop and all those things, and dear Aunt Lavinia is not able. Besides, she's so *old-fashioned!*"

Narcissa had the strong feeling that events and information were getting away from her. She said, "You know, I would be the better for a cup of tea. Is there such a thing in this household?"

Bella said airily, "Oh, yes, indeed, and Kitty has gone to get it. She'll be up in a moment."

Narcissa leaned back against the soft pillows, pulling the comforter up around her shoulders, and examined her charge. Suddenly she realized she was acting as though she were planning to stay here. Such a course did not appeal to her sense of honesty, but it was remarkably attractive to her sense of self-preservation. She decided not to make a decision now but to wait until she saw what happened next.

"Who else is in the household?" she asked curiously.

The answer came, unexpectedly, in the form of a scratch at the door. Miss Lavinia Pinkney entered. She was a plump, very sweet, vague lady, who informed Narcissa that she herself was in charge of the household. Kitty followed her with a cup of hot tea. Narcissa, sipping the strong brew gratefully, prepared to watch Miss Pinkney deal with Bella.

"Bella, my dear, I wonder that you haven't ordered breakfast for Miss Adams. What will she think of this household? It is not the usual thing, of course, for everyone to have breakfast in bed, for it is much too much to ask the maids to do, although they are well enough paid so that one should not hesitate to ask them to do anything. But of course, one does," she concluded vaguely. She glanced around her, and Narcissa had the sudden impression that for all her vagueness, very little escaped the keen eye of Miss Lavinia Pinkney.

"I can quite easily come downstairs," offered Narcissa.

"Not at all," said Miss Lavinia. "Yesterday was a dreadful day, and I am sure you must be soaked to the skin—at least last night you were, and it can't be healthful to leave one's bed quite so early." Miss Lavinia cocked her head, like a small wren. "You don't look like your letter."

Narcissa laughed. "So I have been told."

Miss Pinkney was incapable of holding her tongue. "I want to assure you, Miss Adams—or may I call you Hester?—that we do have a well-run household, and if only Bella would get off the bed, I'm sure you can't like to have her sitting at the foot of the bed, Miss Adams, she jiggles the tea, and, Bella, run down stairs or pull the bell and send for breakfast for Miss Adams, I'm sure she must be starved." Narcissa agreed heartily, if silently. With one hand Miss Pinkney had disposed of Bella and routed Kitty. Now she brought up a chair to sit near Narcissa. She said, "I am sure you will want to get dressed, and I shall send up a maid to help if you wish. No, I see you don't want one. You will be mystified at young Bella's behavior, but she is used to having her own way, sad to say. I do hope it does not extend beyond the bounds of proper behavior, for you must know she is not a bad girl, but sadly headstrong. Her brother, the young Earl, he was a posthumous child, you know, and my sister has been hard put to rear him as befits his station in life. But his tutor seems all right, I suppose, although—but then, if I don't like him, I am sure that it is my fault, you know."

Taking advantage of a momentary slowing in the gentle flow of chatter, Narcissa asked, "How old is the Earl?"

"Merely five. He is so timid that I wonder at the ways of Providence, you know, to give the daughter all the energy and resourcefulness that should by rights belong to a boy. But it is not for us to question, of course. But it must not daunt you, dear Hester, for you will find us a jolly household. Even Rupert."

Miss Pinkney fell silent for a while, for so long Narcissa was moved to prod her gently. "Rupert is the tutor?"

Miss Pinkney favored her with a smile that was vague and sweet, but the look in her eyes was far sharper than her manner. "Oh, no, no, not at all. Rupert Elyot. He is our neighbor, you know, the nephew of the Marquess of Carraford, and I must say to you, Hester, that I am gravely uneasy about young Rupert. *Very* uneasy."

11

Narcissa, over her hearty breakfast, pondered upon what she had learned. Young Bella was in love with Rupert Elyot, the nephew of the Marquess of Carraford, whose lands adjoined the Gaines family holdings. And Isabella herself had confided that she expected soon to be married.

The Marquess of Carraford, mused Narcissa—the man who had pocketed her carriage and horses in Switzerland. A man whose luck had been rising as her father's golden lady had deserted him.

It remained to be seen whether the Marquess had an opinion on his nephew's marriage. She herself would take great pleasure in thwarting Carraford's desires, and the jest would be even more enjoyable were he never to know why!

Leaning back on her pillows and munching toast reflectively, she turned to more immediate concerns. Yesterday at this time she had not yet signed the marriage contracts. She had certainly packed a great deal into the past twenty-four hours. She realized now that she could have dealt with the bridegroom much more easily, by simply feigning illness. Mr. Appercott had a fanatic interest in a healthy wife, for reasons that were only too clear. If she had pretended a series of headaches, Mr. Appercott would doubtless have cried off. But then Sir Maurice, hopelessly in debt to Mr. Appercott, would have made life at Bentham Hall impossible for her.

She took a third buttered scone from the plate and was glad that invention had failed her. Had she seen any other way out, she would not now be ensconced in such luxury. She knew she should confess to the Countess that she was not Hester Adams, but on the other hand, if the Countess needed a Hester Adams, there was none other to take her place.

Narcissa made her way down the broad stairs and into the entrance hall. She hesitated, not knowing her way around, but Jebb, the footman, came to her rescue.

"Miss, Her Ladyship has been asking for you," he said, so shyly that she could hardly hear his voice.

"Oh, I hope she hasn't been waiting too long!" she exclaimed. "Where will I find her, please?"

Jebb, already beet-red, made a strangling sound in his throat and pointed to a door opposite to the Egyptian salon. Amused, Narcissa smiled at him and went to present herself to her employer.

After a word or two of greeting, the Countess came to the point.

"My daughter has the expectation of forming an alliance with one of the great families of the region," explained the Countess, "and I realize—now, my dear, this is a family secret, may I count upon your discretion?"

Narcissa nodded.

But the Countess did not continue at once. She fidgeted with the papers on her desk and finally, not meeting Narcissa's eyes, said, "Well, I see I must. Our name was Pinkney, before I had the good fortune to marry the Earl. He wasn't the Earl then, of course. Lavinia is my younger sister, you know. Our father was in trade, in Liverpool, and there was a great stir when my dear husband told his family he was intending to marry me. Not but what they weren't glad enough of the money," she added sourly. "It took all my dowry to bring the house here into a place fit to live in. But . . . they let Edward marry beneath them, so they said, because there was such a remote chance that he would ever come into the title."

She lapsed into a reminiscent silence, before she continued in an altered voice. "But there it was—a combination of accidents and illnesses that was unbelievable. And here I am, Albinia Pinkney Gaines, Countess of Hapworth, and knowing no more about how to go on than a nodcock."

Narcissa murmured what she hoped was an appropriately sympathetic word. "So that is what you are to do," said the Countess. "Get Bella up to the mark." She eyed Narcissa doubtfully. "I had little hope of you after that letter, but I thought at least I would give you a chance. I was agreeably surprised when you came."

Narcissa was moved to protest. "It seems to me that Miss Gaines has very pretty manners—"

The Countess interrupted. "It's going to take a little more than that, I am afraid. Young Rupert is all right, and he loves my Bella. But that uncle of his is high in the instep, and I pray every night that he stays in France or wherever until we have it all arranged. Bella is fixed on young Rupert, and I'm bound she should have what she wants."

The interview was over after a few more words, and Narcissa had time to reflect upon the enormous task set for her. She could not possibly do it, she thought, and then in a moment her optimism came to the fore, and she decided to give it a try at least. She owed the Countess something, and in truth Lady Hapworth's naïve confession beguiled her. She was to her surprise becoming a great partisan of the Countess and her ambitious plans. It remained to be seen what Bella's view of her future was.

Bella was standing at the door of the morning room. She was wearing a cloak of a deep blue that matched her eyes and dangled a bonnet by its strings.

Narcissa looked at her with approval. She was really a very pretty girl, Narcissa thought. She said, "I'm so glad I found you. I was going to ask you to show me the grounds."

To her surprise Bella seemed reluctant, yet Narcissa was sure she was about to go out herself.

Narcissa had more than a suspicion that Bella had been badly spoiled, and she would have to walk warily and establish her authority step by step. She ignored Bella's hesitation.

When Bella agreed, and they stepped from the open door of the morning room together, Narcissa had her first view of Hapworth Hall by daylight. The house itself, truly very large, stood on top of a rise that she suspected might have been artificial, so perfectly was it formed. But the great trees around it, the ancient beeches and oaks, gave the lie to that idea. They had certainly not been uprooted within the memory of man.

They strolled across the grounds, into the rose

garden, along the edge of what might some day be an ornamental water, and they arrived at the bottom of the hill. There was a small coppice of poplars, forming a charming contrast with the stately trees that surrounded the house itself. These were hardly more than saplings. Their leaves fluttered in the slightest breeze, giving an impression of youth and innocence. It was by chance they arrived there, Narcissa thought at first, until she discovered a young man already standing among the trees. Bella was curiously nervous, glancing sidelong at Narcissa, and Narcissa realized that Bella had made several subtle attempts to draw her back to the house. The young man had not been waiting there by chance. And if Narcissa were not mistaken, this must be Rupert Elyot. Bella introduced him, adding at the end, "You may as well know it, Hester. I am determined to marry Rupert. We are in love, and nothing can stop us."

Rupert came to stand beside Bella and held her hand.

Narcissa tried for a light touch. "You look as though you were standing before the vicar at this moment." She let her eyes drop obviously to the joined hands, and Rupert dropped Bella's hand as if it were hot. He stepped aside, leaving a perceptible space between the two, and Bella looked at him reproachfully.

Narcissa continued. "I wonder that your mother thought it necessary to engage a chaperone when your wedding is all but announced."

Her voice, ending on a rising note, compelled Bella to answer.

"She doesn't know it yet, nor does Rupert's uncle."

Narcissa, feeling immeasurably old, turned to Rupert with lifted eyebrows. "Your uncle?"

"Uncle John is the Marquess of Carraford, but he doesn't care a fig for me. I'm going to marry Bella, no matter what he says!"

"Has he refused permission?"

Disconcerted, Rupert glanced at his feet. "I haven't written him."

Bella broke in. "You *must* help us, Hester. If you could talk to my mother and gain her permission, then we can write to Rupert's uncle!"

Narcissa made a hasty revision in her thoughts. Apparently the girl did not know her mother was heart and soul on her side. Only the Marquess was the unknown quantity.

"Must your uncle give his permission?" ventured Narcissa, feeling her way.

"He is my trustee, and the title and fortune will be mine, for he has no heirs. Nor is he likely to, for you know, he shows no intention of marrying."

"But he cannot keep you from marrying?"

"When I am twenty-five, I am my own man. But until then—"

Bella broke in swiftly. "But you have your mother's house and her estate! We would be able to get along until you come of age!"

Narcissa said gently, "But it would not do, you know, to defy Rupert's guardian when a little patience would serve best."

Bella looked at her chaperone with transparent emotion. "But I *love* him!"

It was time for a firm hand. Narcissa said, "Love or no, this clandestine meeting in the shrubbery is most *common*, and it will not do. Mr. Elyot, I would expect you to know better. Come, Bella. We must return to the house."

Bella and Rupert began to expostulate. Narcissa lifted a quelling eyebrow. "It will not do to discuss this in the shrubbery either," she pointed out. "Mr. Elyot, I should inform you that Bella will not be meeting you in such a really furtive manner again."

She devoutly hoped that she was speaking only the truth. She did not see, noting Bella's determined chin, that she could stop her in any way short of force. It was really a serious matter, this surreptitious meeting, far from the house, out of sight of Bella's mother. If this were to be anything but a juvenile escapade, the couple must have the backing of both families, else it would go ill for them. Narcissa had her own parents to serve as examples for her. It had been an unhappy event when Narcissa's parents ran away and were married. She suddenly felt immeasurably older than the rebellious couple before her. She turned to Rupert and said kindly, "Mr. Elyot, I strongly recommend that you come to terms with your uncle, whatever they might be.

And present yourself to the Countess, and for goodness' sake, have a little decorum about this."

Rupert stepped forward, throwing his hands out in desperate appeal. "The world says my uncle is wicked, and they certainly ought to know, for I don't see him at all. He doesn't care what I do. He cares about nothing but himself. He hasn't been here in Yorkshire for ten years, and I've had only tutors and trustees since then. My uncle is my main trustee; but he turned me over to his attorney, and I haven't seen him since."

Narcissa was appalled, but she rallied enough to say, "You are his only nephew? He must have some feeling."

Rupert said, "I will show you whether he cares or not." She waited, an inquiring look on her face. "I'll write to him at once."

Narcissa said, "I urgently suggest that you do write to him. But for heaven's sake, stop behaving like a pair of village bumpkins!"

She kept her grip firmly upon Bella's arm and steered her resolutely out of the coppice and across the lawn toward the house. Bella, predictably, was on the verge of strong hysterics, giving way to ominous sobbing, a catch in her throat, and certain unmistakable signs of tears to come.

Narcissa dealt with her charge by the simple method of ignoring her. "I must tell your mother about this clandestine meeting, you know, Bella."

Bella cried out, "Oh, please, Hester, please don't! You must know that I have been used to doing very much as I please, but that was before you came. I can see that you are right, for you tell me nothing I didn't already know. Even though I didn't want to admit it, I know I was wrong to see Rupert. Now that you're here and you're taking our side, I won't do it again. Only don't tell Mama, for she will not understand."

Narcissa reflected that there was much truth in what Bella said. From a distance she saw the young Earl and his tutor approaching the house from a different direction. She had only a moment or two to answer Bella's plea and decide what she would do. She made a quick decision. "All right, but I will not make any promises about the next time."

Bella said, tearfully grateful, "Oh, there won't be a next time, Hester. You have my word on that."

Narcissa hoped that was enough. She knew the girl was beguiling and wayward. She was uneasy lest she herself had fallen victim to Bella's charm.

12

The small Earl William, as he approached across the lawn, his tutor trailing after him, held a small wooden sword in his hand and apparently conceived himself in the role of a Crusader. He darted and lunged, swishing his sword manfully across the throat of an imaginary foe and making warlike sounds as he came.

"Such sharp swordplay!" she said, congratulating the small boy as he neared. Suddenly the ferocious Crusader, straddling with stiff legs his imaginary destrier, turned into an appealing small boy.

He gazed earnestly at her. "Do you think so, Miss Adams? Mr. Wayne tells me all the knights are gone and there aren't any more Crusades."

Narcissa shot a sharp glance of disapproval at Charles Wayne. "There are always brave men," she told the boy. "And I know you will be as brave as—as King Richard himself!"

William's face glowed. Narcissa realized she had won his complete devotion. With the intention of turning his thoughts into more modern channels, she went on, "Did you know that you can still see the seaports in Italy where the brave knights set sail for the Holy Land?"

"Really? Mr. Wayne didn't tell me that!" The boy took her hand confidingly. "What does it look like?"

"Well, the Grand Canal—a sort of big river, you know—winds through the city." She described the letter *S* with one hand, to illustrate.

"How do you get across the river?" he demanded practically.

"The Rialto bridge," she informed him. "It's made out of white marble. But you would like the people—they're dressed in such bright colors. There are rope dancers, and jugglers—"

She broke off when she caught Charles Wayne's

speculative eyes on her. She finished lamely, "Someday you'll go to see it, I know you will."

Charles said in a low voice, as the Earl picked up his sword again and described fierce circles in the air, "You must have seen Venice yourself—I hadn't thought a governess would be so well traveled."

She had nearly given herself away. But she retorted tartly, "It's all in books, you know. Or perhaps you don't spend much time reading?"

He was a very poor tutor, she concluded. Certainly, if he stayed long at Hapworth, he would repress young William's exuberance and turn him into a pedestrian, narrow-minded young man, and that would truly be a shame.

She glanced at Bella. The girl might have been alone in the world, for all the attention she paid to her companions.

Charles Wayne might not be up-to-date on his teaching. But Narcissa reflected with a sinking feeling that neither was she.

She longed, as she entered the house with Bella, for counsel from Dilly. Dilly would know exactly what to do with a wayward girl like Bella, and sometimes, especially in the last fifteen minutes, Narcissa had the odd feeling that she spoke with Dilly's voice.

Narcissa had promised not to tell the Countess about the meeting in the coppice. The meeting just past, she guessed, was one of a long series, for the two undoubtedly knew each other well. And this was another thing that bothered Narcissa.

Rupert was far too familiar with Bella for her liking. She was reminded forcefully of the old story of the babes in the woods. She had such a pair on her hands.

Certainly Rupert could do with a year in town, to attain a patina of town bronze, and Bella would be the better for a year in London society. She said as much to Bella when they had regained the house. Bella objected strenuously. "But I don't want to go out in society, nor does Rupert. He has an estate of his own, from his mother's people, and it is our dearest wish to live on that estate, totally rusticated, and never see London."

It was a new concept to Narcissa, who was essentially an urban person, and the idea of long stretches of life on an estate in Yorkshire did not appeal to her. But then, she was not Bella, thank God!

She would be forced to use all her wits to deal with this development. She considered writing and asking Dilly to suggest ways in which she might go on, but it would certainly be an awkward situation to ask Dilly to reply to the name of Hester Adams. It was more than she could manage, to speak to Dilly, that model of rectitude, and explain that she was masquerading under someone else's name. And why.

She could not help feeling that Hester Adams, whoever she might be, needed to be explained, not only to Dilly but to Narcissa herself. Where was Hester?

Having rejected the idea of writing to Dilly, Narcissa was on her own. Her wits cudgeled, she at length came up with the perfect solution. To occupy Bella and also to indicate her sympathy with the girl's ambition, she suggested a great needlework project.

"You will need to have new draperies and new furnishings in that house of Rupert's, always supposing you arrive there. But if you are determined on this, then it would seem to me that you will have much to do to get ready. It will be some time before Rupert hears from his uncle, and the arrangements for your bridal garments will take up much of your time. It is always wise to get a head start on whatever we have to do. I suggest that we start now on certain furnishings for your house."

She went, with Bella's approval, to the Countess— "Don't tell her what it's for!" cried Bella—and got permission to occupy Bella with unexceptionable work. True to her word to Bella, she managed not to arouse the Countess's suspicions. New music and a new needlework project were apparently exactly what the Countess would have suggested herself. So Miss Pinkney, Bella, and Narcissa set off in the travel chaise for a day of shopping. The market town was full of shops serving the surrounding area. After spending most of the morning on their purchases, they found exactly what Narcissa had hoped to find, a needlework plan that would be sufficient to keep Bella occupied for some weeks. There was even a place to buy new music, and they left the stores and went to the inn to have lunch, feeling well satisfied with their morning's work.

After lunch they went to call on the vicar, Mr. Hensley, and his lady. Mrs. Hensley was a comfortable woman, and their daughters, Jane and Elizabeth, were not quite old enough to be out of the schoolroom, but old enough to have garnered a great deal of information about the area, which they were anxious to share with Narcissa, the newcomer.

The vicar's conversation ran more along the lines of instructing Narcissa about the ancient church and its history. Mrs. Hensley and her girls dwelt more on their neighbors, the Stanleys, the Walefords, the Marquess of Carraford, Squire and Mrs. Barker, their son Tom.

Narcissa learned, to an extent larger than she needed to know, about the economic foundation of the Vale of York. Its prosperity was built on sheep and wool. There had been a time when Scarborough was one of the Wool Staples. But extricating Narcissa from the conversation about the vagaries of certain kings, who looked upon the staple as a personal source of funds, Mrs. Hensley returned to the subject that seemed to be dearest to her heart at the moment. The Marquess of Carraford, seemingly, was of far more interest in his absence than some of the neighbors were in their presence. The Marquess was a regular out-and-outer, according to Jane, looking at her father, greatly daring in her use of slang. She was rewarded by a quelling look.

Her father said, "I think we need not gossip about the Marquess. His agent is generous in his support of the church, and I don't know what we would do without him. Surely, Jane, what he does is his own business."

But Jane irrepressibly had one final word: "But it's so interesting to have such a wicked man, and he belongs in our own neighborhood!"

Narcissa was given food for thought, for if the rumor had truth, then Rupert was right in his assessment of his uncle. But uncle was not necessarily like nephew, and she found an opportunity to speak to the vicar later, as he was escorting them to their carriage. She said in an undertone, "But what about young Mr. Elyot? Is he of the same cloth as his uncle?"

The vicar said in all seriousness, recognizing she was not asking idly, "He's a sound young man. He has great potential, I think, but he is sadly lacking in ambition. I lay this to the door of his uncle. There could not be two men more unlike, than Mr. Elyot and the Marquess."

Narcissa, climbing up into the carriage, thought, all to the good.

If Rupert was different from the Marquess, then Bella had apparently chosen well. The ride home from town fortunately passed without event. Bella was seemingly worried about Rupert's uncle. She had been given enough indication that the Marquess was, in fact, a wicked man so that she began to doubt whether or not Rupert could get his uncle's permission to marry.

Narcissa was worried about Bella, her immediate responsibility. She had high hopes of the embroidery, and the music, to keep Bella occupied during the next few weeks, but after that she did not know. She realized, with a sense of amusement, that she expected to be here for that length of time. She had certainly settled down in the last few days at Hapworth, as though she were going to live there forever. Her luck was in, her father would have said, but it was only a matter of time before it turned again. There surely must be some security in life beyond luck, she thought, but there was no way for her to find it.

Miss Pinkney, lulled by the monotonous movement of the coach, drifted into sleep. The coach turned in between the gates and drove up the gravel drive. The change in motion and in the sound of the wheels roused Miss Pinkney, so when they arrived before the door, she was the first to exclaim, "That looks like a hired conveyance! It certainly belongs to nobody we know. Who has come to visit?"

The three of them descended from the coach, and Narcissa gave orders that the parcels were to be brought in. As she went into the front hall, she saw that Evans, the butler, young Jebb, the footman, and even the parlormaid had found business in the front hall. They looked oddly at Narcissa, making her uneasy. Evans said impassively, "Her Ladyship has been asking for you, miss."

He opened the door into the Egyptian salon, and Narcissa entered. The Countess was entertaining the visitor—if entertaining was the right word. Both Lady

Hapworth and the newcomer looked grim, and the defiant light in the eyes of the visitor struck Narcissa like a blow. She was a stranger to Narcissa. Her hair was frizzed in unbecoming curls, and her dress was, while not in the latest mode, being at least two years behind London, no doubt the latest fashion in the north of England, although a little too extreme for Narcissa's taste.

The Countess addressed her. "Let me introduce you to Hester Adams. And since this is Hester Adams, who are you?"

13

At last her deceit had caught up with her!

The real Hester, seemingly unconcerned that she was several days late for her appointment, eyed Narcissa, the impostor, with dislike and—after her gaze had swept Narcissa from head to toe and recognized her quality—a growing fear. She cried, "You've got your nerve, coming here and pretending to be me, after I had the job and all. How did you cotton onto it?"

Narcissa stiffened, although she said pleasantly, "I certainly had no intention of replacing you at first."

Narcissa had assessed the real Hester's character swiftly and made up her mind. If the Countess wished someone to teach Bella how to carry off the responsibilities of being Mr. Elyot's wife, then the real Hester Adams was not up to the mark. Besides, Bella's intelligence, driven by her overpowering emotions, would rout this woman before the week was out. If anyone was capable of meeting Lady Hapworth's demands, it was surely not Hester.

Honesty was the only defense. "I was set down by the coach at Penton Crossroads because there was a mixup in my ticket. I did not have funds enough to continue to my destination, but I certainly had no knowledge then of anyone named Hester Adams or even the first thing about Hapworth. But before I could begin walking to seek shelter, Dawson arrived with the pony cart and told me I was expected."

The Countess's eyes were alight with interest. Narcissa continued with her adventurous tale. "I must tell you that it was cold, stormy, and I was very wet, for the coach windows leaked like sieves. I could not be any more uncomfortable, and when Dawson put my bandbox into the pony cart, I felt there was nothing to do but to go along. He did say I was expected, and I believed that Providence had decided to take care of me."

The Countess turned then to the newcomer and demanded, "How is it you were not on that stage? Your letter gave the precise time."

Hester said with a toss of her ringlets, "Something else came up that I thought might be what I wanted. It was a job in town and not out in the country. But it didn't work out." She invested the word "country" with loathing.

The Countess said, ice dripping from every word, "But you would have left me without any word?"

Hester realized she had made a mistake. She said, "I did try to let you know, but apparently you didn't get my message."

It was so palpable a lie that the Countess did not deign to respond. Instead, she looked at Hester as though she were an unpleasant specimen of nature brought in by her young son, and Hester's fate was sealed. The Countess summoned Evans and instructed him to provide a few coins. "There you are. Travel money, both from town and back. And I suggest you leave at once. Your coachman will be impatient if you linger."

The door had no sooner closed behind the real Hester when the Countess turned to Narcissa and said, "If *that* is Hester Adams, who are you?"

Narcissa said calmly, "Please call me Hester. I am accustomed to it now."

The Countess said, "I should like to know your real name."

Narcissa said slowly, "I confess it sounds like a great coincidence, but my name could easily *be* Hester Adams."

The Countess shook her head sharply. "It's as I said, the first night you came: You don't look like a Hester."

Narcissa said, "There is no accounting for one's parents' tastes in names, is there?"

To her surprise, the Countess laughed aloud. "No, there isn't, for you must know that my first name is Albinia, and I'm as dark as a savage. My sister's name is Lavinia, and that doesn't suit her either. I suppose you could be a Hester, though it is a coincidence."

"But not so exotic"—Narcissa laughed, attempting to

match the Countess's lightened mood—"as Verbena de Vere!"

Lady Hapworth's expression darkened. "Why did you mention that name?"

"I—I have read some of her novels." Narcissa faltered, wondering whether the Countess might disapprove strongly of light reading.

Lady Hapworth changed the subject abruptly. "You do look like someone I have met. I suppose you can't enlighten me as to who it is."

Narcissa said, "I don't know what to tell you, for I don't know whom I resemble."

The Countess said, "How can I trust you if you don't tell me who you are?"

Narcissa countered, "Could you trust the real Hester Adams?"

The Countess laughed again. "I wouldn't trust her as far as I could throw her. She'd nab the silver!"

So it was settled that Narcissa, still called Hester Adams, would stay, and there would be no questions. Indeed, the Countess seemed to have lost interest in Narcissa's real identity, saying suddenly, "I can use this!"

Narcissa was startled and puzzled, but the Countess did not explain. Instead, she said, "I must get to work."

She disappeared into her study, and silence closed around the Countess again. It was the habit of the household to leave her severely alone when she shut herself into her study. Lady Hapworth did not appear for dinner. Later Bella informed Narcissa that she had sent a note to Rupert, asking him to dinner the next day. Narcissa lifted an eyebrow and said, "I think you have not kept your word to me."

Bella said, "But I cannot live without Rupert! I must see him. You have to let him come to dinner!"

Narcissa said, "Your mother must decide. I cannot give you permission to invite someone to dinner. If Rupert is going to continue to be an habitué of this house, it must be with your mother's permission."

Bella cried, "But Mama won't care! I've known Rupert forever, and he has often been here to dinner!"

"Then why," asked Narcissa pointedly, "must you insist on meeting him in the shrubbery? I really cannot understand that unless you are pretending to be a Gothic heroine?"

Bella wailed, "What am I to do?"

Narcissa said calmly, "You must do the way any well-brought-up young lady would. You must ask your mama's permission to invite Mr. Elyot to dinner. If Mr. Elyot intends to ask you for your hand, he must speak to your mother first. Believe me, Bella, nothing else will serve. I will not inform your mother of your previous rendezvous—even though they are shockingly vulgar. But your mother has given me her trust, and I expect you to conform."

Bella informed her chaperone that Rupert had already written to his uncle. "But heaven knows how long it will take to reach him. He hasn't answered yet!"

Narcissa pointed out reasonably, "I think someone said he was in Italy. You cannot expect an answer before three months at the least!"

Bella was inattentive. "He probably threw it in the wastebasket or made a spill of it and lit his cheroot. It would be just like him!"

"How is it you know him so well?"

Bella turned wide, innocent eyes on her. "But Rupert says so!"

Rupert was not an impartial witness to his uncle's character, Narcissa thought, but refrained from making her doubts known. Bella was a mettlesome girl, and the lightest of hands was needed to guide her properly. Narcissa had rather expected a greater show of temperament on the subject of Rupert's uncle John; instead, Bella grew thoughtful.

Lady Hapworth burst in upon them, clearly irritated in the extreme. "How is this? Young Elyot has asked for your hand, Bella, and I—"

"Oh, do not blame Hester!" cried Bella. "She is right. She told me I could not meet Rupert without your permission, and he must state his intentions!"

"Of course," said Lady Hapworth shortly, "but I had expected more time." She looked at Narcissa. "You will be rushed to accomplish your task," she added sourly, "if you can."

Narcissa said more firmly than she felt, "I can. It was my understanding that you are not averse to the match?"

Bella said, "Oh, Mama, say you aren't!"

Grudgingly Lady Hapworth said, "It's all right with me. But I hadn't wanted it out in the open yet."

Narcissa, recognizing that Lady Hapworth's dearest wish was coming true and also believing that she did not wish Bella to know how eagerly she would promote the match, said, "It is still a family secret until it is announced in the *Gazette*. And it will be much more comfortable for everyone to have this understanding."

Bella came to the point. "You did say yes, dear Mama, did you not? You did say yes?"

The Countess looked at her only daughter with softening eyes. "I said *maybe*. It all depends. You'd better go see Rupert."

Bella vanished into the next room, where Miss Pinkney and Rupert were waiting.

"I confess to *you*, Hester," said the Countess when they were alone, "that I am much gratified. This is the match I have long hoped for, although I could wish they were not so bent upon an early marriage.

"Early marriage?" echoed Narcissa. "How soon?"

"I shall insist upon a year," said Lady Hapworth, contemplating the future with pleasure. "Rupert will be of age in a few weeks, as far as marrying is concerned, although his uncle holds the purse strings for another five years. But there is the dowry of Rupert's mother, a handsome piece in itself, although nowhere near the Elyot fortune."

Narcissa frowned. "Then Mr. Elyot is his sole heir?"

"Yes, and Carraford is such an ogre that no woman in her right mind would consider him. He is truly Gothic! So there's no likelihood that the Marquess will marry and set up his nursery. From what Rupert says, he will drink himself to death before long." The Countess turned thoughtful and then, with an air of striving to be totally fair, added, "At least, I don't *know* that he drinks, but certainly he indulges himself in whatever suits his fancy. That I do know!"

Narcissa reflected upon the wicked Marquess. Even the vicar had been hard put to find virtue in his sponsor. She was conscious of curiosity stirring in her—how could any one man be such a monster?

Lady Hapworth interrupted this train of thought. "I confess that you are right, Hester. I should not like

Carraford to get an idea that I threw Bella at Rupert's head, letting him come in and out of the house as though he were a member of the family. Carraford is apt to throw us all a coil, you know, before we're through with this." She stared broodingly into the fire. "You know Rupert has written to his uncle?"

"So I have been informed, just now. But it will be months before he can reply, I should imagine, and we will put the intervening time to good use." Her words were soothing, but her thoughts were chaotic.

"Yes, yes, there is time," said Lady Hapworth absently. "I had word not long ago that he was in Italy— far enough away." She turned to Narcissa and grinned mischievously. The expression made her wholly likable, thought Narcissa, smiling back. "That was when I decided to advertise for Hester Adams—and got you. A great improvement."

She was gone in a moment, and Narcissa, still bemused, heard the study door close firmly. What could the Countess *do* within the closed study that would take hours every day?

14

Carraford, well into his thirties, was indeed not of a mind to marry. He considered himself ugly. It was too far in the past for him to try to remember who had first told him that his nose was too large, that his mouth was badly formed, and that he had an unfortunately jutting jaw. He labored under the delusion that his assortment of features was not attractive to women, and while many women pursued him, he was convinced they wanted only his money and his title. Believing implicitly that his worth lay in his outer advantages—his fortune, which was indeed vast; his title, which was impeccable—he dared not admit any woman to his inner regard. He led an essentially lonely life and defended the shell he had erected around himself by means of a sarcastic and wounding tongue.

He did not realize that he carried himself with great elegance and that his features, taking harmony from the strength of character that lay behind them, had settled down into a look of great distinction. He was a strong man, with an air of authority, and he could not believe it.

Although he spent his days, and his nights, in frivolous pursuits, in gambling, and in other forms of self-indulgence, he did care, surprisingly, about his only nephew.

It was part of his loneliness that he was unable to tell Rupert, or at least give tangible evidence, that he held a powerful affection for the boy. Being unable to express his attachment, he succeeded in conveying just the opposite.

Rupert was as mistaken in his assessment of his uncle's character and feelings as was the Countess. She was also mistaken in believing Carraford to be in Italy.

It was only a few days after he had asked the Count-

ess's permission to pay court to Bella that Rupert
posted up the drive in great haste. Having flung the
reins to Dawson, he burst into the house with scant ceremony. Evans ushered him into the small sitting room
at the back of the house where Miss Pinkney, Narcissa,
and Bella were engaged in laying out the design of the
embroidery project. The Countess was sitting nearby,
wrapped in her own thoughts, when Rupert entered. He
pulled a letter out of an inner pocket, and flourished it
in the air. His first words shattered their peace.

"He's coming home!" His news startled them like a
hawk among the doves.

"Who is?"

"Carraford? How can he?"

"But he wasn't in Italy then!"

"Let me tell you," interrupted Rupert, his eyes still
glazed with shock, and addressing himself to Lady Hapworth. He dared not look at Bella.

The Marquess of Carraford was coming home at
once. For the first time in ten years the house was to be
got ready for its owner's arrival, and Narcissa was consumed by curiosity. At last she would meet the wicked
Marquess face-to-face.

The Countess, her mouth drawn, said with a touch of
bitterness, "He's coming home! I should have known he
would! Just like a Carraford!"

Rupert handed the letter to Narcissa. "Read it!" he
commanded.

The Marquess had written in a strong, lordly hand,
briefly, "Forget the marriage. I'm coming home."

As a straightforward statement of intent it was clear.
But it left a great deal to be desired as to time of arrival, whether or not the Marquess would be amenable
to persuasion, and many other things.

Narcissa at once took the Marquess in dislike. An
odious man, she was sure.

The Countess said, "I will not allow this! He must
not stop the marriage!"

It was an uncomfortable time in the small sitting
room. The walls seemed to close in, for the emotions
that were vibrating in the small space seemed far too
strong for the space.

Into this scene came William, the young Earl. He
was accompanied by his retriever. In one hand William

had a brace of pheasant. His tutor loomed behind him in the doorway, as William explained carefully that he himself had shot the pheasant. His mother said absently, "Very fine. Now, Mr. Wayne, take him away."

But the small boy was bent on confession. "I must tell you, Mama, that it is not so fine. I shot the pheasant, but it was over the fence, beyond the hedge."

The Countess, slowly perceiving that there was import in the news, turned to Mr. Wayne and said, "What is the meaning of this?"

Mr. Wayne, for once, spoke tersely, "He means, Your Ladyship, that these are Carraford pheasants."

Mr. Wayne said, "We got back across the hedge all right, but the steward from Carraford was right behind us. The steward said he'll shoot the dog on sight next time. And I don't doubt but what he will." Mr. Wayne was not through with his confession either. "I doubt not that he will shoot William, too, if the boy persists in throwing his arms around the dog to protect him. He did that today, and it was a near thing."

William said stoutly, "I will stand buff for my dog. He meant no harm."

The Countess was immobile with shock. Narcissa soothed young William and sent him upstairs, suggested to Rupert that he need not stay, and placed Bella in the hands of Miss Pinkney, with strong recommendations of smelling salts—for them both.

Later Charles Wayne sought out Narcissa. "It wasn't my fault," he said, defending himself. "The boy ran ahead, and he was over the fence before I caught up with him. What's a brace of pheasant to Carraford anyway? He hasn't been here for ten years, and I'm sure he doesn't know how many pheasant he has."

Narcissa said, "The boy shouldn't have done it, you know."

Mr. Wayne said, "I couldn't help it. But I don't mind telling you, Miss Adams, that it was a near thing. I thought for a moment the steward was going to shoot young William."

Narcissa scoffed, "The Carraford steward shoot the Earl of Hapworth? That is not likely. But I must say, you could have done better today."

Charles Wayne said stubbornly, "I don't know what all the furor is about. It's not the first time we've gone over the fence. Why should Carraford even hear about it?"

Narcissa pointed out, "You missed the excitement. Of all possible times for this to happen, this is probably the worse. For Carraford, you must know, is on his way home right now."

Mr. Wayne paled. "You mean he's coming here?"

Narcissa said, amused, "Probably to Hapworth in due course, but certainly he's coming to Carraford Hall."

Charles Wayne looked at her in disbelief. Yet it took no more than a moment for his thoughts to revert to himself. "I appreciate your telling me this. We must stick together, you know."

Mr. Wayne was clearly encouraged by Narcissa's listening to him, and his spirits rose.

Narcissa, thinking of Mr. Wayne's futile attempts to instruct young William, said kindly, "You must assert yourself more."

Mr. Wayne said in a rush of gratitude, "I appreciate your interest, Miss Adams; indeed, I do. I value your advice, and I shall study how to repay you."

"No need," said Narcissa, annoyed at the fawning man. "Pray excuse me. I must go to Lady Hapworth."

When she arrived in the study, she found the Countess in a state of great agitation. Miss Pinkney, her mouth pursed as though ready to burst into ineffective tears, stood helplessly by, wringing her hands.

"That man wasn't in Italy at all!" cried the Countess, incensed. "If he could just stay away for six months, the boy would be of age, and Carraford couldn't stop him!"

Narcissa ventured, "But you would not wish him to defy his guardian?"

Lady Hapworth gave evidence of her own practical rearing. Not by namby-pamby conduct had her forebears amassed the fortune that had brought her to Hapworth Hall! She said with consummate shrewdness, "Once the boy is married—legally, of course—his guardian will have to give in on the rest! For Rupert himself will be of age—it's only the Elyot fortune that the Marquess controls after that."

"But the six months?"

The Countess flung out the words: "For six months,

the boy cannot budge without Carraford's approval. But when he is of age, he'll marry my Bella, make no mistake about that!"

Miss Pinkney found her voice. "Hester, dear, we are much concerned lest Bella take one of her notions, don't you know?"

Narcissa, reading Miss Pinkney's thoughts correctly, said, "I shall try to counsel patience, although I promise nothing."

She was prevented from further comment, for suddenly the sound of wheels on the drive came to them in the study, and the three of them ran to the window to look out.

The Countess recognized the panel on the coach first and said sharply, "Carraford! Already!"

Without a word, Miss Pinkney and Narcissa, in harmony, scuttled out of the study. They retreated as far as the morning room, leaving the door ajar.

It was the Countess's turn to bear a marked resemblance to somebody Narcissa could recognize. Standing erect in the study, breathing, as it were, fire from each nostril, her eyes blazing in defiance, the Countess bore a remarkable resemblance to Boadicea, Queen of the ancient Britons!

15

Evans opened the door, and the Marquess of Carraford strode in.

If ever villain strolled onstage, Narcissa thought irreverently, here he was! He was tall and broad-shouldered, elegantly tailored, and with an air of great assurance, but the appearance of a Corinthian was belied by the active malevolence in his eyes as he looked around. He did not try to disguise his angry disapproval of the events that had forced him to come to Yorkshire, interrupting his own diversions in town.

"How cold and unfeeling he looks!" breathed a voice in Narcissa's ear. She turned to see Bella.

"What are you doing here, Bella?" said Narcissa in a fierce whisper. "I thought you were upstairs, lying down!"

"When my whole life is at stake?" wailed Bella. "Never!"

"Please, Bella," pleaded Miss Pinkney. "I can't hear when you are speaking."

"There's nothing to hear," Bella pointed out logically, but she fell silent nonetheless.

The door to the morning room was still open to the hall, but the interview in the study proceeded silently, as far as the listeners in the morning room were concerned.

This was true in the beginning. It was no more than five minutes before a word or two filtered into the hall. The words themselves were not intelligible, but the tone of the voices left nothing to the imagination. The combatants in the study were giving full rein to their emotions. Bella and Narcissa moved across to the door to listen more intently.

At length, the hidden, fascinated listeners crept closer

to the door, without shame. Now the words became un-
derstandable.

Carraford's harsh voice penetrated into the hall. "I
shall not allow my nephew to fall prey to your ambition, laudable though you think it may be. He is heir to
a substantial income that will make him welcome in the
best drawing rooms. His prospects are such that he may
look higher than a Yorkshire miss for a wife!"

"An Earl's daughter, remember!" cried the Countess
shrilly.

There was silence for a moment, and then Carraford
said with deliberate insult, "And a fishwife's daughter,
too, so it seems. You will oblige me by retracting your
permission for this unthinkable marriage."

"I shall not."

By now the Marquess had reached the door to the
hall and opened it, causing a quick scurrying among
the avid listeners to conceal themselves. Pausing in the
doorway, the Marquess snarled, "Very well, then. I
shall be put to the trouble of preventing the marriage."

"You can't!" came the Countess's harsh defiance.

Carraford's smile was slow and full of triumph. "I
hold all the cards, madam, and I know how to play
them."

The quarrel had removed itself from the study to a
larger arena. Even the scope of the subject matter had
been enlarged.

"I do not heed the words of a wastrel!" Lady Hapworth pointed out loudly. "A rake who wallows in the
dregs of vice has nothing to say to the point!"

Carraford stiffened and sneered, "And you want your
daughter allied to my family? How tolerant! Don't you
fear I might seduce her myself?"

The Countess, once more in control and surveying
the damage her sharp tongue had wrought, bit her lip.
"Certainly not. I fancy an Earl's daughter is above your
touch. Besides, my daughter has a very capable
chaperone."

"Then while your tame dragon is on duty, your
daughter has nothing to fear. I envy you your touching
faith."

He had reached the outside door now, and Evans
made haste to hold it open, brushing aside the footman.
"You see to your daughter if you wish. It does not mat-

ter," said the Marquess in farewell, "for Rupert is no longer concerned with any member of *your* family."

The Countess ran to the open door. On the threshold she shouted her valedictory message: "You're worse than a Gothic monster! You're positively *wicked!*"

Evans was not put to the trouble of closing the door, for the Countess slammed it shut behind her departing guest. She turned to Bella. "The marriage is off. I hoped Carraford would be accommodating, but he is worse than I thought."

The Countess delivered an inarticulate sound resembling nothing so much as the growl of a wounded tiger before she stormed back into her study and slammed that door behind her.

She left Narcissa with Bella on her hands, and Narcissa had a dark suspicion that she would earn her salary before the day was through. She managed to coax the girl back into the morning room and close the door upon the servants, palpitating with curiosity.

Bella, hovering, since the news of the Marquess's return had come, on the brink of hysterics, now flung herself with abandon over the edge. Alternately weeping and laughing, sobbing and screaming, Bella gave vent to broken little phrases. Narcissa caught words such as: "I will talk with Carraford! I'll kill myself!"

Narcissa spent a strenuous half hour calming the wretched girl. Much of the emotional storm she could lay to Bella's lack of emotional discipline and her being accustomed to having her own way in all things. But there was an undertone in the tempest that Narcissa did not like. She had a strong suspicion that all this emotional upheaval was symptom of a much deeper commitment to the marriage than she had expected. Isabella might be seventeen, but she had so far given no indication that her mind was not formed, nor her resolution wavering. Narcissa could hope only that the Countess had more control over her daughter than she herself did or that Rupert, impressed by the Marquess and his overwhelming influence, would cry off.

She said as much to the Countess later, after she had put Bella to bed, with a hot brick at her feet, had seen her imbibe two drops of laudanum in a glass of water, and had watched the girl fall into a heavy sleep. The Countess dismissed Bella's condition with a wave of the

hand and said, "I know I can trust you to take care of
her. The old Marquess was just as bad. I had not
thought that young John would be the spit and image
of his father, but so it is. An outrageous temper, and
he's never had to control it!"

Narcissa, bent on furthering Isabella's suit, said, "But
Rupert is different, I think."

The Countess agreed. "Yes, he is much like his
mother's people. I can accept Rupert as a member of
the family, but not the Marquess. And you can see that
the Marquess will come along with the marriage."

"Perhaps Carraford will go away again," Narcissa
ventured.

The Countess said, "Not soon enough. He is a very
dangerous man."

Rupert, surprisingly, would have agreed with Lady
Hapworth. He was more afraid of his uncle than he
would have admitted, having feared him all his life.
Rupert had been left an orphan at an early age, and the
Marquess had taken him into his own custody, saying
that his mother's people would not have the qualifica-
tions to raise the future Marquess. So Carraford had arranged a nursery for the small boy, and after Rupert
had outgrown his nurse, his uncle had provided for a
succession of tutors. He was not accustomed to small
children and scarcely knew how to make himself ad-
mired and respected. And since Rupert had reached the
age of ten, the Marquess had been away. He had seen
Rupert occasionally from time to time, but not at Carraford Hall. So Rupert watched, with the uneasiness of
a stranger, when his uncle returned from his stormy
visit from Hapworth.

While the Marquess of Carraford was noted for an
outrageous temper, no one could claim that he carried
a grudge or that his stormy temper lasted very long. So,
by the time he reached home, he was somewhat recovered.

But Rupert, on tenterhooks with apprehension, was
disturbed. The Marquess entered and said quite kindly,
"Well, Rupert, you have me to thank. I've got you out
of that mess."

Rupert could only echo, "Mess?"

Carraford raised one eyebrow. "Yes, of course. You

certainly didn't want to get involved with the Hapworths, did you?"

He went into the parlor, freshly dusted and made ready for his arrival, and busied himself with his snuffbox. Rupert, surprisingly, found welling up from some unsuspected source from within him a resolution of which even Bella would have been proud. He said, advancing toward his uncle, "You have ruined my life!"

The Marquess, unaware of the white heat that was about to consume Rupert, said only, "Enact me no tragedies! I am weary of this storm of emotion. I find it tiring."

Rupert said, "You think you can come down here, after having been away for ten years, and tell me what I can do."

Carraford said calmly enough, "Why, yes, I do think I can. For you must know I am your trustee, and therefore, I must do my duty to you. This is an ineligible marriage, and I will not permit it."

Rupert doggedly pursued the matter. "I love Bella, and she loves me. Bella says she will be perfectly happy at Mansfield Manor. Bella says we will do fine there, there's enough land to support us, and our wants aren't much."

He continued in this vein for some minutes until the Marquess with one raised eyebrow brought him to a halt.

"There seems to me to be too much of what Bella says," said Carraford. "I can assure you that what Miss Gaines thinks is of little concern to me. But I should like to hear what you think."

He waited with an appearance of calm. He gave little thought to Rupert's defiance, thinking it was only the natural rebellion of a schoolboy, when faced with a game he had lost, some footling plan that had gone astray. Rupert said, "I believe Bella is right."

Carraford, satisfied, said more kindly, "I will tell you what I think then. You need more polish, at least a year in London. There is a certain town bronze that I wish you to acquire. And since the season is already in full swing, I think it would be best if we went first to the Continent. A Grand Tour might be old-fashioned, but I find it is the best way to acquire a knowledge of the world. And then when we return, next spring, we will be ready to enjoy the season to the full."

Rupert stammered, "A Grand Tour?"

Carraford nodded almost carelessly. "I see that I haven't paid enough heed to you as you were growing up. It is a fault past remedy now, but I shall attempt to retrieve my error. I will go with you."

Only Carraford knew what a sacrifice this suggestion entailed. Rupert, having been presented with a year of the Marquess's life, calmly turned it down.

"I want to marry Bella. We can live on the money from my mother's inheritance, and I will not be calling on you for any trust money. I do not need your approval to spend my mother's money, and Mansfield Manor, of course, is mine."

Rupert's sudden revolt aroused Carraford's suspicions. He was not used to the idea that Rupert might be thinking for himself, and he sought in his words an echo of the Countess and probably her daughter. "You think that girl will be satisfied?" said Carraford savagely. "They want money. The Hapworths have been under the hatches this long time! They have an eye on your fortune, don't think they don't!"

The Marquess was speaking out of his own deep conviction, but Rupert resisted. He said, "No, they aren't."

Carraford looked at him blankly. "Aren't what?"

Rupert patiently explained, "The Hapworths aren't under the hatches. There's no sign of penury there at all."

Carraford reflected upon his own impressions of Hapworth Hall when he had been there an hour before. Unfortunately he had been too blinded by his own emotions to look around him, but he did now, vaguely, recall at least a butler and a footman, who were in themselves signs that the Hapworths at least pretended to some prosperity.

Rupert, sensing an advantage, pursued the matter. "Miss Adams seems to be well paid," he said. "At least she isn't the kind to work for nothing. I imagine she commands a good salary. She says, besides, that there is no sign of neglect in the house that she can see. So you see, Uncle John, Bella is not hanging out for a fortune."

Carraford said, "Miss Adams? Who is she? A paragon of judgment, I gather, but I have not met her."

Rupert explained Narcissa's position in the household, and Carraford realized that she was the chaperone Countess had mentioned—her "tame dragon."

It seemed clear that Rupert knew what he was talking about, even though he was distressingly apt to take a woman's ideas and make them his own. But Rupert had given Carraford enough food for thought to keep him for a week. But all Carraford said, in closing the interview, was: "If there is a great love involved here, which I doubt, then such a strong attachment will certainly survive a Grand Tour."

16

"Grand Tour!"

Rupert echoed his uncle's last remark, but at a remove. He was now at Hapworth Hall, where he had posted as soon as he could gracefully leave his uncle's company. Seeking solace with Bella, he was denied an interview with her alone, for Narcissa was true to her word and had no intention of leaving the young couple alone. She was grateful that this interview in the morning room was far more comfortable than standing in ankle-deep leaves in the coppice. It was the only advantage she could see.

Bella, with a look of desperation, said quite quietly, "I will simply die."

Narcissa felt moved to interrupt. "But, Bella, it's only for a year at the most."

Rupert shook his head. "It's not quite that simple, Miss Adams. For after the Grand Tour, my uncle has planned that I should spend a year in town procuring what he calls town bronze."

Rupert began to pace the room. It looked for a moment as though he had forgotten his love, for he paid no attention to Bella, being intent on his own thoughts.

"What good is town bronze, I ask you?"

He did not wait for an answer fortunately, for Narcissa would have been hard put to form a reply. Rupert raced on. "What good is knowing what Paris looks like when all I want to know is what my own sheep look like on my own land?"

Correctly assessing the question as being truly a matter of form, Narcissa resumed her needlework. She kept her head bowed over her work, but from the corner of her eyes she watched Bella and Rupert. Bella's desolate expression was worrisome.

"I've been figuring," said Rupert at last. "My uncle can indeed withhold my Elyot income."

"But not the capital?" interposed Narcissa. With her strong recollections of hungry weeks when her father's luck had departed, she had a powerful sense of the desirability of capital.

"He can spend my capital before I get it," said Rupert flatly. "On travel, for example, or bad investments. He has absolute authority."

Narcissa was shocked. "Surely he wouldn't deliberately *fritter the money away!*"

Bella spoke then sharply. "Rupert's wicked uncle would do *anything!*"

Bella's face grew pale, and she watched Rupert with the fascination of a bird following a prowling cat. Clearly this was a blow of the first water.

At last, realizing that something was expected of her, Narcissa set her needlework aside and addressed herself to Bella. "Now, Bella, it's no use to mourn like this. There is nothing so desperate about waiting for a few years. The time will go by, and if Mr. Elyot can preserve his inheritance by seeming to agree with his uncle's wishes, then there can be no harm in planning for such advantage. For I am persuaded that you would not quite like to live in straitened circumstances. I have seen happiness fly out the window when the bill collector knocks at the door."

"It's nonsense to wait. The money is nothing to me. I just wa-ant Rupert!" The last words rose in a wail, and Narcissa put down her embroidery to deal with her charge. "It's a year, more than a year, and I cannot stand the idea of being without Rupert!"

Narcissa continued her soothing remarks, counseling submission to what could not be changed. But Bella was not convinced.

"You wouldn't give in, I'm persuaded," said Bella.

Bella's observation was acute, Narcissa thought, for indeed, she had not given in when faced with a situation she did not like.

"True enough," admitted Narcissa, "but I see no other course open to you."

Bella, losing her control, gave way to wild sobs. Narcissa spent all her efforts trying to control the girl, to bring her out of her hysterics, and for a long time her efforts were futile. When she looked up at last, she saw Rupert edging toward the door, a very worried frown on his usually pleasant face. Mentally castigating him for his desertion of his professed love, Narcissa went back to Bella and paid no further heed to him.

He had left the house before the Countess entered, whether warned by one of the servants or because Bella's weeping hysterics had penetrated the study wall, Narcissa did not know. But when the Countess was put in possession of the facts, not by Bella, who was incoherent, but by Narcissa, she said briskly, "I am loath, as you know, to agree that Carraford has the right of anything. But in this I do have to agree with him. It would do no harm to have Rupert go away for a year at least, and then we'll see whether or not your feeling is as strong as you claim it is." Lady Hapworth, seeing her dreams floating away on the tide of Carraford's intransigence, yet spoke to Bella tenderly.

Bella said, distraught, "I love him, and if he goes away, I will simply die."

It was more than the excited exaggeration of a young girl, Narcissa thought, worried. These hysterics had gone on longer than any she had ever seen, and while it was a welcome change from the stricken look with which she had greeted Rupert's first words, nonetheless, such a prolonged fit of emotional abandon could not help having a bad effect.

The Countess eyed her only daughter with affection. "Best get your face washed and straighten up, my dear, for what cannot be helped must be endured."

With which sage advice she returned to the study, leaving Narcissa to deal with the aftermath.

At some cost to her own nerves, Narcissa finally managed to get Bella upstairs and quiet. From hysterical weeping she had lapsed into stricken resignation. It was as though Bella had gone somewhere inside herself, leaving only a lifeless outer shell to make its way through life.

At length Narcissa was able to leave the house, and she walked across the lawn. She was seeking nothing but solitude, to feel the cool wind on her fevered brow, and to forget the sound of Bella's wild sobs still loud in her ears.

She was frightened out of her wits to see a man

standing among the trees. It was only Rupert, waiting for her.

"I thought you would never come," he said.

Narcissa said caustically, "I thought I wouldn't either, but you certainly didn't expect me. I never walk here."

Rupert astutely said, "It's simply the closest place for peace and quiet, and I knew you would come."

Narcissa, surprised at his perception, leaned against the trunk of a tree, resting her weary head against its cool bark, and prepared to listen. "But make it short," she begged, "for I have had enough emotional storms to last a lifetime."

Rupert said calmly enough, "That's what I wanted to talk to you about. I cannot bear to see Bella in such a state. And she's right, you know. I think she would die, and I cannot allow it."

Narcissa opened her eyes and looked at him, surprised. This was not the Rupert who had railed like an adolescent against the decrees of his uncle. This was a man on his own. She prepared to listen with more interest.

Rupert continued. "I have decided to take Bella to Gretna Green. My uncle cannot dissolve our marriage after it's taken place."

Narcissa was obscurely disappointed. It was such a mundane and vulgar answer to a real problem. "I had thought better of you, Rupert," she said. "That is no solution at all, and you should know it."

Rupert said, "I confess it is not what I would want to do, but I'm determined on it, you know, and I would not want the Countess to blame you for it. But I did want you to know where we are going."

They argued for some time, and Narcissa became convinced that Rupert's strong doggedness was not the mere stubbornness of a thwarted juvenile. It was the strength of a man who knew what he wanted, and if Rupert thought that Bella would be of more importance in his life than town bronze, so be it.

She felt an optimism that had been lacking until now. She thought that with Bella's devotion and Rupert's strong will, they might well make a match of it. For the first time she believed in the marriage as a desirable thing. Rupert left her in the coppice. His last words only reinforced her opinion: "I will not go on the Grand Tour!"

It was Rupert's last word for some time. There were three days of the most strenuous efforts on Narcissa's part as she tried to rally Bella to a point where she would at least respond. Bella was totally crushed and seemed to have retreated far away. The cook sent up little dainties, to tempt Bella's appetite, but she sat at the table crumbling a piece of bread and eating nothing. Her clothes grew loose, and her face was suddenly thin and wan. After three days the Countess could no longer stand the sight of her daughter.

She called Narcissa into the study. "I cannot see my daughter go downhill this fast. If I could call down a curse on Carraford, I would."

Narcissa thought the Countess was as much to blame as Carraford, for she had agreed with his decision, but she forbore to say anything. The Countess was not waiting for an answer anyway, for she turned to Narcissa abruptly and said, "What do you think of this proposed marriage? Will it work?"

Narcissa, thus invited, told the Countess what she thought. "I believe they have a genuine attachment, one that will outlast any Grand Tour or any separation. I must agree with Rupert that if he wishes to spend his life among his sheep, town bronze will not help him."

The Countess grew thoughtful. "I confess I should like to see Bella with a London season, for there is nothing so delightful to remember in the years to come, but I can see that it would be a waste of money and time. I certainly can't send her looking like a skeleton, and I imagine that in another week she will."

Narcissa, then greatly daring, ventured, "Is there a real objection to the family?"

The Countess said with a curious lack of emotion, "The old Marquess was a stubborn ox. But Rupert's mother's family was good enough."

Suddenly making a decision, she turned to Narcissa and said, "Hester, I want you to do one thing for me. I know you have Bella's interest at heart, and I want you to straighten everything out for me. A side of me apparently arouses Carraford to blind anger, but he may listen to you."

Narcissa revolved the idea in her mind and agreed. "But how can I get him here?"

The Countess said, "Go to him. Take a groom and a maid, and go see him. You are a respectable woman, plainly dressed—although I admit there is nothing submissive about you. But talk to Carraford. Convince him he is wrong—if you can. It's for Bella. Remember that, and I know you will overcome any objections."

Narcissa agreed, but the Countess had one further direction to give her. "Be wary. Don't develop a *tendre* for him. Some foolish women dote on rascals."

Narcissa, consulting her own schemes for the Marquess, said, "I've seen enough of aristocratic tyrants to develop a decided aversion to another one. Never fear!"

17

Narcissa made her plans. It was a matter of some urgency to lift the burden that lay heavily on Bella, and she wasted no time in preparing a scheme to convince Carraford the two young people should marry.

If she could make an excuse of errands in town and *by chance* stop at Carraford Hall, it would be better than her making a visit to the hall on purpose.

Narcissa knew that for Narcissa Bentham, a young woman of family and breeding, it was unheard of to go visit a nobleman at his bachelor hall. But she was merely a governess, at least for the moment. Such niceties of her own behavior should fall before the urgency of Bella's need.

The Countess reinforced her orders. "If it were a question of a young lady—Bella, for instance—then, of course, I should not suggest it. But you must not delude yourself, my dear Hester, for the Marquess is far too high in the instep to toy with a servant. He will probably not even notice your youth or your rather *different* style." She cocked her head on one side, birdlike. "I daresay you have nothing to fear."

Narcissa, dismissed like a kitchen maid, seethed for a few minutes. She hurried up the stairs to fetch her cloak—a warm garment, but not the fur-lined cloak she had had to pawn in London—and hesitated before the mirror. Was she really vain enough to care about her appearance? The face the mirror gave her back was ordinary enough, in the shadow of her bonnet. She tucked a stray curl under the confining ribbon and suddenly laughed. She really *was* vain enough—a fault that must be suppressed!

Bella, seeing that Narcissa was going to town, surprisingly did not ask to go along. Narcissa would have refused anyway, and she did not tell Bella that she intended to stop at Carraford Hall. Narcissa went in the curricle, Dawson, the groom, up behind, and Kitty sitting beside her uneasily. The maid had ventured a question, "Wouldn't it be better to have him drive?"

Narcissa could see that the groom echoed the maid's opinion, but she refused and took the reins. As they headed down the drive, Dawson, watching Narcissa catch the thong of her whip and negotiate the turn at the end of the drive, settled back, knowing that Miss Adams, supposed to be a governess, had somewhere driven, and done it well.

Narcissa had, in fact, driven her own carriage all over the capitals of Europe when her father was in funds. She had even driven a team, keeping all four horses in line so that they moved as one. It felt good to set out again, behind a pair of goers.

Reflecting on Europe, a subject brought up by her feeling the reins in her hands again, she could not agree that traveling across Europe would be good for Rupert. Not that she felt he would fall prey to gambling fever or fall victim to chicanery or be hit over the head by footpads. He might survive all these experiences, but they meant nothing to the ongoing life of an English landowner. While the prospect of allowing a flock of bleating sheep to fill a vision of the future was appalling, yet, if that was what Rupert and Bella wanted, she would see that they got it, as far as her ability carried.

She reached the road into town, and intent on framing the persuasive words she would use to Carraford, she failed to notice a rig coming up behind her.

A solitary driver was overtaking her in his high-perch phaeton. Apparently fancying he was the equal of all the notable whips of London, he decided to pass her, to show that he could drive to a peg. It was a mistake.

A shocked exclamation from the groom alerted Narcissa to the situation. Looking over her shoulder, she was dismayed to see that the phaeton was almost upon her. She moved to the roadside, but not soon enough.

Full of his own self-importance, he failed to negotiate the passage. His wheels locked with hers and sent her curricle into the ditch.

Hot words trembled on her lips. She crawled out from the overturned vehicle and looked to her people.

The groom was laid flat, but she saw quickly that he was only stunned. Kitty was in hysterics, sitting on the grassy bank under the hedge, alternately shrieking and moaning.

"Come, now, Kitty!" cried Narcissa in a bracing tone of voice. "You're not hurt! Suppose the horses had stepped on you. They might yet—if you don't get up directly!"

The threat succeeded. The maid scrambled to her feet and looked around wildly. Narcissa then turned to the culprit.

"I don't know what happened! I'm just dreadfully sorry!" he said, near tears. "I'm Tom Barker."

His apologies were profuse and repetitive, and finally, Narcissa cut them short. "You should look to your horses before they run away," she counseled urgently.

Neither of them, standing in the midst of the wreckage, was aware of a light chaise emerging from the drive down the road. The vehicle, emerging from Carraford's gate, hesitated in the road as the driver took note of the situation. Instead of turning toward town, as had been his intention, he turned his horses and came down to meet the accident victims.

Taking in the situation with one sweeping glance, he gave orders to his groom and to Dawson, now sitting up, looking about him vaguely, and bestowed upon Tom Barker a glance that rocked that young man to his shoes.

At first sight of Carraford, Narcissa was ready to sink into the ground with embarrassment. But she was soon moved to admire the masterly way in which he took charge of the deteriorating situation. How good it was, she mused, to leave one's troubles in the hands of an expert, who was more than capable of overcoming life's obstructions with authority and competence!

Narcissa was not quite sure what happened next. In a very short time the situation was totally mended. Tom Barker was on his way with his pair toward town, and Narcissa stood in the road, while the Marquess's servants, along with Dawson, put the Hapworth curricle back on the road. The groom examined the horses and reported there was no damage, except for a scratch on a leg.

Then the Marquess took time to look at Narcissa.
His eyebrows raised for a moment as he said, "I had
not thought to meet you here."

Then, taking a closer look, he realized his mistake.
"Sorry," he said, "I thought you were someone else.
You have a marked resemblance to someone I know.
Pray forgive me."

Narcissa nodded, her thoughts racing. "Of course,
sir." She must postpone her visit to Carraford to another day. But the Marquess made no move to depart.

This beauty was not the lady he had at first thought
her—he couldn't even think of that lady's name!—but
he held a recollection of languid eyes and a die-away
manner. All the fashion, of course, and a man could
hardly tell one belle from another. The girl standing before him now was vibrant, and spirited, and far more
intriguing than any lady of lassitude he knew.

Narcissa looked steadily up at him, aware that she
was staring at him, but unable to stop. He was not
nearly as ugly as she had been told. She managed to
stammer, "I'm Hester Adams, from Hapworth Hall,
and I am very much obliged to you."

So this was Rupert's Miss Adams! A governess-com-
panion? The Marquess's knowing eye took in her erect
figure, her indefinable air of breeding, and scented a
mystery. Miss Adams was clearly a cut above her
present position.

He said, "You were on your way to town?"

Narcissa responded, "Yes, I had errands to do, but
now, of course, I will have to put them off." She looked
back down the road at Hapworth Hall, clearly judging
how far she must walk.

The Marquess suggested, "I think it would be best
for me to take you on your errands and then restore
you to Hapworth Hall. Get in."

His tone of voice was harsh, and his instructions almost uncivil. She lifted an eyebrow and murmured,
"How dictatorial!"

His expression did not alter. Only the flame leaping
in his eyes told her he was moved. She believed him to
be angry, but in fact, he was gratified that his assessment of her quality was correct. No governess of his
acquaintance would have dared *speak* in answer to his

gruff orders, much less rebuke him! Who was the girl anyway?

He reached his hand down to her and repeated, "Get in."

It was really the only solution, and with alacrity she climbed up into the chaise. Now she welcomed the opportunity to talk to the Marquess, in open surroundings. At least on the road he could not do anything dreadful, unless he chose to pitch her out of the chaise on her head. How much better this was than trying to see him in his own house!

So far, even though he was not aware of the reasoning, the Marquess had turned out to know best! It was all very well for Carraford to deal summarily with menials and cattle, but it was quite a different matter when it came to ordering Narcissa Bentham around! But, she thought honestly, her resentment was too personal. She did not like his tone—treating her as though she were merely another servant! But she was! She laughed inwardly and vowed to remember her position in the future.

She had not had an opportunity before to take note of Lord Carraford's appearance, and she was pleased with it. He was dressed in country buckskins, most suitable for what he must consider the wilds of Yorkshire, and his coat, while superbly tailored, yet lacked the glovelike fit that must have proclaimed the London dandy.

His clothes were no different from what she might have expected of any wellborn, well-informed, and very wealthy gentleman. But it was his indefinable presence that lured her into closer consideration of him. His jaw hardly escaped being termed "heavy," and his lips were perhaps too full to be in the classic line of handsomeness; but there was a virile power emanating from him that affected Narcissa like a strong magnet.

She considered the question thoughtfully. It was his strength, she decided, that drew her to him. She had known so many men who were weak, or self-indulgent, or swept by the whims and vagaries of fashion or their mood. A man who appeared to be a rock of authority was a welcome change.

She shook herself mentally. It might be nice to lean on his strength—she was still wrapped in the warmth of her relief when he appeared just now. But there was always the other side of the coin. A weak man, she knew well, could be persuaded if one knew the key. But a strong man—like the Marquess of Carraford—was apt to be intransigent, obstinate, and altogether inexorable in his roughshod trampling on other people.

For instance, Rupert Elyot, the man's own nephew, was an outstanding victim, Narcissa thought. And, my girl, she told herself, remember that, when you are in danger of succumbing to his charm.

Charm? she thought, and sank lower inside her cloak. The man was appallingly loaded with it!

For his part, Carraford was unaware of Narcissa's close scrutiny. He himself had much to think about, and not least was his long-established fear of being pursued relentlessly, object—matrimony, not for himself, but for his assets.

He could not think that Miss Adams was yet another marriage-inclined female. She could not, for one thing, have foretold that he would return to Yorkshire just now. Yet long experience made him wary, and knowing that flight was always an escape for him, he decided to add to his experience by observation of the tricks the mysterious Miss Adams chose to use.

He was not sure that her name was Adams, for it seemed a remarkably common name for her quality. He started his pair moving again.

She said, "How kind of you to offer to take me to Pocklington. I have a number of purchases to make. If it had not been for that foolish boy, I would be nearly there by now. I have never seen such juvenile driving."

He was thus moved to ask her about the accident, and she favored him with a lively description of Tom Barker's attempt to pass her. "Fortunately no bones were broken, and the horses were not hurt. But you, Lord Carraford, gave young Tom all the rebuke that he needed."

Carraford, after they had driven a couple of miles, repeated her name. "Hester Adams? I do not recall any family named Adams."

She looked at him and said calmly, "There is no reason why you should."

His interest was sparked. She was aloof, and it was, he realized, a new approach. He went on, "My nephew

says you are new to the area. I wonder where I have
seen you before?"

Narcissa said firmly, "You haven't."

She was becoming cautious and realized she must be
on her guard not to give away her real identity. She
was too close, geographically, to her mother's people,
and not far enough from Sir Maurice. It was quite
likely that the Marquess had known her father, even
though she herself had only once seen Carraford in
Europe. But she was too well aware of the prominence
of her mother's family to take a chance.

He asked her how long she had been a governess and
where she had been before she arrived at Hapworth
Hall. She said firmly, with civility and finality, "I am so
satisfied with my employment by the Countess that I
try to forget everything else."

He accepted the rebuke, and conversation moved
into more general channels all the way to town.

They arrived at Pocklington, and he pulled into the
innyard at The Feathers. It was no surprise to Narcissa
that the ostlers came running. She had seen many times
the effect of birth and wealth on those who hoped to be
favorably noticed.

To Narcissa's great surprise the Marquess attended
her on her tour through the Pocklington shops.

How true it was, she reflected, that when one didn't
want to see certain persons they seemed to be on every
corner! She felt exceedingly self-conscious, with the
great Marquess of Carraford walking beside her. As
fate would have it, she saw nearly everyone she knew
in the area. The vicar's wife stopped them, consumed
by curiosity, and flustered when the Marquess spoke to
her.

Beyond the hatmaker's shop, the Marquess murmured, "Behold the mother of our young Jehu!"

The comfortably plump woman approaching bore a
strong resemblance to her son Tom. Narcissa turned to
Carraford, and pleaded, "I pray you not to distress
Mrs. Barker with the story of Tom's excess zeal in
driving."

The Marquess lifted one eyebrow, almost impercep-
tively, and said, "A sorry opinion you must have of me,
to think that I would betray the lad."

Narcissa, forgetting to be circumspect with him, said, "Truly I have no opinion of you at all."

Regretting her tart reply and wishing it had never left her lips, yet she noticed that Mrs. Barker was agog with speculation.

"My goodness, Lord Carraford, imagine meeting you on a village street!" crowed Mrs. Barker. She was a stout woman, dressed in a gown that six months ago might have fitted her. Now it was sadly strained at the seams.

Carraford bowed over her hand. "It is a pleasure to meet you at any place," he murmured. He glanced wickedly from the corner of his eye at Narcissa, who suddenly was in grave danger of bursting into a chuckle. The unexpectedness of her response to his irreverent sense of humor nearly routed her sense of decorum.

But Mrs. Barker's inquiring glance, lingering on Lady Hapworth's new servant, chilled Narcissa at once. The squire's lady had little doubt that Hester Adams was setting her companion's cap for the nonpareil Carraford.

After they had left her, the Marquess said, more kindly than she had heard him speak before, "I pray you do not allow the uninformed speculations of the villagers to distract you. You know, and I know, that it was by pure chance that we met, and I would have been sadly ill-bred had I not offered my assistance."

Narcissa could not reply coherently, for her guilty conscience rose to place a barrier on her tongue. It had not been by chance that she had sought out the Marquess, even though Tom Barker was an unwitting tool.

When her shopping was done, Carraford having ordered all the goods to be sent, he said, "There is no more reason for us to linger in town, I think."

As he steered her back to the inn, she had to agree. She could not expect the Marquess to carry all her parcels. As a matter of fact, she doubted whether he had ever carried a parcel in his life. And since her purchases had been only an excuse in the first place, she forgot them and turned her thoughts to forming her speech, on behalf of Rupert and Bella, to Carraford.

On the way home he made conversational overtures, but she was wrapped in her own thoughts and did not respond. He fell silent. She did not realize that he was somewhat piqued, for he was not used to being ignored. When she did speak, it only reinforced his opinion that she was not listening to him at all.

"I wonder whether you have not been too harsh on your nephew," she began. She dared not look at him, lest his severe frown put her off. She continued, "I cannot see that an extended sojourn in Europe would help Rupert. He is a little old for a Grand Tour, besides."

Carraford's only response was a calm "I think not."

Narcissa returned to her argument. "But if he has such a dislike for the journey, I fear he will get little from it."

The Marquess replied, "Leave that to me."

Her rehearsed speech fell apart, but she salvaged sufficient of it to make it clear that she was seriously questioning the Marquess's judgment. He was not a man to accept such criticism without protest.

"Believe me, I know what's best for my nephew. I fail to see that this concerns you at all."

Narcissa, thus baited, threw caution to the wind. "You certainly know what is best for him, not having seen him for ten years. Rupert says you haven't been down here for a decade, leaving him in the hands of tutors. Surely you haven't been keeping close track of him, or you would have known before this that he had a growing *tendre* for Bella. No, you cannot convince me you have Rupert's welfare at heart."

The Marquess said without visible emotion, "I had not tried to convince you, I think."

His calm assumption that he knew what was best for Rupert and also, judging from his recent behavior, that he knew what was best for Narcissa began to nettle her. She had gained nothing by civility, she thought, and it was time for more strenuous measures.

"You are perhaps the most arrogant man I have ever seen," she told him pleasantly. "I do admit your right to judge what is best for Rupert, even though he is twenty. Nearly of age. But I should like to know, sir, whether you manage the world's affairs?"

It took a visible effort, but he managed to control himself. He said, "Rupert will be the better for travel. He needs polish more than anything else. More, certainly, than he needs a marriage."

Narcissa said, "He is too old. He should have gone abroad when he was sixteen. One who had his welfare at heart should have known that."

Carraford said, his words clipped, "Rupert will go. He will do as I tell him."

Narcissa, irony edging her voice, said, "A fine education he'll get."

"What do you mean?" asked the Marquess with genuine interest.

"If he doesn't lose his money gambling in Paris, then he might easily die of garlic breath in the coaches," responded Narcissa with heat. "Too much *bavaroise*, after an evening of play at Madame Hecquet's, and he'll be too cast away to take in the edifying sights of the city."

She felt the rush of reminiscence sweeping her off her feet and carrying her along in a headlong stream. "Your nephew will be fortunate, indeed, if he does not return home with pockets to let after a month of carnival diversion along the Grand Canal, where all manner of Englishmen have sported. He may well lose his coin in a gaming house, where none cares about the face behind his mask, but only about the gold in his pockets."

"You amaze me," he murmured, with perfect truth.

"It would be different," continued Narcissa, "were he to aspire toward a life at Court, where a knowledge of the art and monuments of Europe are a necessary background to any pretensions to culture, but—" Too late she realized how totally she had given herself away. "But of course," she finished lamely, "you know best."

"I must confess my knowledge, while broad, is not on a par with yours!"

Carraford, to her surprise, grinned with malicious enjoyment. The vivid description she had given of certain of the capitals of Europe, to his own knowledge, was accurate. One might even suspect that the mysterious Miss Adams had firsthand knowledge of such gambling dens. He told her as much. And added, "What a lurid picture you paint! I confess the life of a governess is far more exciting than I was led to believe."

Too late, she saw where her arguments had led her. She was too stunned to say another word, and they traveled all the way to Hapworth Hall in silence.

18

Carraford turned into the drive. He was clearly anxious to erase the impression he had left in her mind. Returning to his initial theme, he said, "I must remove Rupert from the vicinity. If this great love of his for the dashing Miss Gaines is valid, a year's separation will do them no harm." His mouth drawn down into bitter recollection, he added, "I have known separation to work miracles of recovery from a dangerous infatuation. Sometimes the cure even encompasses the healing forgetfulness of the great fortune that engendered the passion at the start!"

"Then it was not worth a candle!" said Narcissa stoutly. "To join a true love and a desire to marry a comfortable income in the same breath is repellent to anyone's sensibilities."

"Do not tell me," he said harshly, "that such a joining does not happen!"

"No, I should not dream of trying to persuade you of anything. But I must tell you I do not see any desire for fortune in the case we are discussing."

"You don't? I wish I had such rosy views of young love. But neither one of these two is fit to be left alone in the rain—without someone to tell them to come in!"

She was becoming angry. "And you have come home, after years away, to tell your nephew that it is raining? How thoughtful of you!"

Carraford's formidable jaw jutted forward. She knew from her sidelong glance that she had pushed him dangerously close to breaking the rein he held on his temper.

"I have employed persons to . . . stand in my place, I suppose you would say," he said finally. "But I should have come myself." The last words were under his breath, as though to himself rather than to his companion. Then, taking a resolve, he spoke firmly to her. "I shall forbid them to see each other. Then, as soon as I can make arrangements, Rupert shall begin his travels."

Narcissa regained her self-assurance and replied with spirit, "That's the best way I know to send them off to Gretna Green." She could see his knuckles turn white on the reins and knew that she had startled him. She was obscurely pleased.

He said with an appearance of calm, "Is that a threat?"

"Not at all," she replied. "I merely state a fact. If you were not so arrogant and headstrong, you would see for yourself."

Again, the Marquess reflected that Miss Adams had a strange way of talking for a governess. All he said was: "They wouldn't dare."

Narcissa, seeing that she had rocked him, pursued her advantage. "An elopement," she said, "would be nearly impossible to prevent. We are not far from Carlisle, as you know, and they could be over the border in a day."

Carraford said, "I see you have looked into the subject. Is it possible that you yourself have suggested this alternative?"

Narcissa, kindling, retorted, "I think you forget, sir, that were Bella to marry I would be without employment. It is not to my advantage to send her across the border."

Carraford said, "I think you are right in that. But I certainly feel that you are sadly in want of principle in abetting an elopement."

She was instantly furious at his assessment of her character. She told him as much, saying, "Every reason would tell you that I am not abetting such a harum-scarum scheme! The Countess would be dismayed, I would be unemployed, and Rupert would be in your bad graces. The last in itself should be sufficient to discourage them. But then, I suppose that whatever he does would result in your disapproval, so sometime he must make his own way."

Carraford remarked, "I do know that the Countess is overly ambitious and would doubtless stop at nothing to ally her family with the Elyots. But I have no basis to judge your principle or want of it, since we have only met today." His altered tone was almost an apology, and she was moved.

But he was clearly inviting her to tell more about her background, about her upbringing, and she realized that she had given away too much of her past. In speaking of gambling in Europe, she had revealed far more than she realized. She recognized now that the Marquess was a very dangerous man. She was beginning to worry lest he penetrate too far. There was no reason why he should pursue the subject, for she was a lowly governess, yet she instinctively realized that she must guard herself.

With sarcasm, she retorted, "I can see why an alliance with a young boy, barely out of his teens and with such want of spirit that he cringes and cries off at the first sign of opposition, would be totally desirable. I must make up my mind to abet Miss Gaines at every opportunity. It would be wrong in me to dissuade her from such felicity, don't you agree?"

She looked up at him with a bland expression that did not mislead him for a moment. Mendaciously he said, "I cannot abide a playful woman!"

"I should inform you," she said gently, "that Miss Gaines is not playful."

"Deadly serious, I take it?" he said. "Then I shall expect you to teach her better." Suddenly he laughed. "I must admit it is amusing—"

"You are entertained?" she asked suspiciously.

"I must admit that the Countess has more *flair* than I had supposed, to introduce into her household, in such an intimate position, a young lady who is so well acquainted with certain pitfalls that lie in wait for the neophyte in society."

Her cheeks slowly flushed. How rash she had been, to talk to a stranger as though she were his equal! She was perturbed even more about her lack of proper decorum as a mere companion speaking freely to a man of exalted status—no matter how irritated he made her!

She *must* guard her tongue, lest he penetrate too deeply into her identity and circumstances. He was a dangerous man! Summoning her defenses, she said brightly, "But I am persuaded there can be no better mentor to a young man than you, sir, for you would know—"

Too late, she realized that her words would be fatally provocative. His eyes glinted dangerously as he finished the sentence for her. "Know all that is to be avoided!"

The only defense she could summon was a bright, cheerful attitude. An attitude that told him, "You know best," was the best answer she could think of. "I do wish you success, in your Gothic way. I doubt that you could sustain a defeat, for you have so little experience."

A glint in his eye told her that her taunt had struck home, but he said, "I want you to promise to restrain that girl and keep her from eloping with my nephew. Surely this is a reasonable request."

Narcissa, eyes glittering, retorted, "I am no jailer, and I shall not bother myself to promise you anything." By this time they had arrived at the front drive, and without waiting for him to help her, she leaped down to the ground.

Carraford looked down at her, eyes blazing, and said, "Then you insist in helping them elope to Gretna?"

Narcissa said, "I *thought* you were not listening. For I made no such statement. I suggest that you look to your nephew, for you have fewer scruples than I do about interfering in someone else's life." She glared up at him, realizing with some dismay that she had lost her argument, and said tartly, "Don't let your horses stand." She turned and walked up the steps to the front door.

Evans opened the door, and she went inside. Evans, consumed by curiosity, allowed himself a quick look at the Marquess. He was glad that he himself did not serve in the household of Carraford, for eyes that could blaze with hot anger, as His Lordship's did just now, could also be expected to search out shortcomings of the most trivial kind.

The Marquess himself, setting his horses in motion again and whipping them up down the drive, had much to think about. His affection for his nephew was strong, but he recognized with justice that Rupert had reached the age of twenty with very little interference from his uncle and guardian. But the rub, thought Carraford, was that he had to hear of his shortcomings from a slip of a girl with dark blue eyes who—far from being impressed by his title and his fortune—seemed more than ordinarily critical of his actions, past and present.

He had thought that novelty no longer existed for a man who had, in fact, tasted most of the vices that Narcissa had mentioned. A *ridotto* in Venice was as familiar to him as the back of his hand. He was positive that the governess had not been in Venice when he had been, for he would have noticed her. But she had no business to have been in such a place at all!

A *ridotto* was a gaming house, usually an apartment in a nobleman's house. Nobody but the aristocrats kept the bank there, and the tourists furnished the profits. A *ridotto* was a place where one might meet a masked lady, somebody's wife who attended in disguise and mingled with the ladies of pleasure throughout the establishment, the center of the wild life of Venice, and was a well-known kind of resort on the Grand Tour.

How could a young lady, for the governess was obviously gently born, be so familiar with such a place? Had she been one of the ladies of pleasure, or had she lost her fortune gambling? Either one was as unlikely as the other, and Carraford could not make up his mind.

He was steeped in deep thought and almost missed his own gateposts. He was trying to track down the elusive memory of someone whose name he could not recall. His first thought when he had first seen Miss Adams was that she was someone else! But he could not now for the life of him remember who it was. It was only a face that he remembered, and there was no name attached to it.

The first thing that he was sure of was that her name was not Hester Adams. It was a governessy sort of a name and did not seem to fit her. As he turned his chaise over to his groom and went up the front steps of his house, another thought occurred to him. Throughout the afternoon, which had passed more quickly than he could have believed time to flow, not once had she tried to flirt with him. Not once had she given any indication that she thought of him as a man, not to say a desirable match.

It was an interesting experience, he thought, an experience out of the ordinary. His butler took his cloak, and he moved almost without thinking into his library.

A fire was burning there, and he moved to stand before it. He looked down into the flames as though seeking inspiration, and then suddenly another thought came to him.

It came to him that if she had been forced to assume a name that was not hers, quite possibly there must be a strong reason for it.

The governess was not a woman of feeble intellect, and he recognized that reason dictated her actions. She was not one to flit about the countryside without a purpose. And the fact that she used a name that was in all likelihood not her own, and beyond that was so mysterious about her antecedents, led him to probe for the underlying cause. And all he could think of was that she might be in trouble, hiding from—the authorities? He could not believe she was of criminal bent. But it was possible that she might be glad of a friend.

He made a decision to stay awhile in Yorkshire. He told himself, I'm interested only in solving the mystery that surrounds that young lady. But a deeper motive, which he did not yet admit, was a strong wish to see whether she needed help and to stand by in case she did.

19

The next morning Carraford woke to find his resolve strengthened overnight.

Carraford had a devious mind. A hunter never revealed himself at once to his prey, but, instead, stalked it from a blind downwind. He suspected that a person of the governess's resourcefulness, honed to a fine point by her need for secrecy, would be skittish as an untrained foal, and he must take great care not to startle her into running away.

Asking for Rupert at breakfast, he was told that Mr. Rupert had left the house and had not said where he was going. Nor, added the butler, when he would return. Carraford dismissed his servant with a nod and reflected. The suggestion of Miss Adams, that Rupert and Bella might run off to Gretna Green, had rocked him as much as she hoped it would. He could not believe that Rupert would deliberately take such drastic measures without exploring his influence with his uncle further. Certainly Carraford had expected far more argument from Rupert than he had so far received.

He had developed a strong respect for Miss Adams's common sense. If she suggested that an elopement might be in the wind, then it behooved him to prevent such a disaster. He restrained an impulse—yesterday he would have given way to it—to gallop to Hapworth Hall and demand to know what was going on.

Today, massaging his chin thoughtfully, he strolled with an appearance of casualness toward the stables. If Rupert were going to elope, he would have taken the traveling chaise or even the heavy coach. But both were in the coach house, as polished as though they were going to be run out this moment to have the horses put to. But at least Rupert was not driving one of them. Of course, Carraford reflected, the couple could always elope in one of the Hapworth vehicles, but surely it was more conventional for the prospective groom to furnish the transportation!

Carraford decided that Rupert was simply avoiding him, and he was in a sense relieved. He dressed carefully and rode over to Hapworth Hall. His mood was lighter, almost as though his anger had been forgotten. He was not a changeable man, but his goal had altered. When he had ridden up from London, his only purpose had been to bring Rupert into line with a short rein, if necessary, and wrench the boy away from his insidious surroundings.

But now he began to think that he had done Rupert an injustice—not only in the matter of Isabella Gaines but in his own management of the boy's life. If Rupert had, in fact, grown up to wish to be a responsible landholder, it was no thanks to the Marquess, by either precept or example.

He must make amends to Rupert and set the boy's affairs on a straight course. He would not admit that part of his reward would be not only a sense of duty done but also—if he were lucky!—a smile of approval in a certain pair of eyes.

Lucky! He was reluctant to admit the significance of his choice of words. He told himself, and almost believed it, that it was only curiosity about the mystery he conceived surrounding the governess, her wayward manners, and his own ability to search out the truth that guided him now. Curiosity—and nothing else.

When he arrived at Hapworth Hall, he asked for the Countess. While he was being ushered into the small salon to wait, his eyes strayed up the stairs. Miss Adams was not in sight.

But Miss Pinkney was, and she hastened across the hall to join Carraford in the small gold and white salon. Carraford was a tall man, broad of shoulder, and altogether too huge to fit into the dainty French-decorated room. Miss Pinkney, valiant in the crisis, tried her best.

"Pray sit down, sir," she said with a breathless rush, "I think you'll find that chair—no, no, not that one, this one—most comfortable. Although I do hope . . . but it is not usual for us to have visitors of such size— of such *elegance*, I mean—and dear Rupert is always afraid to sit in these chairs, and of course he is not so—so *broad* as you. I imagine he must take after his mother's people, don't you think? But then, he is always so welcome here that we do not stand on ceremony with him, I assure you. . . ."

Her voice dwindled away as she realized that of all subjects she might have chosen, the familiarity of Rupert with this household was perhaps the last that a prudent woman would have hit upon.

Carraford took pity upon her. "I truly cannot stay long, Miss Pinkney, and shall not take a chance of rendering myself comfortable." He eyed the spindly-legged chairs with dislike. But he suddenly realized that the furniture in this room was quite new and expensive. Perhaps Rupert was right—the Gaines family had fallen into prosperity!

As he was about to take his leave with all the civility he could muster, the Countess arrived. Carraford, whose manners when he chose could be meticulous, took care to ask about all the members of the household. He even contrived to ask about Miss Adams. Here he congratulated himself on his cleverness. He pronounced Miss Adams's name as though he were aware she were in disguise.

"How fortunate you are," murmured the Marquess, "to have chanced upon a young lady of such experience."

The Countess was intrigued. "I find no fault in her," she said neutrally. "But I am surprised, Carraford, that you have even noticed the girl."

Smoothly he quieted ruffled waters. "Only my curiosity," he said blandly, "to see what kind of influence your daughter has felt over the years."

"Miss Adams has been with us only two weeks."

He raised his eyebrows in honest surprise. "But such a great deal of experience for one so young," he said.

The Countess was nettled. "It is my daughter, Isabella, whose happiness is my concern," she pointed out. "And when the marriage takes place, then Miss Adams will, no doubt, travel on. I shall give her good references, of course, unless I find I have been much mistaken in her quality."

"As she had good references when she came." It was an invitation to the Countess to confide in him. Surely she could see that Hester Adams displayed only an outer shell at Hapworth Hall, and the Countess must know what lay beneath. But if she did, she was not planning to share her knowledge with Carraford.

Abruptly changing the subject, Lady Hapworth said, "This is a farewell visit? You plan to return to London?"

"No," Carraford responded. "I feel that I must witness for myself the great devotion between these two young people, and that will require my staying in the vicinity for some time. I must confess I should wish to see for myself whether Miss Adams was right. She claims that there is a strong attachment between your daughter and my nephew. I am not sure that she is right. Miss Adams spoke as though she had known your daughter for a long time before her employment."

The Countess said crisply, "Hester Adams came in answer to an advertisement. She is not a governess; she is my daughter's chaperone and companion. I find her of eminent quality, well bred, and full of common sense beyond her years."

Carraford agreed, for his opinion was much the same. He also to himself added the one quality that he wished she had less of, at least for the moment: discretion.

Carraford said, before he left, with a touch of wistfulness in his voice, "I wish I knew your daughter better."

While his words were not true, they were reasonable, and the Countess agreed at once. "I shall give a dinner party. You will wish to renew old friendships, and you will also see how well the youngsters comport themselves, how very mature they are!"

If Carraford looked forward with less than enthusiasm to becoming reacquainted with neighbors he had nearly forgotten, the feeling was not visible on his features.

He took his meticulous leave, well satisfied with his first step. He had made sure, by a roundabout way, that his continued residence at Carraford Hall would be accepted and that at least once he would be sure of meeting the elusive Miss Adams again.

It was easy enough for the Countess to say she would have a dinner party. Her method of entertainment was quite simple. One said one would have a dinner party, and then one turned the problem over to Miss Pinkney. Narcissa was asked to help with the guest list, and Bella, after it was pointed out to her that this would be good training for her own household, entered vigorously into the planning.

There were to be at least four removes and a dozen and a half of side dishes. A rump of beef à la Mantua, prawns, asparagus, a saddle of mutton, and peaches from the greenhouse—and each dish required Miss Pinkney's personal attention, which, in the event, became Hester's attention, for Miss Pinkney developed a *migraine* under stress.

Rupert, in and out of the house as a familiar of the family, informed them all that his uncle had only postponed the projected trip to Europe.

Charles Wayne, eyes lighting up at the prospect, cornered Narcissa. "You think there's a chance for me to go along?" he demanded. "As Mr. Elyot's tutor, of course?"

Narcissa managed not to express her astonishment. Instead, she objected, "I imagine that you might find it a trying task to guide a young man through the museums and handle the luggage and the conveyances, and the schedule of post routes, and the languages required at the different inns."

She had expected Wayne to appear chagrined, for she was positive he had no sense of the scope of what was called a bear leader. She sometimes considered that even the young Earl was beyond the capabilities of the pale young man with a nervous habit of licking his lips before venturing into speech.

But Mr. Wayne said, "There is nothing to learning foreign languages, and Mr. Elyot is a gentleman who would not be inclined to base company, I am sure." He looked nervously around him before continuing in a lowered voice. "I must tell you that I have taken steps to remove myself from this position. It does not give me sufficient room to expand my ideas of educating the young." He squared his shoulders impressively. "I am seeking another place."

"I wish you well," she said with more warmth than she felt, because she was sorry for him, deeming him a miserable misfit. If he was sufficiently energetic to seek another position, then she hoped for his success.

Narcissa, thinking privately that he was no worse than many of the tutors who had gone along with other young men she had seen in Europe, nonetheless thought that it would be Rupert who would have to keep an eye on Charles Wayne.

She returned to her reflections on Carraford. She could not doubt that Carraford's change in attitude was in large part due to her.

She was looking forward to seeing him again at the dinner party. She wanted to thank him, for one thing, for his indulgence toward the young people. But perhaps he would think that was presumptuous in her, to arrogate to herself the cause for his change of mind.

She rehearsed small speeches, pretty in themselves, and cast them aside as soon as she had thought about them. She ended up thinking, I will not even mention it to him. Besides, it was foolish to think that the Marquess of Carraford would pay any attention to a governess who attended the dinner merely as a companion to the daughter of the house. Narcissa would be present at the function only on sufferance. Yet she was anticipating the event as though she were the guest of honor.

The plans for the dinner proceeded. New dresses must be obtained, wine provided, music arranged, and flowers decided upon. The costs rose daily and, to Narcissa's mind, astronomically. Anxious, she sought out the Countess and explained her worry.

With a wave of the hand the Countess said, "Please don't bother me with it now, for I must get this off to London." She waved vaguely at the desk, but since she explained no further and had clearly forgotten the question, Narcissa left.

Narcissa indulged herself to the extent of a new scarf to drape around her shoulders. She purposely did not think of new clothing, for she had had only a slight advance on her salary so far, and as a matter of strict discipline she insisted upon the quiet garb of a paid companion.

At last, although she had for a while thought that it would never come and at other times wished it would never come, the night of the party arrived. The Marquess of Carraford, surprisingly, was among the first to arrive. Rupert was with him, and after they had made their bows to the hostess, to Miss Pinkney, and to Isabella, Carraford left the receiving line and moved into another room. Here, his eye falling upon Narcissa, he came at once to her side.

"I should imagine that you have much to do with the elegance of the rooms tonight."

Narcissa bit back the strong wish to tell him everything she had done and elicit his approval of her efforts. But she said only, "The Countess's staff has worked valiantly."

A small silence fell between them, until the Marquess spoke again. "I have come to watch the devoted pair in the transport of affections which you have assured me is theirs."

Narcissa, recognizing in time his provocative tone, responded only, "I hope they have sufficient deportment to moderate their behavior in public."

The Marquess, amused, said, "Then am I to understand that you have witnessed their transports in private?"

Narcissa, nettled, said, "You understand no such thing. They both have behaved with the utmost propriety."

Carraford said irrepressibly, "Young people in love forget propriety. Such has been my observation. I suppose you, too, have noticed the fact."

Narcissa replied oppressively, "I must be guided by your greater experience."

He glanced away, but not before she saw the amusement lurking in his eyes. She followed his glance to Rupert and Isabella, talking quite properly with Mrs. Hensley. She could not help noticing, however, that there was an aura surrounding the two that enclosed them in a world of their own—that while outwardly they moved and talked and behaved decorously, inwardly they were supremely aware only of each other.

A small gasp escaped her, and Carraford turned to smile. "Quite transparent, are they not?" His voice was gentle as he noted the dark circles under her eyes. He had no doubt but that the entire burden of this entertainment had fallen upon her slender shoulders. He could not help that—not now—but he could perhaps take another burden from her. "Do not concern yourself," he said almost tenderly, "about the children. I shall see to them."

Imperceptibly relaxing against the back of her chair, she watched him make his way across the room and join Mrs. Hensley and her young companions. It was a sacrifice on his part, she had little doubt, but how grateful she was!

Resisting the temptation to bait Narcissa further, Carraford had moved off, for he did not wish his conversation with her to be remarked. It was only civil to speak to her for a few moments, but any prolonged conversation must give rise to speculation. Carraford had not seen his near neighbors for years; but he fancied he knew their inordinate curiosity, and he would not subject either Narcissa or himself to their scrutiny.

At length dinner was served, and Narcissa sat down unobtrusively toward the middle of the table, removed by the squire's son, Tom Barker, the ham-handed driver, from Isabella. She had arranged the seating and purposely set Rupert at the far end of the table. Isabella and Rupert would carry on no private conversation under her eye.

There were times when Narcissa was hard put to recall that she herself was only twenty. Watching Bella's starry eyes and seeing Rupert watch her down the long table without caring for the consequences, she felt immeasurably older than her years. The six years spent on the Continent and the two months spent at her grandfather's had given her a maturity that showed in her carriage, in her air of authority, and even in her attitude of mind, although she was not aware of the latter.

Eventually dinner was finished, and the guests moved into the drawing rooms. Narcissa, seeing that her charge was still under the watchful eye of the Marquess, could find an unobtrusive chair near a window standing open to catch the cool air and close her eyes. Never had she been so weary!

A voice behind her mentioned a prominent family in Scarborough. "Old Lady Holland is pretty far gone," said the voice, which Narcissa did not recognize. "She's worn out her son's wife and runs the rest of the family a merry chase—a terror, so I've heard."

Another voice agreed. "No wonder her daughter thought even that wastrel was better than staying at home!"

It took a few moments for Narcissa to realize that

the unseen speakers were referring to her own family—her mother and her "wastrel" father. But she could not ask questions, and the speakers changed their subject. It was little enough news—only that old Lady Holland, her grandmother, was very ill. And she had learned that from the caretaker in London. How long ago that had been! Less than three months on the calendar—but at least a lifetime and a half to her!

Far more to the point, she realized, was the fact that Carraford's eyes had rested on her through nearly the entire dinner. Whenever she looked up, to see if she could read his expression on contemplating "the devoted pair," she caught his glance on her. Yet she was sure that so unobtrusive was his manner that no one else was aware of his scrutiny. In fact, she began to believe that she had imagined it. She did not wish the Marquess to spend his time looking at her, for sooner or later, he would insist on knowing who she was.

Narcissa turned her thoughts to Bella. The girl's manners were flawless; she spoke kindly to Tom Barker on her left and then, at an appropriate moment, turned to her neighbor on the right. Narcissa had no fault to find with Isabella, or with Rupert, as a matter of fact. Although he seemed unusually silent, he seemed to speak civilly when spoken to.

Later in the evening Charles Wayne, the young Earl's tutor, entered. Having finished his duties to his charge, he was allowed to mingle with the guests, and it was quite soon apparent that he did so with purpose. He nodded to Narcissa as he went past, and within moments she saw him standing quite as if by accident next to Carraford. He spoke rather at length to the Marquess, and she was pleased to see that Carraford at least did not snub him. She was irritated with Charles, for he was clearly trying to ingratiate himself with the highest-ranking guest.

She was as sure as though she were standing beside the two men that she knew the substance of the conversation. Mr. Wayne was certainly attempting to secure the Marquess's interest in employing the tutor as a companion to young Rupert on his travels in Europe. An odd recollection came into her mind of a young Englishman she and her father had met, in Genoa. He was full of the iniquities of his English servant, and a few of his impassioned phrases swam into her mind: "He demands more comforts than I do; he cannot sleep in the beds; he cannot drink the wine—I am more his servant than he is mine!" The criticisms could apply equally to Charles Wayne, she believed.

At length, although she thought it would never end, the party came to a close. She was much relieved to think that nothing unpleasant had happened, and Carraford had been civility itself. He managed a word with her before he left and said quietly, "I will not precipitate any elopement. I do not intend to drag Rupert away, so you may rest easy on that score."

He held her hand a trifle longer than she thought was necessary, but she forgot to withdraw it. He smiled down at her, a look in his eyes that no lady of recent years had been privileged to see. He added, "You may trust me on this." She felt a strong tug toward him, one that she would have to examine later, but her thought, although she did not express it, was simple: I would *like* above all things to trust him.

20

It was the day after the dinner.

Narcissa felt as though she were victim of a shipwreck, now tossed upon the shore.

She had been strong in her arguments to Carraford, persuading him that there was a genuine love uniting Bella and Rupert. The dinner, in the eyes of both the Countess and the Marquess, was expected to provide proof of the attachment and to convince him that Bella was indeed the wife he should choose for his nephew.

The preparations for dinner, with its attendant strains, had borne heavily upon Narcissa. She had at once to keep her eye upon Bella, whose tendency to send for Rupert at every juncture kept her chaperone busy, and to turn Miss Pinkney's vague instructions into reality.

And all the time she wondered whether she was right in becoming such a partisan of Bella and Rupert. The Marquess had much more experience than she had, and presumably he was able to read events with more acumen. At any rate, the burden of proof seemed to be hers, and now, midmorning of the day following the successful dinner, she believed he had been persuaded.

But her memory dwelt longest on his kindness to her, his offering to keep an eye on Bella for her, his *understanding*—usually lacking in gentlemen of her acquaintance—of the difficulties and the strains of her position.

She was on her way to the kitchen, to congratulate the cook and her staff for their efforts toward making the event the success that it was, when she was waylaid, in the short hall leading to the servants' wing, by Charles Wayne.

She was growing to dislike the young tutor, for no reason she could discover. It could be, she reflected, his assumption of easy familiarity, taking for granted that her origin had been as lowly as his. With a shock she realized that she was harboring the essence of snobbery. She resolved to smother the vice at its start!

As a result, she greeted the tutor with excessive kindliness. "Did you enjoy the evening? I imagine there has not been a press of the kind at Hapworth Hall for many years. Lady Hapworth must have paid off every social obligation for a generation!"

"Quite likely," said Mr. Wayne with a grimace. "How much did she spend on the entertainment?"

Narcissa said coolly, "I could not say."

He laughed. "You could, no doubt, but you won't. And I don't blame you. Her Ladyship would soon send you packing if you told tales, and then how would you snare your aristocratic friend?"

"I don't know what you mean!"

"Well, if you wish to keep your secrets, I should not pry, I suppose. But what I should really like to know is: When is the Marquess leaving for Europe?"

"I understood he has postponed his trip indefinitely."

Charles Wayne chewed his underlip meditatively. He blocked the passageway so that Narcissa could not get past him, and she was forced to wait. "He was very kind, you know," said Wayne. "I asked him about traveling with young Mr. Elyot, and the Marquess said he would think about it."

"Well, then, you have done as much as you can, haven't you?"

He was not satisfied. "Perhaps as much as *I* can, but certainly *you* are in a position to help me."

"How is that?" she said, surprised.

"You can put in a good word for me."

"With *Rupert?*"

"With His Lordship. I do hope that they depart before my letter comes. You know I told you I was seeking another post? I expect to hear momentarily on that. And I shall take it, I think. But if the Marquess were to employ me, then, of course, that is the position I should like."

"I suggest," said Narcissa, suddenly weary of the tutor and his machinations, "that you ask Lord Carraford himself. I have no idea of what his plans are."

"No? Then I suggest you consider your own position."

She stared at him in sheer astonishment. "Whatever do you mean?"

"You are at present in his confidence, of course. But don't count on that familiarity to endure."

"You are totally mistaken!"

"Not in his confidence? You surprise me, Miss Adams. When I myself saw him deep in conversation with you last night. And besides, he could hardly take his eyes from you all evening."

Anger held her speechless. When she found her tongue, she exclaimed, "You are unfair! The Marquess and I have never exchanged more than a few words, and nothing of a personal nature has passed between us!"

Wayne's smile was a knowing smirk. He knew what he knew, his attitude said, and nothing she could say would change that. "Well, if you won't tell me, you won't. But I should think you would have a feeling for a fellow servant."

Narcissa said, her eyes narrowed, "I don't consider myself a servant."

Wayne said, "No doubt you consider yourself a prospective Marchioness!"

It was time to call a halt to this, she thought, and she told him icily, "I think you've said enough—"

He broke in. "I feel it is my duty to give you a word of advice. Don't get ideas above your station. His Lordship is a notorious rake, and any woman who succumbs to his attractions—I can't understand what they are, but you will know—is more than a fool. She would be in the suds before she knew it."

She didn't remember later what she said, for anger blinded her and made her heedless. But she spoke to such effect that Wayne scuttled away, leaving her with the strong suspicion that she had given away more than one clue to her real feelings.

She promised herself to behave with more discretion. The tug toward Carraford that she had felt last night, indeed, had felt from the beginning, the tug that could draw her irresistibly into his orbit, was a feeling that she would have to fight against. She alternated between a lowering notion that Charles Wayne was right, for she had noticed that Carraford was watching her during dinner, and the knowledge that she was more than susceptible to the charms of the Marquess. He had more than his share, she believed—no man should combine worldly advantages with such personal magnetism. She could so easily turn to him as though he were an anchor in a sea of uncertainties.

What Charles Wayne did not know was that she was sufficiently wellborn to be eligible as the Marchioness of Carraford.

While her thoughts, totally out of control, ran along the lines of marriage, she was sure Carraford's did not. His unexpected concern had insinuated itself through chinks in her armor, so to speak, and she hardly knew when it had happened.

But one thing was certain: She could not go to the Hollands now, for eventually she would meet Carraford. The Hollands would say, she believed, that she had come to them only to establish her identity to trap the Marquess. Her pride sank from any such interpretation being attached to her natural desire to be united with her mother's family.

Besides, if she were *then* to meet Carraford, on easier terms, and he smiled ironically and departed, she had a dark suspicion that she would carry the scar the rest of her life.

She could not risk such an outcome.

And if she went to the Hollands, they could be disgusted with her for not accepting their silence as final. Whichever way she turned, to tell Carraford or to tell the Hollands that she existed and that she was kin to them, there were pitfalls. There was nothing for it but to be even more cautious in keeping her secret. The best way to do that, she realized without enthusiasm, was to avoid Carraford entirely. It was an easier resolve to make than to keep.

The vicar and his wife invited Bella, Miss Pinkney, and Narcissa to lunch.

"Now we can settle down to a comfortable prose," said Mrs. Hensley, leading the way from the dining room to her small drawing room. "Mr. Hensley may just leave us if he does not wish to listen." She raised an eyebrow archly at her husband.

The vicar said with a smile, "I think I had best remain, lest the gossip get too far out of hand."

The two were on exceedingly comfortable terms with each other, and Narcissa enjoyed the relaxed air that pervaded the house. But soon her serenity was marred.

Mrs. Hensley, with a sidelong glance at Narcissa, addressed Miss Pinkney. "I understand you are to have a wedding in your family. All the village is talking of it. They say that the Marquess came home especially to give his blessing to the two young people. Miss Gaines, I am sorry to put you to the blush. It is so pleasant to see young people so modest, is it not?"

Bella shot a pleading look at Narcissa, but surprisingly it was Miss Pinkney who rose to the occasion. "It is not at all settled, Mrs. Hensley, and I fear that our dear Bella is much too young to marry." She favored them all with a sweet smile and added, "I trust you will not listen to any rumors about the Marquess. His temper, of course, is well known to his friends, but I assure you we pay no heed to his threats. Just words, don't you know, and not at all to be considered."

Narcissa listened, appalled, while Miss Pinkney bared the inner counsel of the residents of Hapworth Hall. Bella was ready to sink into the floor with embarrassment, as Miss Pinkney continued, saying, devastatingly, "It is thanks to our Miss Adams, you know, that dear Rupert's trip has been postponed, at least for a little while. I should like to see Rupert's Grand Tour become a honeymoon, don't you agree?"

"Miss Adams?" repeated Mrs. Hensley. "I had not thought you had such power over a total stranger. But surely your influence is all to the good, and we must be grateful." She eyed Narcissa with speculation.

Narcissa protested weakly, "I had nothing to do with his decision, nothing at all."

Mrs. Hensley smiled knowingly. "We all are aware of the havoc a pair of bright eyes can wreak, are we not? My dear husband often says—"

Her dear husband broke in with a masterly clearing of his throat. "My dear, we need not go into that," he rebuked her dryly. "Besides, I may point out to you that the Marquess himself is just now approaching our front entrance. I shall go receive him myself."

The Marquess was ushered in and evinced surprised

pleasure at seeing them. Mrs. Hensley fluttered a welcome; but his manners were exquisite, and immediately she was at her ease.

Carraford sat uneasily on the chair just vacated for him by Mr. Hensley. "Pray do not put yourself out," said the Marquess, "for I chanced only to be passing this way and on an impulse dropped in." He looked across at Narcissa and added with a bland expression, "I had no idea that you were entertaining such charming guests."

Narcissa rejected such a false statement out of hand, for the carriage outside had the Countess's crest on the panels, and the Marquess must have been seriously absentminded if he had failed to observe that.

Mrs. Hensley, her thoughts busy with the conjectures that had been fostered by Miss Pinkney's indiscreet remarks, fortified by Narcissa's obvious confusion, fell silent.

Narcissa, fully aware of the tenor of Mrs. Hensley's thoughts, decided to withdraw as gracefully as she could from an untenable situation. Signaling Miss Pinkney, she rose to take leave of the vicar and his wife.

Carraford, rising punctiliously to his feet, bowed to the departing guests. Narcissa, following Miss Pinkney and Bella, caught his eye as she passed him. She was gratified to notice a glint of chagrin that boded ill for the future. But for now she swept past him, savoring her small triumph. For the Marquess could not in decency leave the Hensleys for half an hour, and she was positive he would find their unalloyed flattery a sore trial!

Suddenly Carraford seemed to be everywhere. The Countess did not have a chaplain in residence, so that any members of the household who wished to go to church had to attend St. Mark's in the village. Narcissa and Bella and Miss Pinkney did so, but to Narcissa's surprise, Carraford was among the worshipers. He managed a few words with them at the close of the service, before they rattled off in the chaise to Hapworth Hall.

Narcissa was becoming nettled at the constant appearance of Carraford, almost as though he sensed her wish to avoid him. She believed he was trying to make an assessment of Bella as a bride for his nephew, but he made only a civil effort to speak to Bella. In fact, he spoke mostly to Narcissa, and when he was not speaking to her, she found that he was, if not watching her, at least sensitive to her moods.

To think that a man of Carraford's rank and intelligence had a wish to talk to her was flattering indeed. Although she began to dread the sight of his approaching her, because of the tumult of her own senses and the confusing tenor of her thoughts, eventually there came a time when she knew unalloyed joy at the sight of his tall, elegant figure.

Bella developed a toothache. After two days of constant and vocal misery, she at length agreed to be taken to the tooth drawer in Market Weighton. The expedition turned into a serious undertaking before they finished.

Miss Pinkney, of course, went along, as did Narcissa. Rupert, beside himself at the sight of his beloved in agony, insisted on accompanying her, making the coach more than a little crowded, but there was nothing for it. Bella clung like a limpet to his hand. Rupert was quietly defiant, and Narcissa and Miss Pinkney simply did not try to separate them.

It was a long way to Market Weighton. By the time they left the tooth drawer Bella's pain was somewhat relieved. He had given her several drops of laudanum to deaden the pain, and while it served its purpose, it made her drowsy. There had been no chance for a small luncheon, for Bella's plight was too serious for them to leave her.

At length, Narcissa decided that they must immediately travel back to Hapworth Hall. By this time Bella was too ill and feverish to sit up. She was assisted to lie at full length on the front-facing seat. The prospect of Miss Pinkney, Rupert, and Narcissa crowded together on the back-facing seat for the endless journey back to Hapworth Hall was daunting.

Narcissa wondered whether Rupert could be persuaded to sit on the box with the coachman. The two grooms could double up at the back.

Rupert gave strong signs of resisting any separation from Bella. Miss Pinkney's temper, usually kind and vague, rapidly deteriorated in the absence of lunch. She was feeling distinctly peckish, and her irritability was apt to increase seriously before they got home.

It was at this juncture that the Marquess of Carraford drove into the innyard. Narcissa, upon seeing him and realizing that he was pulling to a halt beside them, said, "Oh, how good of you to come! How glad I am to see you!"

The Marquess, preserving calm, said only, "I'm gratified. You must know that I am more than willing to put myself at your service, Miss Adams. How can I be of assistance?"

She began to explain; but he signaled to his groom, who ran to the heads of the horses, and the Marquess stepped down to stand beside Narcissa. With one sweeping glance he took in the situation. Bella lay on the seat, moaning. Miss Pinkney eyed the narrow back-facing seat apprehensively. Rupert had eyes only for Bella.

Scarcely knowing how it was accomplished, Narcissa saw that within moments the situation was sorted out. Rupert was allowed to ride with his beloved Bella, and Miss Pinkney sat beside him to preserve the proprieties. Narcissa was swiftly handed into the curricle, and Carraford mounted beside her. His groom swung up behind them. Carraford held his pair back until the lumbering coach had waddled through the gate and onto the street and then sent the curricle to follow.

Carraford said virtuously, "You see, I have taken care of the proprieties as far as you are concerned also, for there can be no objection to your traveling in an open vehicle with my groom behind."

Narcissa said, "I must also expect that you are not of a mind to seduce a mere governess."

The Marquess laughed, saying, "Not a governess, I believe. More a companion. Companions are not off my list."

She bit her lip in vexation. She had asked for that kind of remark, and she feared that she had given away her own ambivalent feelings toward him. They traveled in silence, keeping the coach ahead of them well within sight, for as Carraford said, "We must be at hand in case the situation ahead becomes untenable."

Narcissa, amused, cried, "How cruel! You have imprisoned Rupert in the carriage, knowing that he is seeing Bella at her worst!"

Carraford said indulgently, "How did you expect me to remove him? I could not forcibly peel him away, could I?"

Narcissa giggled.

Carraford, encouraged at his success in making her laugh, continued. "I told you I would not precipitate an elopement. It is my design now to have Rupert see exactly what he can expect. He must be thoroughly exposed to the worst. I think the vows run 'in sickness and in health'."

Narcissa informed him, "He is utterly devoted. I have had to revise my opinion of him, for I had not expected such constancy from him."

"You have a low opinion of men in general then?"

"It has been my observation, sir, that men are inclined to vanish completely in the face of any unpleasantness."

Carraford was stirred by her simple statement that spoke volumes, clearly the distillation of many incidents when Miss Adams was left to pay the piper. His imagination drew on a vast experience of what his companion called "unpleasantness," and worse, and he marveled at the courage that could bring her through, unembittered.

Narcissa returned to the subject she thought must interest him. She said, "Rupert is utterly devoted, as you have seen. He didn't flinch even when Bella cried out when she lost her tooth."

Carraford said, "Spare me the details. I have no doubt that Rupert will favor me with many a description of how brave she is and how pathetic her suffering was, and while I shall have to listen to it, at least I don't have to anticipate it."

Narcissa said, "I beg your pardon. But my excuse is that Bella's suffering has been very much on my mind for the last three days."

Carraford nodded. "I suspect you have had a hard time. Could you not now enjoy a small respite?"

Narcissa was burningly conscious of his kindness. The air, as they bowled along in the well-sprung curricle, was pleasant on her cheeks. It was more than pleasant to be aware of her virile companion, to feel his concern for her well-being, to realize that for a short space of time Carraford had deftly relieved her of her onerous responsibilities. With him in charge, she knew, she need only ride along, knowing he would take care of anything that came up.

Yet she felt impelled to protest, "As always, you know what is best for everyone."

Carraford objected. "Not at all. You must agree that Rupert should be given every opportunity to see what life with Bella will be like. He must have every chance to draw back, before anything so final as an elopement or even an announcement in the *Gazette.* If he is to sustain disillusion, you must agree that it is better if it happens now, rather than later. If he is not leg-shackled, he can recover."

They rode in silence for some time before he added, "Don't you agree?"

When she still didn't answer, he persisted. "I'm sure disillusion has come to you. And one gets over it, doesn't one?"

If she had glanced at him, she would have seen that his face was drawn into lines of bitterness; but her eyes were full of tears, and she could barely see the ears of the horses ahead. She was remembering—remembering too much.

She remembered Sir Maurice and her disillusionment for her grandfather. There had been her hopes of the Hollands, who had proved faithless to the family tie. She even remembered a young man in Germany for whom she had developed a strong attachment. He was a gambler, and because his luck was out, he had drunk himself to death.

All that kind of disillusion, she agreed, one could get over. But what upset her now, so that her voice was unsteady and she dared not trust it to answer, was the tone of Carraford's voice, a gentleness that she had not suspected in him and a note of concern that threatened to overwhelm her.

Carraford unobtrusively took note of her distress. With great thoughtfulness, he soon moved the conversation into more impersonal channels, and the rest of the drive was passed in such mutual pleasure that Narcissa was surprised that they reached Hapworth House in such a short time.

"It took twice as long on our way," she said shyly.

Carraford gave her a smile of great charm. "But then you were worried over your charge. That is always anxious."

She agreed. But, she knew, it was Carraford's companionship that had sent the time flying!

21

Carraford, back in his own study, reflected on the events of the day. He was now surer than ever that Miss Hester Adams—surely not her name—was involved in a mystery. Her plight seemed to be sorely distressing. He had not missed the trembling of her lips and the somber reflections that had troubled her this afternoon.

If disillusion had come her way, she was not yet over it. While time might cure disillusion, it was possible that her problem had not yet been resolved.

He had made every effort to gain Narcissa's trust. The times over the past two weeks that he had seen her—at the vicar's, on the road, calling on the Countess—had been not at all by chance. He was making a determined campaign to obtain—he was not quite sure what.

He was realistic enough to know that his reaction to the winsome miss with the dark blue eyes was not his usual one. He did not view her as a possible conquest, nor was he repelled by a reaction all too familiar, of assessing his person and then deciding that title and fortune were sufficient to overlook his lack of attractiveness.

It had been his experience that first a young lady—or her ambitious mama—took note of his ill-assorted features and then, on second thought, remembered his assets.

Not Miss Adams!

She treated him as though she were as wellborn as he, and his observation conceded that she might well be right. She pointed out his faults—not without a spicy word or two—without fear.

For the rest, when they could treat on neutral ground, she was a delightful companion, with a well-in-

formed mind—too well informed on certain subjects!
She was blessed with common sense and a courage that
shone through her simplest actions.

I'm babbling like a schoolboy! he thought with
chagrin. But even so, laying Miss Adams's charms
aside, he was convinced that some trouble had come to
her and still distressed her. He could perhaps, if she
would only trust him, take care of her wrongs, whatever they might be—since he was convinced that position and money cured most ills.

Even this afternoon's expedition to Market Weighton
had been a carefully planned expedition. Rupert had informed him of Bella's impending journey, and Carraford, without confiding in Rupert, thought it would
be a good idea to find himself in Market Weighton. He
had no idea that the situation would turn out the way
as it had, but where Narcissa was, there he thought it
would be well to be also.

He felt he had made some strides in obtaining Narcissa's confidence, and he wished she would trust him
all the way. Even if he could not lift the cloud that surrounded her, at least he could share it with her. He
thought, that afternoon, she had almost come to the
point of telling him who she was and what troubled
her—almost, but not quite.

An alien emotion stirred him, one he had not felt for
many years. If he looked at it, he might recognize it,
but since he was not ready to admit he was in love,
head over heels, for the first time since he had been in
school, he carefully refrained from considering it. Instead, he simply told himself he wished to help her out
of whatever scrape she was in.

For any woman of such obvious good breeding to
appear in an obscure household in Yorkshire, under a
name that he was positive was assumed, argued the
presence of more than ordinary trouble.

Rupert returned from Hapworth Hall and at once
came to his uncle's study. "Uncle John, I want to thank
you," said the young man, rousing his uncle from his
deep reverie.

"For what?" said Carraford blankly.

"How good you were to come to Market Weighton
and remove Miss Adams! Although," he said reflectively, "it would have been more to the point to remove

Miss Pinkney. I vow her moans in sympathy were worse than my dear Bella's!"

Carraford grimaced. "That's what you would have wished on me? Thank you, I am too wily a bird to be caught in *that* snare!"

Rupert grinned. "Bella will be better now that she is home. The ride was anguish for her, but she never complained, not even when the tooth drawer brought out his tools!"

"Spare me the details," said his uncle. "I have seen one or two tooth drawings in my day." It was light conversation, but Carraford was struck by the accuracy of Miss Adams's observations. Rupert had indeed stood firm in the face of an unpleasant scene and displayed a maturity that was astonishing, because unexpected. Carraford would have to revise some of his opinions.

After Rupert left, Carraford's thoughts turned to some reflections on the Hapworth household. If Narcissa's trouble were connected with the household, he could deal with it easily. There was that idiotic tutor, Charles Wayne, who had approached him about traveling with Rupert on the Continent. Carraford had a strong inclination to tell the Countess of his disloyalty. There must be some way, and he would find it, to warn the tutor away from Miss Adams. He had seen him making sheep's eyes at Narcissa, and the sight had stirred anger in Carraford. There was one thing he could do for Narcissa, and that was to remove Wayne from her vicinity. Or at least render him harmless.

Bella, Narcissa's charge, was, according to Carraford, headstrong and basically self-centered. He had judged her on the basis of other women he had met, and since he had taken almost every woman in dislike, Bella was no exception. He had not been impressed by Bella's suffering that afternoon, for surely having a tooth drawn was something that most people managed to survive.

He was still determined that Rupert have some wider experience and not simply marry Bella because she was the only woman he had come in contact with. But he had given his word to Narcissa not to cause an elopement, and he would keep it. An elopement could only add to Miss Adams's troubles.

Miss Pinkney, in his opinion, was a cipher. One couldn't count on her for much, and he dismissed her out of hand. The Countess herself was a strange, selfish, and somewhat malicious woman. Then came another thought. Where did the Countess get her money? For there was obviously money at Hapworth Hall. The Gaines family, according to rumor, had scarcely a feather to fly with. After the Earl died, leaving an unborn son, the family had sold the house in London and retired to the country.

The mystery surrounding the money was one that didn't truly concern Carraford. But perhaps that was part of Narcissa's problem. He could not dismiss the Hapworth money out of hand.

The result of his systematic cogitation on the subject of those persons surrounding the governess had one result. The girl was alone and friendless, except for him.

He truly could not continue to rely on running into Miss Adams by chance. Bella's toothache had been fortunate—for the Marquess!—but he must take a more active role in the governess's affairs. It took only a few minutes to decide upon his next step.

He would give a dinner party!

He owed it to his neighbors, he told himself, rehearsing the details of his scheme. He surely should return the Countess's friendly entertainment. . . .

But his devious plans included far more than the dinner party. He went the next day to Hapworth Hall. His ostensible reason was to inquire about the health of Miss Gaines. Being reassured that she was recovering, he changed the subject. "I have in mind to give a dinner party, to repay your kind hospitality," said the Marquess, "but I find that I am without means of making the arrangements. I wondered whether I might borrow your Miss Adams, to help me plan my dinner party."

The Countess had come to a mistrustful truce with the Marquess. She had not forgotten his calling her "fishwife" at the onset of their renewed acquaintance. It rang too near the truth for her to forgive easily. Since her merchant antecedents had already caused her so many insults from her late husband's family, she was acutely conscious of any slurs upon her breeding.

She could not fathom Carraford's turnabout. From being the greatest monster of all time, he now stood in her drawing room totally at ease, his coat fitting superbly, his boots with a mirror-gloss finish, and smiled at her. She didn't trust him an inch.

"Miss Adams?" echoed the Countess. "I should think, if you wished to become better acquainted with my daughter, that you would wish to see how *she* conducts herself in managing a household."

The Marquess permitted himself a slight smile. "My dear Lady Hapworth, we both know that an efficient household runs itself, provided one has chosen a proper factotum. I have not the slightest doubt that you would see to the selection of a butler in your daughter's house, or at least a housekeeper, who would know how to go on." He caught the triumphant glint in Lady Hapworth's eyes and decided to dampen her hopes. "Whomever," he added, "Miss Gaines marries."

Grudgingly the Countess admitted that he was right. "I shall, of course, always be interested in my daughter's affairs." She could not resist a telling thrust. "And not simply arrive at a time of crisis, to upset everybody."

"May I expect Miss Adams?" said the Marquess, ignoring her peevish words.

He had made a mistake. The Countess was no fool, and she found his iteration of Hester's name suspicious. Why had the Marquess, who scarcely knew the girl, become so insistent on her aid? Lady Hapworth, until she could consider the matter further, simply evaded the issue. She said with every appearance of truth, "I fear that Miss Adams is not the person you require. I should like to offer you Miss Pinkney, my sister, you know, who planned my own dinner party. You are very kind to say that the arrangements were elegant, and I feel sure that you may trust Lavinia to do as well for you."

Carraford lifted his eyebrows. "It was my understanding that Miss Adams planned the arrangements?"

The Countess, nettled, said, "I can't think what gave you that idea! Surely Miss Adams herself did not tell you so? I had not believed her to be untruthful."

Realizing that he was doing more harm than good, the Marquess retreated. "I should certainly be grateful for any help you can send to me."

The Countess, wishing to get her daughter's marriage arranged securely, said, "I hope that after your dinner party we can send the announcement to the *Gazette*. Shall I leave that in your hands? Or can I take the burden from you?"

The Marquess was conscious of a growing dislike for the Countess. He did not look forward with any pleasure to the prospect of being connected by marriage with her, for she struck him forcibly as a forward, ill-bred, match-making mama, who would stop at little to ensure her offspring's security.

A week ago he would have blasted the Countess with a well-chosen phrase, designed to demolish her pretensions. He would even have said *never* would such a marriage receive his consent. But the Marquess was a changed man.

No longer was he concerned with his nephew's marriage. He could wish for a better match perhaps; but after all, the girl *was* an Earl's daughter, and if Rupert could not loose himself from the silken bonds of infatuation, it was no more than many another well-padded heir had faced. Carraford, intrigued by the mystery of Hester Adams and more than a little enmeshed in silken bonds himself, was intent now on disguising his own interest.

"You have the new *Gazette*," he said idly and picked it up from the library table.

"Yes," said the Countess shortly, "and I shall expect to see *a certain announcement* quite soon."

He scarcely knew what happened next. His eye fell by chance upon an item in the column where deaths of prominent persons were reported. His eyes fastened upon the words, the one name, and he stood thunderstruck. His thoughts were milling chaotically.

The *Gazette* item announced the death of Lady Holland, the mother of the present Baron. *Now* he knew at least part of the mystery of Narcissa. If she was not a Holland, even a by-blow, then he was bereft of his senses. He dropped the newspaper on the table and left the Countess only with the barest of courtesies.

He had been startled that first day by Hester's resemblance to someone he knew. Surprise had jolted words of recognition from him, yet even then he could not put a name to the face he thought he knew.

Now it all came back to him. He had seen the dowager Lady Holland, an ancient lady of perhaps ninety years, taking the waters. Just now he could not remember where. But tending the old baroness was a granddaughter—what was her name? It came to him— *Julia*. And Julia and the enigmatic Miss Adams looked enough alike to be sisters!

He was totally bemused, and his discovery kept him company all the way down the drive.

22

Happily unaware that the wall of secrecy she had maintained around her had been breached, Narcissa was strolling in the park surrounding Hapworth Hall. She was out of sight of the house and had wandered along some of the bypaths through the woods. At length, worrying at having her skirt caught by brambles, she emerged onto the drive, close to the outside gates.

She scarcely knew where she was. Her thoughts were keeping her miserable company, and she had originally set out from the house to be alone.

Her situation here at Hapworth Hall was becoming more precarious. It seemed a foregone conclusion that Isabella would not for long need the services of a chaperone. She thought she knew all the signs. The Countess was anxious for the alliance, and Carraford seemed to have given up his strong opposition to the marriage. And as Bella had said, the first day of Narcissa's stay here, a married woman would not need a chaperone.

Narcissa was very near to being unemployed. She had spent only a small part of her wages, and it was a comfortable thought that the money was piling up, for her use when worse came to worst.

That time had come more quickly than she had expected. The ride home with Carraford the day before had given her the unwelcome realization that her position was equivocal, to say the least. Carraford was far too curious, far too perceptive of her moods, and she suspected that she had told him more than she had said. She could not understand his motives, for surely he could have no interest in her as a person!

There were two things that she must fear from Carraford. One was that he would penetrate her disguise and immediately would inform her mother's people that she was here. She was reluctant to have her existence brought once more to their attention. She did not wish a stranger, like Carraford, to run to her family with the news that he had found her. She could not help feeling that the Hollands would look with disfavor upon any gambit—so they would term it—to bring her to their attention again.

But it was the second fear that bothered her more. It was her own far from equivocal feeling toward Carraford. She was uneasily aware that he was a dangerously attractive man, and in her present state of insecurity, she recognized that she was only too prone to listen to his blandishments.

And of course, that would not do.

There was no question in her mind that she would have to leave Hapworth Hall in the foreseeable future. With Isabella married, she must seek other employment. There was no choice to be given her—she would have to seek another governess's position.

She was sure that the Countess would give her letters of recommendation, and since the letters would be written on behalf of Hester Adams, Narcissa began to feel that she must say farewell forever to her own identity. She must continue living as Hester Adams, and all of a sudden she realized that there was no name on earth she detested more.

So intent had she been on her own thoughts that she saw with a start that Charles Wayne and the young Earl were approaching up the driveway. She had been avoiding the tutor as much as she could and dreaded being alone with him even for a moment. But there was no escaping it. They had seen her and now were hastening toward her.

She greeted them civilly. "Where have you been all day?" she asked young William kindly.

He cast a dark glance at his mentor. "Mr. Wayne wouldn't let me hunt. But now that the Marquess is just about related to us, I don't see why I can't shoot at his pheasants!"

"It's very wrong to shoot someone else's game! It's called poaching—"

"Not if I'm an Earl!" cried the boy stoutly. "Mr. Wayne doesn't let me do anything!"

He ran up the drive. Mr. Wayne, instead of following his charge, grimaced sourly. "You can see what my life is like," he complained to Narcissa. "But I'm not taking this any longer." Narcissa was faced with the choice of returning to the house in company with him or of continuing on alone to the road. She took a step away from the house.

Mr. Wayne reached out a hand to catch her sleeve. "Please don't go," he said urgently. "It is my great good fortune to find you alone. I have wished to talk to you seriously, ever since yesterday, and I had not dared hope that the opportunity would arise so soon. I want to tell you, for I know this will concern you as nearly as it does me, that I have a new position. I will be leaving Hapworth Hall very soon."

Narcissa said, "That is certainly good news for you. I wish you well. Where is it?"

Wayne's face lit up as he said, "I have been offered a position in a school in Derbyshire. It's run by an old school friend of mine, and he's asked me to come and help him. I will be leaving as soon as the Countess releases me."

"For your sake, I hope that will be soon."

She turned to stroll up the drive toward the house. But Charles Wayne was not yet finished. "I am glad that you are interested, for you know that you, too, will have to leave Hapworth Hall very soon. I would like to have you go as my wife."

Narcissa stopped in her tracks. She could not believe that she heard aright, yet she knew that the word "wife" had certainly been spoken. She turned to him and looked into his face. She did not even try to hide her shock.

Seeing that he expected an answer, she said with a lamentable lack of civility, "I cannot. You know I cannot."

Charles Wayne, far from being the bland, rabbitlike person she had believed, now began to show signs of anger. Ugly red blotches appeared on his face, and his lips tightened. "I suppose you think you're too good for me! Well, let me tell you that marriage to me, no matter how you feel about, is better than a slip on the shoulder from Carraford! You know he is intent on disgracing you, and I offer you the only honorable way out."

Narcissa said, with returning spirit, "Pray do not give any heed to my position, for I do not see that it concerns you. I told you I cannot marry you, and that is the limit of your concern."

Charles Wayne said, "I suppose you would rather give in to Carraford!"

Narcissa said, "There is no chance of that!"

But the idea and Charles Wayne's importunities had overset her. She was trembling with anger. Not only was she shocked at the manner of Charles Wayne's proposal of marriage, but she was also dismayed to find that in her heart, unbidden, was the realization that disgrace was all Carraford had to offer. And she was even more upset to find that she looked almost kindly upon the prospect.

This would never do! Her eyes filled with tears. She was frantic, longing to run and hide in her room, to cry her heart out, and then—realistically—to pack her bags and leave!

She turned blindly again toward the house, but the thunder of approaching hooves stayed her. Someone was coming from the house, his horse galloping, at a thundering pace. Charles Wayne reached out to grab her wrist. Perhaps his purpose was merely to remove her from the path of the oncoming rider, but in her upset state of mind that possibility did not occur to her. She pulled away, angrily, just as the rider came into view. What Carraford saw, bemused as he was with the revelation that had just come to him, was the girl on his mind fighting off an unwelcome suitor. He reined up abruptly and slid to the ground. His eyes blazed with contempt for the young man before him and a sure sympathy for Narcissa, but his voice was bland when he spoke. "I see that I came just in time, Miss Adams. I seem to rescue you quite often."

Narcissa could only retort sharply, "I suppose you think this, too, is my fault!"

Carraford said, "On the contrary, I see it is the error of this very callow young man, who has been asking me for a position as bear leader for my nephew. I should tell you, Wayne, that I find this behavior, forc-

ing yourself upon a defenseless woman, a contemptible
act. I could, of course, not countenance your staying at
Hapworth Hall, in charge of an impressionable young
boy, any longer. I would be quite concerned, were I
the Countess, about the influence your sad lack of judgment would have over her heir."

Wayne, in a mixture of fright and resentment, tried
to speak. "I only was trying—"

Narcissa broke in. "Oh, please, do not disclose this
incident to Lady Hapworth! No harm has been done,
and my own position is equivocal."

"Not above scandal," agreed Charles Wayne, recovering his spirit. "For my intentions, Your Lordship, are
far more honorable than some I could mention."

Carraford seemed to recede to a measurable distance.
"I trust you will not be so misguided as to pursue this
line of thought. Miss Adams has saved your reputation
this time, but I really cannot vouch for the consequences if there happened to be another incident of the
sort." His voice dripped ice, and even Narcissa could
feel the chill.

Charles Wayne was not devoid of dignity. "I must inform Your Lordship that there is no need to relate this
incident to the Countess. I have a new position, and I
will take it up two weeks hence." He turned to Narcissa
and bowed slightly. "I shall speak with you again, if I
may, when I shall hope you have reflected further on
our conversation."

"There is no need for reflection," said Narcissa.

Mr. Wayne hesitated, then, glancing defiantly at the
Marquess, started up the gravel driveway toward the
house, leaving Narcissa and Carraford alone.

Now that he had had his eyes opened, Carraford
could see Holland characteristics written all over into
Narcissa's face. How could he have missed her strong
resemblance to Julia Holland? More to the point, how
close a relation was Narcissa? Surely a cousin, but although he thought he knew all members of that family,
Narcissa must come from a forgotten branch. His
memory tickled him with the hint of some long-ago
scandal in the family, but just now he could not lay
mental hands on it.

What was a member of that great family of Hollands

doing here at Hapworth Hall? It was an even a more intriguing mystery, now that he had solved part of it!

Narcissa, unaware of the thoughts that were milling through Carraford's brain, was stammering her thanks. She was grateful for his rescue, although she sank in embarrassment at the thought it was Carraford, once again, who had performed that office. Besides, she was trembling, not with belated emotion or disgust with Charles Wayne, but with the realization that her feelings for Carraford were indeed powerful. She wondered whether she would ever recover from them—and the only recourse she had was to flight.

Carraford was talking to her, saying, with a great deal of assurance, "You shall not endure that man any longer. If he stays longer than two weeks, he must be sent away."

Narcissa said, "He really didn't bother me."

Carraford said, "That is such a palpable untruth that I shall not even try to deny it. You are still trembling, and I would not have had this happen for a good deal. I shall see to it that the man does not bother you anymore."

Narcissa, overcoming her agitation and retorting with spirit, said, "You know, I suppose, what is best for everybody! Even a lowly tutor, whose existence you are hardly aware of. Yet you solve his problems, direct his destiny, as though you had a right to interfere."

Carraford, maintaining his composure with some difficulty, quirked an eyebrow and said, "You are quite right. I must not interfere with the destiny of that young man. Whatever he does is of no concern to us." He added, with a note in his voice that had not been heard by a female for some years, "Let us forget him. I know what is best for you."

She stared up at him and saw that the anger in his eyes was gone. Instead, there was a new look in his eyes, one that she was not able to understand, but that just the same gave her a feeling that was entirely pleasurable. "For me?" It was an inane answer, but she did not seem to be in control of her faculties.

He smiled down at her and repeated, "For you, Miss—Adams? Can that be right? For I know who you are."

Narcissa felt the color drain from her face, and she swayed. She might have fallen had he not reached a hand out to steady her. She was so distraught that she did not realize that he allowed his hand to linger on her elbow long after the need for it was past.

"Oh, no, you couldn't!"

"Oh, but I could!" retorted Carraford. "Your reasons for denying relationship to that family are quite beyond my understanding. I have never heard of any connection of theirs by the name of Adams. I wonder why you would hit upon such a ridiculous name."

He was talking more to give her an opportunity to recover her composure than from a quest for information. He had the knowledge he needed for the moment. All he could hope for was that she would—faced with the fact that he already knew much—confide the whole truth to him.

Even an illegitimate connection with the straitlaced Hollands would not have stunned him as much as her response to him.

She could not answer at once because of the strange lump in her throat. No one had talked to her in such a fashion for a long time. Even her father had never noticed her thoughts, her feelings, in the same way this man did. "Oh, I am completely undone!" The words were wrung from her as though by force, and she did not mean entirely the penetration of her identity.

Carraford let the storm of her emotions blow itself out and then said, "I wish you will trust me. Is there something I can do?"

Somewhere a rustle sounded in the shrubbery—probably a bird, thought Narcissa's wayward mind.

She looked up at him, her eyes drenched in tears. "Oh, please do not tell the Countess! She has asked me who I was and I would not tell her!"

Carraford said, "I think you know I am not the kind of man who would betray you. You may trust me not to tell anyone until you give me the word to do so. In fact, you may trust me in *all* things."

He stood watching her, a queer, hungry look in his eyes. If she had turned to him that moment, saying that she did trust him, he would have seized her in his arms and promised her anything she wanted. But she did not, and he could not understand that her dilemma was caused by her wanting too much to trust him.

She was within seconds of throwing herself upon him, saying that she trusted him with her life. She returned to sanity, as she termed it, just in time. There was nothing he could do to help her. Her problem was not so much knowing who she was as knowing how she would live. And the only thing she could ask for would be money. She would die first!

She turned again to him and said in a faltering tone, "You spoke of that family. Perhaps you are mistaken?"

"No," he said, "I am not mistaken. You are a member of the Holland family, for your resemblance to Julia Holland is unmistakable. You could be twin sisters."

There it was! Sir Maurice told her she was no Bentham. Apparently she was entirely Holland, and it had brought her to her undoing. She said with perfect truth, "I never heard of her."

If she were torn between her two motives, of longing to trust him and a need to preserve her integrity, not to reveal her poverty, Carraford, too, was torn. He had realized, as recently as yesterday, that he had fallen in love for the first time in more than a decade. And this, he strongly suspected, would be the last time. He longed to protect her, to have the legal right to surround her with his formidable authority, and to keep her safe from whatever threatened her. But he was still not ready to make an offer unless she would believe in him. He set great store by his need for her to turn to him in complete trust. Although in his mind he was totally committed, for Carraford never did anything in a halfhearted fashion, he knew he must penetrate her need for help before he could present her with another problem—that of accepting him.

He said once again, "I want to help you in any way that I can. Only tell me how!"

Narcissa, confused to distraction by the conflicting tides of emotion that swept her, could remember only the tutor's warning—that Carraford, if he could, would propose not marriage, but what was called *carte blanche*. And more to herself than to Carraford she moaned, "Oh, I can't! I could never—"

He said in a voice that turned her bones to jelly, "You cannot be happy in that house, with that idiotic young man dogging your footsteps, catering to that foolish woman and her silly daughter."

She forced herself to answer. "The Countess has been very kind to me. She helped me when I had no place to go." It was an admission she had not intended to make to him, that she had been destitute, but his concern drew her past discretion. Looking up at him, she knew she must explain further. "I had made a mistake on the coach fare, and the driver set me down at a place called Penton Crossroads—do you know it?"

He nodded shortly.

"And by chance Lady Hapworth's groom came to meet me."

"Or," said Carraford, "the real Hester Adams. I fail to see any sign of excess kindness."

"She let me stay," said Narcissa simply. "I have a roof and enough to eat. So you see—"

Harshly he interrupted. "And pay for it by drudgery ten times over! I have eyes in my head! I wish—"

He fell silent for so long that his horse, puzzled by the long wait, moved against him, suggesting they move on. Failing to get the expected response, the animal began cropping grass noisily.

"I wish to take care of you," said Carraford.

She gasped at the bald statement. Her astonishment knew no bounds. She could only stammer, "Wh-what?"

"You are miserable here, or will be, when that minx gets her way and leaves home. You will be much happier with me—"

As a proposal of marriage, it lacked a good deal. To Narcissa, it was irresistibly reminiscent of Charles Wayne's warning: "You're a fool to think anything else."

Her cheeks burned. How dare he think she would run off with him—or anyone else! There was no mention of love or marriage—simply the calm assumption of an arrogant man who had always carried all before him. This time he was wrong.

"Lord Carraford," she said, her voice faltering in spite of every effort to keep it steady, "I cannot accept your most *generous* offer. I am quite happy here, and at least my standing here is honest, honorable—"

To her surprise the Marquess was full of mirth, his shoulders shaking and his eyes brimming with amusement. "You *idiot*," he said fondly. "I mean, marry me. Did you think—anything else?"

Her eyes blinked with tears. "No, of course not," she lied.

"Best stick to the truth," he said shrewdly. Then, after a moment, he turned sober again. "But you have not answered me."

She could not look at him. She would have to respond, but her thoughts were turbulent and her emotions trembled on her lips. "I—I cannot," she said at last in a muffled voice. "Believe me, I am sensible of the great honor—"

"Fustian!" he exploded. "Why cannot you marry me?"

He had never before offered marriage—at least not for fifteen years. He had, when he came to it, no deftness in the manner of it. He almost asked her whether she considered him too ugly, but he dared not.

"There are things," she began, tears thickening her voice, "you cannot know, you must not, truly you must not—" She was incoherent, but she could not help it. "I can't, I can't!"

He was silent for a few moments. Then, in an altered tone, he said, "I shall not trouble you again. If you change your mind, send word to me. I will come."

He rode off then, leaving her to wring her hands in distraction.

She would have even been more upset had she known what was going on in his mind.

Surprisingly he was not chagrined. Miss Adams—to call her by the only name he knew—was not easily to be won over. He had been too precipitate; he had proved too overbearing; his anxiousness to be of help had been misunderstood. He must take care the next time—

But should there be a next time?

What did she have in her past that impelled her to refuse an offer of honorable marriage? Surely his position was sufficiently exalted to overcome the ordinary objections that might arise. If she were a member of the Holland family born, as it were, on the wrong side of the blanket, then the stigma of illegitimacy might cling to her. But John Elyot, Marquess of Carraford, gave not a fig for any breath of scandal. But then it came to his mind that there was one scandal that even Carraford's name could not overcome.

Suppose that the girl had really been a part of the *ridotto* set in Venice? Suppose she knew that wherever she went in the world the dishonor of her past would linger, tainting all the rest of her life?

He brought up his horse sharply. He needed to think and slowed his mount to a walk. He could not believe that a girl with as lively a mind, as forthright a spirit, as Hester had ever been an inmate of a Venice *ridotto*. She was too innocent, too unspoiled! He fancied himself a judge of the infamous. No Cyprian ever fooled him for a moment. He could not believe Hester had been shamed—yet *something* lay deep in those dark blue eyes, a pervading sadness that she could not hide.

If she were truly a part of the *ridotto* set in Venice, this might explain her reluctance to trust him. If she had belonged to that very fast and immoral group, then she would have long since decided not to trust anyone.

But if she had been a part of that group, then he was convinced it had not been her fault. First, however, he must know who she was, in exact detail. Only then could he trace her back to find out what lay so heavily upon her mind.

By the time he had arrived at his own front door he had decided the next step to take. He did know this: If she had been a member of that fast set, it would in all probability make her ineligible to be his wife in the eyes of society. In his own eyes, he knew he wanted no other woman. But if Rupert were allowed to marry Bella and the succession were assured, then the Marquess could wed whom he liked. And the woman calling herself Hester Adams was the wife he wanted above all things.

For the first time in his life he was genuinely worried. He had thought, in his simplicity, that the mere offer of his hand and fortune would be sufficient to unlock her secret. But he had failed. Now, more than ever, he was convinced that she needed help. And he was determined that *his* was the help she would have!

But possibly her refusal had nothing to do with her secret past, whatever it was? Possibly—and there was precedent enough for this!—she simply did not like him!

And then *what would he ever do?*

By the time he walked through his own front entrance his face was set once again in grim lines, which his butler noted with great dismay.

If Carraford could have seen his love at that moment, the question of whether or not she liked him would have sunk into the oblivion it deserved. By the time she had regained her own room she realized that she was head over heels in love with a man whose position and influence made it impossible for her to confide in him. There was no question but that if she told him her situation, he would think she was after his fortune. He had said enough on the subject of fortune hunters, even though his remarks were leveled at Bella, to give her any confidence that he would overlook such a fault in her.

The tutor's poison, she realized, was already at work. Carraford knows now, she thought, who I am. At least he is on the right scent, knowing that I am related to the Hollands. If he told them, they would be furious with Narcissa, she thought, for trying to use him to worm her way back into the family.

He had said she could trust him, and she ached to do so. She had only instinct to tell her that he was entirely trustworthy. She wished then that she had gone to Scarborough to introduce herself to the Hollands in person. Now she was unable to do so, unless she could forestall the Marquess of Carraford.

She had never been so confused in her life. And at the fringe of her distracted mind sat an imp, crying a warning.

"You saw how quickly, and with what little concern, he routed the tutor? Much as one waves away a bothersome gnat!"

She retorted to her imp, "But he would not hurt me!"

"Besides," cried the jeering imp, "what happened to the scheme for getting your own back—the carriage and horses your father lost in Lausanne?"

She had entirely forgotten her first impulses, she realized. At base, she knew that her father's fatal flaw lay in his belief that luck would favor him—and her father, had he won from the Marquess, would have had no regrets whatever.

"I didn't truly mean it," she confessed to her other self.

"Then why did you refuse him?"

"I don't know."

The conversation was over. She sternly quelled the imp in her mind, but the thought that she had spurned Carraford's offer of help, and refused his offer of marriage, drew her into a morass of remorse.

23

She had been more than foolish. The Marquess had, in past days, filled her waking thoughts and had stridden masterfully through her dreams. He was amazingly attractive, she thought, with his air of distinction and his keen mind. He had a kind of lively appreciation of the absurd that matched her own, and his company was delightfully stimulating.

And she had been such a fool!

Were she to construct for herself an ideal man, Carraford would come very near the mark. And he had offered her marriage. She could not fathom why she had stammered, shrunk back like the veriest school miss. She recalled every moment of their encounter along the drive. And she dwelt longest on the mask he had set back in place on his features when he had understood that she was rejecting him. She had been privileged to see the real John Elyot, released from the strict discipline that ruled his public behavior. She suspected rightly that few people had ever seen the true character of the man, his tenderness to her, his concern, and his surprising understanding of her situation. He had paid her the highest honor in exposing his thoughts to her, presenting her with his vulnerability, as it were—and she had spurned it.

But he had said—she remembered toward morning—that if she were to call him, he would come. She was not too proud to admit she was wrong, not too puffed up to send an apology to him, to confess her unaccountable stupidity in throwing away what could be her life's happiness.

She could not believe that she had marred her future with one idiotic, unaccountable, *stupid* blunder. Surely he was a man of his word. If he had promised her he would come, then he was certain to come galloping up the driveway within the hour.

It was not his fault that she was so surprised that her wits went scampering, that her first thought was to say she could not believe he truly meant *her!* At the first opportunity this morning she would send a note to him. . . . She slept at once.

Rupert came in shortly after breakfast was over with an announcement that his uncle, erratic as usual, had left early that morning, and no one but the sleepy groom had seen him go. The Marquess had left no word where he was going or when he would be back.

Narcissa's coffee cup trembled in her hand, and she set it down quickly. If Carraford had left, he was beyond doubt angry at her, and she felt as lonely, suddenly, as though she were the only one left on the face of the earth. She could not give vent to her feelings, but Bella was under no such restraint. She was frankly dismayed. "Perhaps he's gone to make arrangements for your Grand Tour across Europe," she exclaimed. "Perhaps he's gone to—"

Rupert interrupted her. "I told you I wouldn't go on that tour, and that's what I meant." Rupert, already a member of the family in his mind, poured himself another cup of coffee and sat down beside Bella. "I told you I wouldn't go, and I told you we would be married at once. Just trust me, and you'll see it all work out. Besides," he added to the company assembled around the table, "He wasn't angry with me."

The Countess interrupted. "Is your uncle always angry? I confess it must have been a relief to the community that he has been away for ten years, and although I had not expected him to leave quite so soon, nonetheless it is an advantage not to expect his scowling face at the door."

Rupert protested, "He is not always angry! In fact he has been much more good-natured this visit than any time I remember. But something certainly happened to upset him."

Bella said sharply, "It wasn't anything I had to do with. I didn't even see him all yesterday."

The others hastily followed Bella's example, in clearing their own skirts of blame over the Marquess's quixotic and inexplicable change of plans.

"He was asking me about a dinner party he had planned," remarked the Countess, "only yesterday afternoon. It certainly seemed to me that he had settled down for a long stay."

Even Miss Pinkney pointed out that she had not seen the Marquess either. "I do not think," she said, "that the dear Marquess would be so ungentlemanly, for he has been well brought up, his manners I find exquisite, that he would leave without a word to us, for he surely must know how soon we will be nearly connected."

The Countess favored her sister with a speaking glance and returned to worry the subject as a spaniel worries a bone.

"He came to see me, and I did ask him how soon he was going to put the announcement in the *Gazette*," she mused. "He did not seem upset about that. He picked up the newspaper—and suddenly he threw it down and fled."

"Dear Albinia," said Lavinia Pinkney, "You really have used the wrong word. Carraford would not flee."

"Well," retorted the Countess, "there certainly was something on his mind. He went out of here as though ten thousand devils were at his heels."

Narcissa could agree to that, for the thundering of his horse's hooves down the drive was still vivid in her mind. She fell into wild surmise. He had had that interview with her, and he had seemed calm enough until he left. She had no doubt but that she was at least part of the subject that had upset him. But he had told her to trust him, and then he had left without a word! She could think only that he had left the country quickly so as not to be available to her if she were to trust him. Or, she thought, even if she had changed her mind. It was not like him, instinct told her, to offer help and then leave before she had a chance to ask it. So much for counting on him for help!

But William had come into the room, followed by his tutor, in time to hear part of the conversation. In his clear voice, he piped, "It was Miss Adams's fault. I know that!"

William expanded under the fascinated stares of his elders. For once, he was the center of pleasurable attention, and he swaggered slightly, knowing he was not engaged in culpable deeds.

Repeating his arresting news, he cried, "It was Bella's governess who threw Carraford into a tantrum!"

Bella cried, "You never liked Hester!"

"What has that got to do with it?" wondered William. "I know what I saw!"

Miss Pinkney turned shrewd. "Now, William, you must tell us what you saw, don't you know! It would be wrong to tease us."

Rupert said, with real curiosity, "But first, William, tell us how you saw—whatever it was that you saw. Where were you?"

William realized that his part, put badly, was subject to unwelcome discipline, but aware of all eyes upon him, he realized that there was no backtracking. Besides, he sensed that his behavior was of less importance than usual. He confessed.

"I hid in the shrubbery," he said, conscious of his naughtiness in doing so, but assuming a mantle of virtue. "I watched Mr. Wayne. He talked to Miss Adams for a long time. He sent me away to play, but I didn't. I hid in the bushes and watched them. He talked to her for a long time and they got mad," related the Earl. "It was after that the Marquess came, and he talked a long time, too."

Conscious of rectitude in unburdening his soul of something that was damaging to someone else, William folded his arms and stared sturdily at his mother.

The Countess said, "I thought you didn't tell stories like that anymore."

She turned to the boy's tutor and said, "I had hoped that you had restrained the boy's imagination in a more effective fashion than seems to have been done."

But Charles Wayne, presented with the opportunity of a lifetime, stood up for the young Earl. "He is telling the exact truth, Your Ladyship," began Wayne, "because I too saw them. The Marquess stopped and talked for a long time with Miss Adams." Here he shot her a malicious glance. "And I must admit that I was surprised, for I took great care to warn Miss Adams about Carraford's evil intentions."

Rupert, stung, leaped to his feet. "I will not hear such scandalous remarks from you!"

The Countess waved him to silence and insisted that Charles Wayne continue. By the time he had finished

Carraford was portrayed as a wicked Gothic villain, and Narcissa was portrayed as a foolishly naïve girl.

Such was her punishment for scorning Charles Wayne's offer, his glance at her seemed to say.

Once the Countess had digested the information which Charles Wayne laid before her, she moved quickly to straightening out her household. Dismissing Charles Wayne and beckoning Narcissa to follow her, she moved into her study, where she closed the door behind them.

Standing behind her huge desk, the Countess stared at Narcissa. "Now, Hester Adams, you have a few things to explain to me."

Narcissa, convinced that any explanation was futile against the lies of Charles Wayne, said, "I suppose it is useless to tell you that Mr. Wayne has given you the wrong interpretation."

The Countess said, "I deal in facts, and I shall ask you only this: Were the facts that Charles Wayne told us true?"

Narcissa, reflecting upon the events of yesterday, had to admit that they were. "You have been kind to me, and I should like you to know the truth. I did stop and talk to Charles Wayne, for there was no other way to return to the house without him. The Marquess did talk to me, but I do not see how Mr. Wayne could have heard anything that Carraford said to me. I would not expect a tutor to teach his young charge to lurk and eavesdrop. He must have been too far away to hear our words."

"So there was something to hear," said the Countess.

Narcissa's anger was rising dangerously. She opened her mouth to protest indignantly, but the Countess swept on. "I imagine your distress at my learning of your delinquency is genuine. If you talked at length with Carraford, it does not matter whether you were overheard. I am shocked at your assumption of intimacy with the Marquess. I expected you to champion Bella's cause and not advance your own interests. How long have you entertained this *tendre* for a man so completely above your touch? I wonder. Don't answer me—I wish to hear no lies. You surely cannot expect to marry him. Or do you? You truly have so little gratitude to me that you would even entertain the thought of marrying him? I cannot help feeling that this smacks of treason!"

Narcissa lifted her hand in a small gesture of bewilderment. "I do not plan to marry Carraford." How could she when he had vanished? "But if I did, I fail to see how this is a concern of yours?"

The Countess said icily, "I suppose you can't see that if you married the Marquess and produced a son, you would cut Rupert out of the title? Rupert has every right to expect Carraford's vast fortune to come to him."

"But you cannot have considered well. Even if I refused to marry Carraford, can you prevent him from marrying any other woman of his acquaintance? I do not understand how that could be accomplished."

"Besides that," cried the Countess, as though she had not spoken at all, "I know that you are not Hester Adams. I was willing to give you a chance to prove yourself. Well, you have indeed proved yourself—a wicked scheming woman! I wonder why you changed your name and wouldn't tell me your real name. I suspect you are guilty of some terrible crime. Who knows but that we all may be murdered in our beds!"

The Countess swept on like a river in flood, rehearsing a calendar of felony that she could not truly believe in. Narcissa began to protest, to explain that Charles Wayne had only malice in his heart.

"Mr. Wayne," said Narcissa with scorn, "must read novels in his leisure time. The Marquess and his evil intentions, you know. I confess your remarks resemble a bad novel by Verbena de Vere."

The Countess grew markedly silent. "Verbena de Vere does not write bad novels," she said oppressively after a moment.

"Perhaps not bad," continued Narcissa heedlessly, "but certainly ridiculous ones!"

Lady Hapworth, her eyes cold, placed her hand upon some papers on her desk. "Do you see this, Miss Adams?" she said, patting the stack of paper with significance. "This pays your salary. It keeps this household running well. It buys the furniture, runs the farms, provides the coal for your fire, and clothes us all."

The Countess lifted the top sheet and read it aloud: "THEODOSIA, OR THE WICKED MARQUESS, by

Verbena de Vere." She fixed her penetrating dark eyes on Narcissa. "Miss Adams, *I* am Verbena de Vere."

Shock held Narcissa speechless. It all fell into place—Lady Hapworth's outrageous imagination, for one. She could believe anything, since her writing constantly strained credulity. Lady Hapworth saw nothing unusual about a governess playing her charge false or setting her cap for a wicked Marquess.

Narcissa sank into a chair and covered her face with her hands. The absurdity of this interview threatened to send her into whooping hysterics, and she was forced to deal strenuously with her ill-timed merriment. Besides, it was not all that amusing at bottom. Remembering her astonishing interview with Carraford, she sobered.

"There is nothing for me to say," she told her employer. "I am resigning at once. You need not fear my machinations against Bella, Lady Hapworth. I am resigning my post at once."

Lady Hapworth protested. "Not before you tell me who you really are!"

"I am sorry," said Narcissa, "but you really must construct your own plots without any help from me! If you would be good enough to have my wages ready in the morning, I shall leave at once."

"Are you sure you aren't too proud to take Verbena de Vere's money?" said the Countess, still smarting under Narcissa's criticism.

Narcissa said swiftly, "No more than you are to write the books!"

The Countess said steadily, "I'll have your wages ready in the morning." Then, aware of a lurking affection for the girl, she said in a different tone, "Where will you go?"

Narcissa replied sweetly, "I have until morning to make up my mind."

24

By the next morning she had swallowed her pride. It had a bitter taste, but then, so did destitution. It was small consolation to reflect that, if she had accepted the Marquess's offer, she would still be faced with the need to leave Hapworth Hall at once. The Countess could not have been more unreasonable if Narcissa had, in fact, informed her of Carraford's intentions.

The Marquess had decamped—and she was glad she had not accepted the offer of his hand. She had at least been spared the final humiliation. Now she could console herself with the possibility that had she not rejected him, he might not have fled so precipitately.

By afternoon, when she had taken her leave of Isabella and Miss Pinkney, and boarded the stagecoach at Pocklington with a ticket reading—this time she checked!—to Scarborough, she was relieved to see the last of Hapworth Hall and Carraford Hall.

Scarborough lay ahead. It was remotely possible that the Hollands would take her in, acknowledging the relationship—only remotely, possible, she reminded herself, but it was the only choice left to her.

The route led northwest to Stamford Bridge, where she changed coaches and looked about her for half an hour while waiting for the coach for the east. The River Derwent was still quite narrow here. The Saxon bridge no longer existed. She tried to amuse herself by visualizing the marching men of King Harold joining in battle with Earl Tostig in the fateful year of William the Conqueror's invasion, but the gallant fighting armies were routed by the simplest of questions.

What will I say to the Hollands? rang in Narcissa's mind, excluding all else.

She tested countless introductions: "Your letter must have got lost in the mail, but here I am," or, "Do you have a position open as governess, or kitchen maid, or housekeeper?"

There was no easy way to thrust herself upon her mother's family under the circumstances. But Carraford had jolted her more than he suspected, and not with his offer of marriage. It was the great resemblance he found in her features to those of the Hollands. And while he had taken three weeks to discover her identity, it might not take others that long.

She would either have to remain Hester Adams, moving from one ill-paid drudging position to another or have to come to terms with the Hollands. She could not forever fend off people who would say, "You remind me of someone—let me think!"

Perhaps, she thought, they did not receive my letter. "I could say that I expected their letter was lost in the mail," she murmured, leaning over the bridge railing. "As it could have been. Or I could simply say, I am destitute, help me!"

She had still not formed the right phrases when she was summoned to board the east-bound coach. They passed through Malton and then settled down to the long run to the sea.

She fingered the money in her pocket. The Countess's idea of wages had been far from generous. "Considering your betrayal of my interests, I really should withhold half your wages, to teach you a lesson," Lady Hapworth had said. "But it will be worth a good deal to be rid of you. You will not expect me, I am sure, to give you a reference."

Narcissa had enough in her pocket for a skimpy week's lodging. She would never seek out Dilly. Dilly, the dearest person on earth, the only person in the world who truly loved her. Narcissa's lips tightened as she remembered the Marquess. He surely had not!

She could live a week in Scarborough if she were *excessively* thrifty. She would scour the town for a position *after* she had presented herself at the Holland doorstep. At least, she thought with a sore twinge, she would run no risk of meeting Carraford here, for she had not the slightest doubt in the world that he had fled headlong to lose himself in the delights of London and to forget at once his foolhardy offer to a mere governess.

But Dilly—Dilly would share her last crust with her. She would not settle down on Dilly, for she was sure that Dilly's means were more straitened than hers. Even Dilly's move, a couple of years ago, must have been to cheaper lodgings. She had not had word from her since.

When she descended from the coach in Scarborough, she was immediately assailed by the strong briny odor of the air. Scarborough was on the coast of the North Sea, and the inexorable wind blew steadily from the ocean. Behind the town she had traveled over the high moors and broad valleys of obvious prosperity. They reminded her of Mr. Appercott's snug farm in the valley, comfortable, even wealthy, but not for her.

She left her bandbox at the inn where the stagecoach set down and booked a room for the night, under her own name. She had taken the coach using the name of Hester Adams, since that was the name she was known by in Pocklington. But she could not live forever as Hester Adams, and Carraford had taught her that her resemblance to the Holland family was too marked to go without comment. She did not wish the Hollands to hear of her existence from someone else or even to feel that she was trading on her resemblance to make her way. She wished for once and for all to be straight with her mother's family. As soon as she arrived in Scarborough, she flung her identity as Hester Adams to the wind. That name had vanished forever.

She sought directions and made her way toward Holland House. As she walked, not too fast, she tried to picture her arrival. Would they take her in? They would recognize, if Sir Maurice and Carraford had spoken true, that she belonged to them. They *might* take her in.

Narcissa, with more of her father's gambling instinct in her than she was willing to acknowledge, thought that perhaps her luck would turn up. She devised all manner of explanations for the Hollands' seeming neglect. Perhaps the letter got lost. Perhaps she had not addressed it right, or no one was home—

Her mind mused on in these romantic ramblings, and she realized that the Bentham gambling blood had surfaced, as it usually did at an awkward time.

The street where Holland House stood was a street of immensely prosperous houses. The iron railings in front, the three stories of pale stone facing the street were much like the ones she had seen in London. If they had added a small park in the center, the houses around it would be indistinguishable from those at Grosvenor Square.

These houses were built on the proceeds of the wool industry. The sheep that dotted the high moors, the sheep that grazed along the roads—all these gave wool and lambs to England, and on that foundation, these houses raised their prosperous faces.

Face to face with such obvious signs of wealth, she realized that she did not know that her mother's family possessed great fortune. Her heart, bolstered to this point by her hopes and dreams, suddenly failed her. She could not face the possible insults, the turning away of someone with greedy pretensions, as they must think.

She paused at the top of the street and looked to the east. From the height where she stood she could see the long reach of the sea, stretching north and south from the ruined castle on the tip of Scarborough's peninsula. To the north the coast faded into shadows as the sun descended toward the west.

The tangy salt air was sharp in her nostrils, and she filled her lungs with it. How many times, she wondered, had her mother stood just here and breathed as deeply of the sea's breath? Did she ever miss the clean, scouring wind after she left it behind, all for love?

Tears stung her eyes—tears of regret for all that had been and was now past. Her mother's short life, her father's unhappy death. Lord Carraford—

How clearly she could see his face, his odd smile when he teased her, his naked, vulnerable openness when he had offered himself to her!

She blinked back the tears. She had hurt him, she was sure. But his flight, leaving her unprotected and bewildered, had dealt her a blow she would never forgive.

"I'll come at once if you change your mind!" he had promised her—and incontinently had fled into oblivion—or, more probably, to the bright lights of London and languishing Paphians!

She wondered where her pride had gone and thought it must have been drowned in her need. She crossed the street before she got to Holland House. Strolling along the sidewalk opposite, she tried to still the wild beating of her heart and to get herself in to a frame of mind where she could decide either to leave the street, and make her way without the Hollands, or to present herself to her family.

She was nearly opposite the great house when she noticed a coach standing before the door. She stopped short and peered at the panel. She believed she recognized the team of grays, standing impatiently before the door. The coachman she did not know, for Carraford always drove himself. But she certainly knew the Carraford arms on the panel. It was Carraford's coach! She was too late!

Now her decision was made for her. She could not approach the Hollands, not on the heels of Carraford!

The simple fact that he had got to the Hollands before she had wiped away any pretense she might have of making herself known to them. But more than that, it was her abject misery when she considered his deceit, his false promises. He had run as fast as his cattle would carry him to betray her presence to the Hollands. To tell her family that she was in Yorkshire, even to laugh with them at her plight!

He must, by now, know that the Hollands had cast her mother off and wished to have nothing to do with her. She was positive that at this moment the Marquess and Julia Holland were sitting cozily over a dish of tea, commiserating insincerely over the foolish governess who had turned down fortune and title.

If the Marquess had been wounded by her refusal, he had certainly chosen the best way possible to strike back. For of course she could not now intrude herself—a fortune hunter, the Hollands would say. What the Marquess might say, she could not bear to think.

She stumbled away, around a corner, scarcely noticing where she went. She wandered for a long time before the tears stopped flowing and she could see where she was.

She could not face the Hollands, but in truth, it was Carraford she dared not meet. She dreaded the thought of his cold eyes looking at her, knowing that she had refused his offer of help.

She ached to see his dear face once more, at least to explain that she did not hold him in repugnance. But the certainty that the expression in his eyes, warm and stirring only two days ago, must have turned cold and contemptuous made her tongue cleave to the roof of her mouth and gave her a very queasy feeling in the region of her stomach.

She turned down street after street, not knowing one corner from another and hurrying as fast as she could. She wanted to be far away from Holland House by the time the Marquess of Carraford descended the steps and mounted his coach. At last, feeling a stitch in her side and realizing that she must be miles from Holland House by this time, she slowed her swift pace. She began to feel faint. She had not bothered to eat when she got off the coach. She had been too anxious to get to the Hollands before her courage ran out, but it all had been in vain.

Now aware that the sun was westering and that soon she would walk in deep blue twilight, she began to return to herself. She stopped to look about her. She was in a street of narrow houses, with narrow areaways and railings protecting them. The tall, slender facades looked impersonally down upon her, and it seemed to her heated imagination as though they were staring over her head, snubbing the lost intruder at their feet.

She was lost. She looked behind her at the way she had come, and ahead. Neither direction showed her any sign of activity. Just now, though, a woman hurried toward her down the walk. When she drew closer, Narcissa reached a hand out to stop her.

"Please, ma'am," said Narcissa, "can you tell me—"

The woman slowed but did not stop. "You look clean enough, but best get off this street," she said sharply, "before the watch takes you up. This is a respectable neighborhood, this is, and I do wonder at your nerve."

She stepped around Narcissa, gathering her skirts close to her in one hand, the other hand clamping firmly upon her reticule. Narcissa's cheeks burned.

"I'm not a—a woman of the streets," she would have said, but her audience had quickened her step and was already out of hearing.

The encounter was daunting in the extreme. Narcissa automatically reached up to straighten her bonnet. She was out of breath from her headlong flight through the strange streets, and now she was agonizingly hungry. Her knees shook, from lack of food and from fatigue. She must wander on until she found a main thoroughfare or someone who could direct her—

Suddenly she could not abide the idea of returning to the inn, to eat a solitary supper and weep the night away in a cold bedroom. Almost a child again, she knew only one source of comfort, Dilly. Dilly would soothe her, let her weep her heart out, and—*she wanted Dilly!*

She fumbled in her purse. The address on Dilly's last letter was two years old, and anything could have happened in the meantime. Dilly could have moved again or, being past middle age, could have departed this life.

She took the worn letter to a beam of light streaming out of an uncurtained window ahead. She was trying to make out the tiny letters—she had never written Dilly at this new lodging house, for Alfred Bentham's luck was momentarily out, and they were moving quickly from one irate landlord to another—when she heard footsteps approaching.

Wary of rebuff, she steeled herself for insult and stopped him.

"Can you tell me where I can find Rawdon Street?"

The man approached her, and in the light she saw that he looked like someone's grandfather—a kindly grandfather, she amended, not like Sir Maurice.

"We-ell," he said slowly, "let me see. It is that way, five streets over—" He gave her directions, augmented by a sweeping hand, and finished, "Shall I take you there myself?"

"Oh, no, sir," she said quickly. "I am sure with such excellent directions I can find my way easily."

She did not wait to find out his intentions. She had had sufficient hint given her by the woman who passed previously. She hurried down the street and was relieved not to hear footsteps following her.

It was a long way. Five streets over and then, following the numbers, another half mile. She truly had reached the end of her endurance. Glancing at the buildings lining the street, she saw that they looked prosperous indeed, and certainly there was not a lodging house in the block. The kindly-appearing man had misled her!

Hopelessly lost before, she was now equally lost and at least a mile farther away. Her head swam, and her thoughts fled, jostling each other as they vanished—she could not think what to do.

Her steps faltered. She closed her eyes against sudden dizziness. Without thinking she reached out for help, and her fingers closed upon the iron railing beside the walk. The support steadied her. She resisted a strong inclination to sink to her knees on the sidewalk and give way to violent weeping.

The moment would pass, she hoped desperately. With both hands she clung to the railing and, vacantly, looked up at the houses.

She was dreaming! She must be. She had gone beyond the border of reason. . . .

She was looking up at a clean gray-stone building. Three stories, curtained windows on each floor, a shiny black door with a gold knocker—

And beside the knocker a discreet bronze plaque which read "Miss Dilworth's Academy for Young Ladies."

That was all, a neat and dignified metal plate. Dilly had always wanted a school, and Narcissa's childhood ambition had been to help her gain it. Now here she was, standing on the threshold of the school that Dilly had finally got.

She could not take it all in at once. She was still standing amazed when the door opened and Dilly herself stood on the doorstep.

"Narcissa! Can it be? You? Oh, my dear child, what have they done to you?"

It was a welcome that nearly overset her. Dilly threw her arms around her, pulled her up the steps and inside, chattering like a wren all the time.

"What are you doing here? How did you find me? Where have you been? I didn't think you were in England!"

It was fortunate that Dilly did not expect an answer to her myriad of questions, for Narcissa could not have answered even one. In moments she was seated in the snuggest of parlors, with a dish of strong tea in her hand. Dilly sat down opposite and poured herself a cup.

"Now then, my child, I've talked a great deal, and you haven't said a word. But you know you couldn't be more welcome in my house than if you were my own child. Indeed, I feel that you were the only child I ever had. Now, tell me how long you can stay."

Tears blinded Narcissa, for such kindness and such love had been remote from her hopes only a quarter of an hour before. Then she had been so desperate that she was not even sure where she would spend the night. Now here she was, being fed tea, and little sandwiches, a fire leaping in the grate, and her dear Dilly opposite her, her face beaming with affection and warmth.

"May I have more tea, please?" asked Narcissa.

"Of course, my dear, and another small cake, please do. I have never been quite so shocked, you know, as when I found you on my doorstep. It is such a romantic idea—and I confess that there have been many times when I quite *ached* to open my door and find you there."

"And here I am." Narcissa smiled. It quite took her back, sitting at tea with dear Dilly, before a cozy fire. "I had not expected to come, you know."

"But why ever not?"

"Because, dear Dilly, I am pockets to let, you know."

Dilly did not seem surprised. Nor, after that first shocked cry of recognition, had she evinced wonder at the state of her dear Narcissa—disheveled, clearly at the limits of her strength, and shockingly pale. Dilly covered her alarm with the creature comforts and was gratified to see color creep back into the girl's cheeks and that queer, flat look disappear from her eyes.

"Your father?"

"Died. I should have written you, but I had no idea of where I should be in the future."

Dilly, content to let Narcissa tell her story in her own way, leaned back and watched the play of firelight on her features. "Your father's people?"

"Only a rather grim old man, Sir Maurice. He sent for me, and I went there, but, Dilly, it was the absolute end of the earth—in more than one way!"

She told Dilly about Mr. Appercott. "I could not

agree to that," said Narcissa simply and added more lightly, "He didn't have a book in his house!"

Dilly snorted in a ladylike fashion. "I should say not. But perhaps, if the arrangement had been made in a more genteel fashion?"

"No."

The word was quiet, but it did not satisfy Dilly. She had learned to know the young Narcissa through and through and, since then, had been exposed to a great many young ladies in her academy. If Dilly was not mistaken, there was a man at the back of the sadness in the girl's eyes—a man who, according to Miss Dilworth, must be blind or he would have carried off this altogether *sterling* girl!

She prompted, "And then you came directly here? But you spoke of May at your grandfather's, and it is the end of August!"

Narcissa, assured of sympathy, told the rest of the story. She glossed over the bad times, like the sight of the coach receding into the distance on Penton Crossroads, and omitted entirely any mention of the Marquess of Carraford. But Dilly had not nourished the growing Narcissa in her early years without knowing that young lady very well. She suspected that there was somebody—Dilly insisted in her mind on thinking of somebody with a capital *S*—but she also decided that when Narcissa was ready to talk about it, she would. It would in many ways explain the clear desperation that haunted Narcissa.

Just now she told Narcissa, in answer to her question, about the school. She had got an inheritance she had not expected. She had never known the Hollands, so it was entirely without any help from them that she was able to start her school. She said with a twinkle, "I charge outrageous prices, and I have to turn away pupils every year. It is most satisfactory."

Narcissa said, "What do you teach?"

"My teachers teach drawing, music, the use of the globes, and other things that a young lady would need. I turn out a finished product that would be at home in any drawing room. You see I am quoting from my own prospectus."

Dilly laughed then, a contagious giggle, that was music to Narcissa's ears.

"No languages?"

Dilly did not answer directly. Instead, she said, "What are your plans, my dear? Are you at leisure?"

At leisure! It was a small phrase to describe Narcissa's present condition and her future plans. But the mood had been broken. "It's a long story," she said, "and I must not trespass on your kindness any longer."

Dilly's eyes flashed. "Trespass is not a word I wish to hear on your lips again," she said severely. "What I have is yours, you must know that." She eyed Narcissa and astutely guessed her thoughts. "You thought, of course, that I had nothing. Well, my dear, Providence has been very good to me, and not the least has been your arrival on my doorstep. Now, my dear, where is your bandbox?"

Narcissa told her. "But if you will give me directions—"

"I shall not. It is a most unsuitable place for you to stay. I shall send for your luggage at once, and I think you will find the small room adjoining my sitting room most comfortable."

Tears welled up in Narcissa's eyes. How total the change had been! From sinking into a despairing heap on the sidewalk, without more than a few coins in her pocket, and with only the bleakest of prospects ahead, she had come to a place of warmth, and food, and shelter, and, most of all, a loving kindness that went beyond price.

"My dear Narcissa, do not thank me. For I promise you, I shall get my money's worth out of you!" Her eyes twinkled with amusement. "Now, not another word out of me shall you get. We shall have supper later, and then you will want to seek your bed early. And in the morning we shall talk."

"But—"

"No buts. I must leave you for a few minutes now, for I have a few duties to discharge at this time of day. The tea is still hot, and you must have another cup!"

With a brisk rustle of skirts, she was gone, and Narcissa was alone. She eyed the last cake on the plate and decided it looked forlorn, so she ate it. The unparalleled reversal in her fortunes—at least until tomorrow—was too much to comprehend. With the heat of the fire and after her exertions of the day, sudden peace of mind swept over her like a wave from the North Sea, and abruptly she was asleep.

25

Mademoiselle Annette Duprée, Miss Dilworth's French mistress, had, only a week before, fallen ill. Mr. Merton, the Scarborough doctor who cared for the Academy's residents, deemed it best to send her to a specialist in London.

"I have just returned from accompanying her there," said Dilly, "and if you had come a day sooner, I should not have been here to welcome you."

"To save my life," said Narcissa sincerely. "I do not know what I would have done!"

"But Providence has watched over us both," remarked Dilly. "I do not see that we can doubt it. For I was here, and you came in answer to prayer."

Narcissa raised her eyebrows. "You knew I was coming?"

"Of course not." Miss Dilworth answered the skepticism in Narcissa's question. "But I do need, most desperately, an instructress in French. And you are free to accept, I surmise?"

Free to accept! Narcissa took only a second to consider. "I agree, dear Dilly. An answer to prayer."

"Madamoiselle Duprée will not be back before Christmas," Dilly informed her, "so we have three months to make arrangements for—what happens next."

Dilly, certain as she was that a man lay at the bottom of Narcissa's troubles, had great faith in the healing power of time. She herself had had firsthand experience long ago, and she had found that the passage of months and years, altered one's memories so that the unhappy incidents were almost unrecognizable. But Narcissa would have to learn that for herself.

So Narcissa, with unbounded gratitude, began the term in Miss Dilworth's school. Her French, while colloquial and fluent, yet needed brushing up on grammar and formal vocabulary, and her evenings were filled with study. It was the best possible remedy for her depression of spirits.

The school was not a fashionable one, but in two years Miss Dilworth's Academy had earned an enviable reputation. It did not cater to the children of the well-born. Instead—in Scarborough there was a great demand for this kind of school—she took the daughters of wool merchants, prosperous farmers, and the rich shipbuilding families whose shipyards lay along the inner harbor.

The building that Dilly had bought with her inheritance was a narrow one, no more than thirty feet wide. It rose to three stories. Other houses shared the walls on either side. The top floor was given over to rooms for the faculty. Narcissa moved into one of the bedrooms. The second floor contained the dormitory, dining room, and infirmary, for those students who did not live in Scarborough, but stayed at school for the term. The ground floor was given over to classrooms and Miss Dilworth's own suite of rooms at the back. Also on the first floor was a large reception room where the girls entertained their parents and were free to gather on Sunday afternoons after church.

Narcissa was at first shy among so many girls. Although she was used to dealing with strangers, the concentration of so many females was daunting. She had merely a half day to glance over the assigned work before she met her first class.

Only the vivid recollection of her black despair when she had arrived at Dilly's door sustained her. Anything was better than that!

Underneath her conscious thoughts lurked a grayness that blanketed all it touched. The blanket held in it alternating disgust at herself for having believed Carraford and, once she had begun to trust him, for having had that trust dashed to such a depth. She could never forgive him for running to the Hollands, as soon as he had penetrated her alias, to tell them—and then she came to a full stop.

What would he tell them? That she had designs on him? The Marquess was well able to handle any grasping female! Would he warn them against her, informing them that a penniless "connection" would without doubt arrive on their doorstep, sooner or later? Or— and this was the darkest surmise of all—would he have decided to pursue Julia Holland, having been reminded of her charms by Narcissa's apparent resemblance?

It was fruitless to speculate, yet she could not help it. For if she did not consider Carraford and his motives, reprehensible though they were, there was nothing else to consider. It was strange to be alive at twenty, yet dead. There was no more purpose in life, and the bleak days and years that lay ahead could not be endured.

She turned away from the desolation she saw and returned to remembering, with increasing emphasis on his virtues, which grew mightily, even as his vices paled into oblivion.

The sea of faces that met her on that first day soon resolved into distinct identities: Kitty Ross, a Scottish lass with carrot-red hair and a generous mouth; Margaret Dakin, dark and gravely sweet; Hilda Foster, whose lively spirit covered her lack of intellect. These were the senior students, whose knowledge of French, in books, was equal to hers. But the language as it was spoken, ah, there she had them!

After two or three weeks Narcissa began to feel at home. Her days settled into a routine of teaching French, taking over the demands of certain study areas, and learning to know the teachers and the students. Dilly, a wise woman indeed, realized what Narcissa needed was hard work for a while. If there was Somebody in Narcissa's past, she was trying valiantly to forget him, and Dilly knew exactly how that was to be done. One's days must be so full there was no chance to brood and so exhausted that the nights were filled with dreamless sleep. She did not hesitate to demand more and more of Narcissa.

Narcissa responded, insensibly, by beginning to forget the months just past. Even Carraford, although he occupied a place which could not be dislodged, did not fill her every thought. Instead, the thought of him ran through her days like sad, funeral music, which cannot be forgotten.

She became involved in the life around her, and before long it was Charlotte Wright who filled her thoughts. Charlotte was brought to the school by her father. Narcissa interviewed Mr. Wright when they arrived.

Mr. Wright's red cheeks and stocky figure reminded her irresistibly of Lucius Appercott. But where Mr. Appercott had been confident, full of his own importance, and bawdy, Mr. Wright was full of respect and decency and an honest desire to do what he could to ease his daughter's way.

He sat on the edge of the chair opposite Narcissa and looked at his great red hands as though they had an identity of their own. With an air of not knowing quite what to do with them, he finally placed them carefully, one on each knee, and addressed Narcissa.

"My girl, don't you see, has had a hard time of it. She was mortally fond of her ma, and it was a hard blow when she took sick that way and died. I didn't hardly know what to do."

His honest bewilderment was greatly appealing, and he gazed trustfully at Narcissa as though she could produce a solution out of a desk drawer.

"Does Charlotte have any brothers or sisters?" asked Narcissa.

"No, she was our only chick. It's gone hard with her, but I don't mind telling you I'm at my wits' end. She's trying hard not to show it, but I can tell it's eating away inside. But I thought, don't you see"—he inched forward on his chair and addressed Narcissa in confidential tones—"that if she had something new to think about, she'd do better. And besides that, we might even move to town and set her up, so to speak, in the way of society."

Impulsively Narcissa asked, "Would you like that?"

He hesitated. "To tell you the right of it, I'd dislike it mightily. I'm not much for a lot of people, don't you see. Give me my stock and my people to work the land, and that's all I need. Seems like the good God put us all where we should like it best."

The core of Mr. Wright was honest, solid, and grateful for his lot in life. No man should ask more, thought Narcissa, respecting him. That should teach me a lesson!

Mr. Wright rose. "So if you could sort of put her in the way of doing things right, then I'd be obliged." He held out a huge hand and she put her own in it.

"We'll do our best, Mr. Wright," she promised. "We will let you know how she goes on."

"I'd be happy," he said simply, and was gone.

He left Charlotte in Narcissa's hands, and Narcissa took pity on the motherless child. Charlotte was shy and obviously unused to city life. Narcissa started her on her school routine, and then, as work piled upon her, she gave no further thought to the girl. Not until Dilly pointed out that Charlotte was copying Narcissa in every way that she could did Narcissa begin to look again at the child.

She had been in school two weeks and still, as far as Narcissa could tell, had not exchanged more than a sentence or two with anyone. She began to notice then that the other girls continued to go along in their own ways, exchanging confidences and planning their suppers, but Charlotte was not included. Narcissa could hardly blame them, for girls of middling age were not notorious for their kindness, and Charlotte was an unprepossessing girl. But the loneliness in her eyes reached Narcissa and stirred her deeply.

Narcissa managed to drop a hint to Margaret Dakin. "She's just lost her mother, you know, and is feeling it sadly."

To her surprise, the usually serene girl said, "But that's no excuse to tell us all we're not worth her trouble!"

Shocked, Narcissa answered, "She can't do that!"

"She does, Miss Bentham. To hear her tell it, we don't do anything right!" Margaret laughed. "There is one exception, I believe."

"Who is that?" demanded Narcissa, thinking she was about to learn the key to helping Charlotte.

"I'm sorry, Miss Bentham," Margaret said, retreating, "I am probably mistaken."

At the end of the first week in October a carrier brought a huge box addressed to Charlotte Wright. A crowd of girls surrounded her, miraculously informed about the possibility of treats, as she opened the box. Narcissa marveled at the way news sped through the halls, seemingly in the very air.

"What is in it? Oh, do hurry, Charlotte, open it up! Do you think it's cakes?"

It was indeed cakes, and big red apples polished till

they shone, and a dozen carefully packed peaches. A basket of Damson plums filled half the bottom of the box. Fresh fruit was always a treat, and all eyes lit up greedily.

"Charlotte, aren't you pleased?" asked Narcissa, noting that the recipient of the delicacies frowned at the note in her hand.

"My father sent them," she announced. "He says we should enjoy ourselves eating it all up." Her voice was unnecessarily loud in the small room. She gave the box a little shove with both hands. "Enjoy it, girls."

Without another word she scurried from the room.

"What's the matter with her?" cried Kitty. "Isn't she going to come back?"

Hilda said, "She told us to enoy it, didn't she? Well, I'm going to!" She reached for a plum just as Narcissa hurried after Charlotte.

Narcissa found Charlotte seated with a book open on her lap in the students' library. "What's the trouble?" she asked the girl. "Not hungry? I hope the girls leave something for you."

Charlotte did not respond to Narcissa's coaxing. "I am behind on my geography, and Miss Landon is so strict!" Narcissa, after a few more words, was forced to leave the girl alone.

That night Narcissa was awakened by the sound of weeping. It sounded as though it were coming from the floor just below, and she hurried to put on her robe and find her slippers. Tying the sash of her robe around her, she stumbled along the hall to the stairs leading down to the next floor. The girls were not allowed to close their doors, so she could stand at the foot of the stairs and listen. From the far end of the dormitory came a peaceful snore, and there was heavy breathing somewhere close at hand. The girls slept well, all but one. Now she could tell that the sobbing came from the first door on her left, the room where Charlotte Wright slept. Narcissa approached the bed. The girl was curled up, sobbing into her pillow, trying to stifle the sound. Narcissa sat on the edge of the bed and stroked the brown hair until Charlotte's sobs quieted, and she gulped once noisily.

Narcissa kept her voice down, so as not to disturb the others. "What's the trouble, Charlotte? Are you ill?"

Charlotte shook her head. By patient questioning Narcissa elicited the fact that Charlotte was simply homesick. So homesick she could die! she told Narcissa.

It was not the first homesick girl Narcissa had seen, and in fact, she herself had suffered from bouts of homesickness for a home she had never had; but she had not seen a nostalgic longing as desperate as this. Gently she soothed her. "Your father wants you to be educated. You don't want to disappoint him? He is such a kind man, and he has only your interests at heart."

Charlotte said in a muffled tone, "I know that, but I want to go home."

Narcissa talked a long time. Finally, she was rewarded by a promise from Charlotte that she would try to stick it out. "For your father's sake," insisted Narcissa. "He wants you to be an educated lady."

Charlotte said, "I don't ever want to be an educated lady. I want to go home."

In the end the girl fell into a heavy sleep, exhausted by her emotional storm. She had promised she would stay, Narcissa reflected, climbing the stairs to her own room, but she had not promised to be happy!

26

If hard work was Dilly's prescription to rout depression, it succeeded. Narcissa found that there was no time for introspection at Miss Dilworth's. The teachers were paid well, but they earned every penny.

Her days were full, and even if they had not been, there was a sufficient number of sudden emergencies, both real and fancied, to take up any slack time.

The school day began before daylight as the autumn came on them. There were exercises before the open windows, for Miss Dilworth believed in fresh air. The three teachers taught a variety of subjects. There was French, Greek, and Latin. There was mathematics, history, music, both vocal and instrumental, and instruction in dancing once a week. Miss Dilworth's school was an advanced institution of learning, for the curriculum included a smattering of geography and botany. Narcissa's teaching day ended after supper, when the girls were sent to their rooms to study. Narcissa herself went to her room to learn enough to conduct the next day's classes. She had been asked to teach French, but she was asked to help on other subjects.

Miss Dilworth insisted on the highest standards of learning. "For of what use is it to know only half-truths? The young mind is at its most impressionable age now, and I should be shamed to send my girls out into the world, where they may rise, you know, into fashion, and have them betrayed by an inferior education."

So the girls—and their teachers—were imbued with the precepts of, for example, Lindley Murray's *English Grammar,* and Narcissa became accustomed to hearing the younger pupils muttering to themselves, "The concord of verbs and pronouns with nouns of multitude or

signifying many . . . not without regard to the import
of the word as conveying unity or plurality of idea."

Miss Landon, the science instructress, was a woman
of uncertain age and a steely disposition. She brooked
no lapses in her students, but to do her justice, she did
not teach in the manner of Mrs. Marcet's *Conversa-
tions*, but from a thorough love of her precise subjects.

The other teacher was Miss Cathcart, nearer Narcissa's age, whose efforts were spent in getting—as she
said—"ham-handed daughters of farmers to draw a
pine tree with delicacy, totally impossible, of course,
but I keep trying!"

The use of the globes was advocated, and even a ladylike knowledge of botany was taught—mostly to
make the girls, so it was claimed, "agreeable companions for a man of sense." Narcissa suppressed a wayward grin at the thought of John Elyot, Marquess of
Carraford, and undoubtedly a man of sense, maintaining his temper with a school miss informing him where
nutmegs grow.

But Carraford, a man of sense, had returned to his
natural milieu, she supposed, in London. She did not
recover her spirits again that day.

The weather turned in mid-October. The change was
heralded by her waking to thick gray fog pressing
against the windows, so thickly that she could not see
beyond the doorstep.

"It's like living inside a box!" she exclaimed.

Miss Cathcart looked up curiously. "Haven't you
spent a winter in this climate? You have no idea—this
isn't really bad weather, you know."

Narcissa, vainly trying to penetrate the thick curtain
beyond the pane, exclaimed, "What do you call bad
weather then?"

Miss Cathcart, pleased at being the bearer of bad
news, said, "This is only sea fret. But it's the Purple
Wind, you know, wind from the east over the sea."

"Purple Wind?"

"An old Celtic term. I don't know why it's called
that, unless it turns your lips and fingers purple." Miss
Cathcart joined Narcissa at the window, looking out on
the tiny backyard and the coal sheds and stables behind
the row of houses. At least, she looked in their direc-

tion. There was nothing but woolly fog to be seen. "If we're not in for trouble, I don't know *anything!*"

"You mean bad weather?"

"More than that. I'm half Scottish, you know. And fey. I see things." She shuddered and began to talk brightly of something else.

By the next day the fog had thinned, and Narcissa thought the aspect was even worse, for the fog had turned into long, thin wisps that looked like ghostly fingers trailing past the windows. The girls were restless, even though all of them had grown up in this region and fogs were not new to them.

But Narcissa, laden with the deep sense of loss that lived with her always, even when she was, on the surface at least, engrossed in explaining the French subjunctive imperfect tense, jumped at the slightest sound. It was *unnatural,* she thought, a fog that stayed so long.

After the fog burned off, there was a half day of clear, very cold wind, off the sea, and then the first storm of the season rolled in.

Wet snow fell softly against the windows and piled up on the sill. The damp seeped through the cracks around the doors and chilled Narcissa to the bone. And the first coughs were heard in the classrooms.

From somewhere had come an infection, a cold beginning with chills, turning into fever, and accompanied by sore throat and cough. One girl after another fell victim to the ailment, and some of the smaller children failed to recover as fast as Miss Dilworth would like.

Mr. Merton, the doctor, came every day, shaking his head and leaving vials of evil-smelling medicines. At last, Dilly was forced to suspend classes.

Narcissa, seeking her out to ask about supplies for the kitchen, found her with her head in her hands, sitting forlornly at her desk.

"Is it that bad?" cried Narcissa. "Shall you have to give up the school?"

Dilly looked up and, seeing Narcissa, smiled. "No, it is not a question of money. We shall, of course, adjust the tuition charges, but I've planned for just such an emergency. No, it is only my foolish head, aching, as though I didn't have enough to think about."

Narcissa came to lay her hand on Dilly's forehead.

"Hot!" she exclaimed. "Dear Dilly, you must get to bed. You have caught the infection."

Dilly had not thought of that. "I am never ill. I shall be all right, my dear. Just a foolish headache."

"I should drag you to bed if you do not go by yourself. Please, Dilly, we cannot afford to have you disabled."

Dilly responded slowly, as though from a great distance. "I dare not give in." She clenched her fist and brought it down emphatically on the desk. "I *cannot* be ill!"

Narcissa regarded her for a moment and then seemed to agree. "All right, but I *can* see that you are not bothered by small things."

Narcissa closed the door softly behind her. The doctor was due on his regular visit in an hour, and perhaps he could accomplish what she could not.

The doctor could. "It's bed for you, Miss Dilsworth, and I do not care to hear any argument. You have a good right arm here in Miss Bentham—I have your own word for that, you recall. I shall be in to see you tomorrow, and you are to eat naught but a bit of broth this night."

He glared fiercely at Dilly, and at last she gave in. "I suppose if you are determined—"

Mr. Merton said firmly, "I am."

Dilly was secretly grateful that the decision was made for her. She took a dose of green medicine. She let Narcissa help her into bed and said, "I rely on you to do what is best," as she pulled up the coverlet and was at once asleep.

Three of the smaller girls, recovering too slowly, she thought would be better at home. Mr. Merton agreed. "Not because they are not getting proper care here," he assured her, "but because you can't do everything."

"Oh, but I don't," Narcissa pointed out. "The other teachers and some of the girls themselves help a great deal. And of course, they all have been ill themselves."

Mr. Merton nodded. "And if you're not careful, you will be down just as Miss Dilworth is."

There was no adequate answer. Miss Landon had arrived in time to hear the last words, and she said bracingly after the doctor had left, "It is a marvel the way you have taken over what needs to be done. I wonder whether it is not time to resume classes? It will take the girls' minds off themselves."

With the girls occupied, Narcissa had more time to care for the half dozen who remained really ill. Kitty Ross and Margaret Dakin were past the worst stage, and Narcissa brought them worn copies of *The Fairchild Family* and *Popular Tales* to beguile their time.

Even though these favorites had long ago been read over and over, opening the books again was like seeing old friends come to visit, so Margaret said.

Narcissa, while not ill, became thinner, so that her clothes were loose around the waist, and she fell into bed at midnight exhausted.

Out of this unexpected siege of illness, Charlotte Wright found herself. She helped Narcissa with her nursing duties and proved very apt. While they were making up fresh beds, she confided in Narcissa. "I really don't care a bit about book learning. All the letters get mixed up in my head, and I can't seem to straighten them out. What good will it do me to know the duties of the Justices of the Peace or the way the ancient Brahmins lived? I'll never see an ancient Brahmin in my whole life, do you think? I can't really see that I need to know how to read, more than enough to sign my name. For you must know that in the Vale of Pickering, where we live, I know enough about hens, and the garden, and herbs, and the baking, and the churning, so that we live nice. And I want to go home."

Once started, Charlotte could not stop in her reminiscences of the Vale. Blue and pink morning glories climbed around the door. She recalled with tenderness all the plants in the door yard, love-lies-bleeding, love-in-a-mist. So vivid a memory did she have, and such a ripe gift of expression, Narcissa could almost see the prosperous house in the Vale.

Narcissa all but forgot the Hollands. Her path and that of the wealthy Hollands never crossed. She remembered that Carraford had spoken of her remarkable resemblance to Julia Holland, but now, her memory blunted by the passage of time, she had come to believe that he had exaggerated. His fancying a likeness was simply a conversational gambit, designed to amuse himself while forced to visit his country estates. He had come to untangle Rupert's affairs and had soon become bored—hence his flirtation with the governess.

Narcissa could not read any other message into his actions. He had not even bothered with Rupert's marriage after he realized how deeply he had let himself become enmeshed with her. He had truly offered marriage, and there could be no drawing back on the part of a man of honor. Hence Carraford's hasty departure.

She could not imagine why he had gone to Holland House, unless it was to warn the family that she might appear and wish their help in holding him to his offer. She had not thought of it at first, but now this explanation seemed both simple and accurate.

Carraford had gone out of her life, it was certain. He had left behind an aching void that she would always feel. It was as though half of her had been wrenched away, leaving a grievous wound behind. Too late, she loved him.

One day she could bear to think of him. But that day had not yet come. In the meantime, though, her salvation lay in the many tasks that lay to her hand. With Dilly still keeping her room and still too frail to make decisions, Narcissa's reflective moments were banished.

And at last came the day when the infirmary was empty, the beds were neatly made up, and the floors and walls were scrubbed clean of infection.

Miss Dilworth, probably from having resisted treatment of her illness for too long, still could not summon enough strength to leave her room. Narcissa visited her several times a day, bringing her small tidbits of news, but Dilly was too weak to enjoy them.

Narcissa promised the older girls that on the first sunny day she would take them on a historic tour of the city. When that day dawned, she was not allowed to forget it. So, seeing that they all were carefully wrapped up and putting on her own warm cloak, she took the girls out. The day was fine, the sun glinted on the sea making millions of diamonds, and the wind was comparatively calm. They walked to the peninsula of high land, shaped like a hammer, projecting eastward into the sea, separating the waters into the north bay and the south bay. Along the south bay, so her girls told her, many of them lived, for they were members of the wealthy shipbuilding families. The town itself fringed both bays and extended inland.

Scarborough's peninsula was a natural stronghold, for it commanded a view of great scope, both north and south. The Romans had been, as far as anyone knew, the first to recognize the point's military advantage, for they built a watchtower, one of a series of stations to signal the approach of Saxon raiders.

After the Romans left, the ruins were burned, hundreds of years later, as a signal by Harold Hardrada, announcing his invasion of the land. The town of Scarborough was merely a fishing village even in the eleventh century, but Harold of Norway burned the town to prove his mastery.

The hill remained unoccupied until the Normans built the foundations of an austere fort, finished and enlarged by later kings. The castle was now in picturesque ruins. The keep itself, built by Henry II in the twelfth century, stood well back from the cliff's edge, but the curtain wall displayed great gaps, where the sea had undermined it. The tower, where George Fox had spent some involuntary time, still stood on the brink of the headland.

"Did you know, Miss Bentham," said Kitty Ross, pleased to be able to instruct her mentor, "that Scarborough was named for the Vikings? At least, for one particular Viking."

"His name was Scarborough?" inquired Narcissa doubtfully.

"No, ma'am." Kitty giggled. "His real name was Thorgils, but he was called Skarthi. For his harelip, you know."

"What else?" prodded Margaret. "Or don't you know anymore?"

Kitty said, without shame, "I read that just yesterday. But I don't know any more."

"Then Miss Bentham will tell us what we need to know," said Margaret virtuously.

Dutifully Narcissa imparted the history of the castle to the girls—a history she, too, had just read yesterday—but she took more note of the soaring kestrels, the eiders bobbing like corks in the harbor below, and the constant motion of the water. Far out near the horizon a fishing boat labored. And, acutely, the thought possessed her that her mother knew this land, this coast, well. How strange it was that she herself should, through diverse ways, come to Scarborough!

The stiff, clean breeze reminded her that she must shepherd her convalescent girls back to shelter. She took another long look from the headland as they turned back toward the town.

It had been two centuries since two mineral springs had been discovered along the south shore of the peninsula. A hostelry had been built encompassing the springs, but it had never gained the tourist popularity of other spas, Bath or Harrogate. Perhaps the weather was too bracing for invalids. As they turned back from the castle ruins, she could see, behind the town to the west, the high moors rising, purple against the afternoon sky. From this distance, they presented an unbroken line. She knew, however, that when one drew closer, broad valleys opened up to view. One such, toward the south, was called the Vale of Pickering. And it was a farm somewhere in that well-watered, fertile valley that Charlotte Wright called home.

They reached the intersection near Miss Dilworth's school. They stopped at the crossing, to await the passage of a carriage drawn by four high-stepping black horses. It was an imposing vehicle, paint glistening in the afternoon sun. It clearly belonged to someone of consequence. One of the girls enlightened Narcissa.

She cried out, with the pleasure of recognition, "Miss Bentham, it's Lady Holland!"

27

Narcissa, hearing Lady Holland's name, was startled out of her wits. If she had had a second's warning, she would have averted her face, but as it was, she was unable to keep from staring at the approaching carriage. As it passed, the occupants of the carriage were no more than a yard away from her. The middle-aged lady, nearly smothered in furs, peered nearsightedly out the carriage window and gave no sign of recognition.

It would have been strange if she had recognized Narcissa, for it was a chance meeting, and neither was prepared for it. Narcissa thought later that she had seen a jerky movement from the shadowy figure beyond Lady Holland, but she could not be sure. She was so stunned by the encounter that all that she could remember later was that Lady Holland was about the same age that her mother would have been, swathed in furs, as remote as though she lived on top of a mountain.

Narcissa hardly knew how she got her girls back to Miss Dilworth's. The walk passed in confusion of mind, and she could hope only that none of the girls noticed her reaction. Judging from their total immersion in their own affairs, she believed later, she had escaped without notice.

Even Dilly, when Narcissa went in to report on her outing, noticed nothing amiss. Dilly seemed a little better this evening.

"I am getting stronger. I must," said Dilly, "for you are taking too much on yourself. You are so thin. I had not expected to be such a burden to you when I asked you to stay. But I will confess, my dear, that you have been a lifesaver to me. I must have closed the school if you had not been here."

It was small enough return, Narcissa told her, for all the affection and encouragement that Dilly had given her over the years. When she returned to her room, where she could reflect at leisure, she could make nothing of the encounter with Lady Holland.

Lady Holland, clearly, had not noticed any resemblance between Narcissa and her own family. On the other hand, judging from the vague way in which Lady Holland looked out on the world, Narcissa suspected that the world passed her by as a nearsighted blur.

But the other occupant of the carriage, she could not bring to mind clearly. There was something about the other passenger that teased her mind, but she could not remember what it could be. She finally dismissed the shadow as, in all likelihood, Lady Holland's maid.

At any rate, she now had proof that satisfied her that her resemblance to the family was not as marked as Carraford insisted. She went to the mirror, holding a small candle up so that she could see. She thought, with dismay, that even Carraford would not recognize her now, for her face was almost gaunt. It was not because of hunger, but only that there was so much work to be done, and the unaccustomed responsibilities lay heavily on her.

As she climbed into bed later, her mischievous self rose to confront her with a tableau that amused her. What if Lady Holland had recognized her? What if she had stopped the carriage and demanded to know who Narcissa was? Or, even worse, suppose she had delivered a royal snub on the street, in front of Narcissa's companions?

The vision was amusing for only a moment. She would have had to leave the school before Dilly was recovered. She could not stay without casting discredit on Miss Dilworth. And since the school was the life and soul of her dear Dilly, she would have had to renounce any connection with it.

Sometime that night Narcissa was awakened by a tap on her door. Rousing, she thrust her arms into the sleeves of her robe as she opened the door.

Nabby, the maid, wailed, "Please, miss, could you come? It's Miss Charlotte, and I've got her to the infirmary, she's sick, but she won't get into bed, and I can't make her, and she's awful sick!"

Wide awake now, Narcissa said, "I'll come at once." Pausing only to find her slippers, she hurried down to the floor below. Charlotte had, on her own, crawled into bed and pulled the covers up to her ears.

Narcissa placed her hand on the girl's forehead and almost snatched it away, so hot with fever was it.

She stayed with Charlotte the rest of the night. The girl was restless and spoke in her fever of chickens and sheep. Narcissa was sure that were Charlotte to go home, she would immediately begin to recover.

Sometime during that long vigil, something, perhaps a shadow cast by a candle on the wall, cleared the teasing thought that had lingered at the edge of her mind. It was there before her, brought by her memory, in full detail. The shadowy figure in the carriage beyond Lady Holland, she now remembered, wore furs.

No maid would wear furs! So the companion of Lady Holland was also gently born. Perhaps, she thought with a sinking feeling, it was, in fact, the Julia Holland that Carraford had spoken of!

Julia could have seen her, even might have recognized her, since she stood in full light upon the curb, so close to the carriage that she could have reached out and touched it.

If there was the marked resemblance to Julia that Carraford had insisted upon, then Narcissa's presence so near to the Hollands was known. What would Julia do? Would she send at once for her or even come to see her?

Narcissa's fancy vanished with a thud. Julia could not know where she lived and would, in all likelihood, not put herself to the trouble of finding her. There was a great gulf between them, Narcissa was forced to recognize, and Julia was doubtless not inclined to bridge it.

But the wistful hope clung—what if she did?

The days went by, dragging their heels, and there was no word from the Hollands. She was forced to conclude that she had erected a dream castle on a foundation of sand.

No word from Them, she phrased it to herself, and that's that, my girl. Forget them—after all, you never knew Them to begin with.

Charlotte's listlessness could not be beguiled away by any device that came to Narcissa's frantic mind. In only a week Charlotte seemed to fade visibly. Mr. Merton was cheerful until he stood in the corridor with Narcissa.

"I cannot give her more medicine, for there is nothing that I can find wrong with her."

"An affliction of the lungs, perhaps?" Narcissa voiced her dread.

"No, lungs are sound. If I didn't know better, I'd suspect a secret love affair." He glared at Narcissa as though she were to blame. "That's been known to send a girl into a decline."

Narcissa was lost in thought. "I believe I know, then, what to do," she told the doctor.

"Don't tell me it *is* a love affair!"

"Well, in a way, yes," Narcissa told him. "Love comes in all forms, you know."

That evening, with Dilly's languid permission, Narcissa sat at the big desk in the office and drew paper and pen toward her. She nibbled on the pen for a few reflective moments, and then began to write:

> My dear sir,
>
> I regret that I must tell you that your daughter, Charlotte, has fallen ill. While her recovery seems assured, it does not progress as the surgeon would like. It is his thought [here she wrote falsely] that the child is suffering from a wish to convalesce at her home, among dear and familiar things. . . .

When the missive had been duly dispatched, she basked in the consciousness of a deed well done. The result would be, she believed, to return Charlotte to her home, where she longed to be, and Mr. Wright, honest and anxious, would give up his idea of educating Charlotte for a world a cut above her. As Charlotte had said, what good would it do the wife of a prosperous sheepman to know where nutmegs grow?

Mr. Wright arrived the next afternoon. Narcissa received him in Dilly's office. Smiling at him, she begged him to sit down.

"You will wish to see Charlotte at once, I know," she began.

She was exceedingly glad to see him. He was sturdy and honest, believing in the good intentions of the world and giving more than he received. One could rely on him to the last breath, she thought, if, of course, one's cause was just. And above all else, she was sure, was his inarticulate love for his daughter.

"Aye, I shall. But first I want to thank you for taking the time to write me. I've been wondering how my girl was getting on."

Narcissa wished she had written sooner. "She was getting on well, so we thought," she explained. "We have had quite a few girls ill, and Charlotte is no worse than the others. She was such a great help when the worst of the trouble kept us busy, and perhaps she overdid. If that is the case, then I am guilty, for she was so needed I let her do as much as she liked in the infirmary."

"It is always her way," he said with simple pride. "She must go at things hammer and tongs, you might say. And a handier girl in a sickroom I've never seen."

"You do not surprise me." She leaned forward. "Before you see her, Mr. Wright, I should like to ask you to consider one thing. Some girls do not have a bent toward learning, in the strict sense of books and classes."

"And you are saying that my Charlotte is one like that?"

"She has so many virtues, such a talent for more domestic arts, such as nursing—"

"And not book learning," interrupted Mr. Wright heavily. He looked at his hands, splayed on his knees in his favorite pose, and sighed. He was silent for some moments. "Aye," he said at last, "I think I knew it all the time. I wanted her to have everything I could give her, you know."

"I have grown very fond of Charlotte," said Narcissa deliberately, "and I do not like to see her unhappy, as she has been here."

Mr. Wright got to his feet and stood, turning his hat around and around in his blunt fingers. "Could I see my girl now?"

"Of course." Narcissa moved ahead of him to the door. She ventured, "Shall you tell her she is going home?"

His disappointment at the failure of his plans was

clear in his weathered face, but he said, "Aye, I'll tell her."

Narcissa gave him a dazzling smile. "She will be so happy!"

Mr. Wright drew his mouth down and then, reluctantly, began to smile. "Aye, Miss Bentham, I'll be right happy, too! I've missed her like—like my life!"

"Tell her so, Mr. Wright," recommended Narcissa, and took him to the infirmary.

She left them alone, and they talked for a long time. When she went back later, Charlotte was lying peacefully back on the pillows, her hand firmly held in her father's. Mr. Wright looked up at Narcissa. "I was shocked, I admit, when I saw how thin my girl was, but she tells me you've taken great care of her."

"I'm glad she is doing so well."

"She'll be going home with me at Christmastide," he said, "to stay."

Charlotte sat up abruptly and said, "Really, Father? Will you let me stay home? Oh, I can't wait! Let us go now! You might not be able to get back at Christmas, if the roads are full of snow! Please, Father——"

"You could have the right of it," he admitted, "but us Wrights never give up on something we've started. You'll finish the term, and then I'll take you home."

It was only two weeks until the Christmas holidays. Charlotte was, with some difficulty, restrained from dressing immediately and convinced that she must wait. In order to pacify her, Mr. Wright announced that he would give a Christmas party at the school for all the girls. "They've been kind to my Charlotte. It's only right we should pay them back with a farewell party."

Narcissa had told Charlotte that the two weeks would fly past, but they dragged leadenly for Narcissa. By the time the last day of the term arrived she was in a lower mood even than she had been when she watched the coach lights disappear down the road at Penton Crossroads.

This afternoon all the girls would be going their separate ways to their homes, where loving families waited for them. Dilly would be well enough to pick up the reins of the school by the time the next term began, and today Mademoiselle Duprée had written the news that she was totally recovered and would return by New Year's Day.

There was no place for Narcissa anymore at Miss Dilworth's school.

28

The sounds of laughter and a snatch of song reached her, and she knew the party was getting under way. The festive mood of holiday and happiness set against her, but she must make an appearance.

The front room of the school was hung with pine boughs and holly wreaths. The girls, she thought wryly, put far more energy into decorating the room for the party than they had on French or geography. But then, she thought philosophically, they would no doubt decorate many a room in the future, but the geography books would gather inches of dust.

She slipped unobtrusively into the room and found next to the door an armchair of beechwood, its japanned back ornamented by an Oriental figure in gilt. The chair had once been in high fashion, but it was far from comfortable. Yet soon she was lost again in her reveries.

Dilly was enthroned in the dark green velvet chair, her feet propped on a low stool, a lap robe tucked in around her ankles. She was still pale, but a glow of contentment shone in her face as she watched her girls, laughing and happy.

It was strange, she thought, to consider the cycle of the years, from Christmas to Christmas. Now she could recall the holidays of her childhood, when both her parents had been alive and Dilly had taken such affectionate care of her in the nursery.

Later on, when she had advanced to the schoolroom, she was allowed to help with the Christmas preparations, and the holiday merrymaking was a part of her childhood that she would not for the world give up. But when her mother died, all those Christmases were gone. Dilly had to find a new position and eventually retired to her place in Scarborough. Her father took Narcissa on his travels with him to Europe, for the simple reason that there was no one to leave her with.

Her Christmases on the Continent all seemed to string together in one long panorama of alien customs, snow on the steep roofs in Heidelberg, the clear, cold air along the Seine in Paris. Always seeking warmth, they spent several Christmases in the south of Italy.

Here, and now, Father Christmas, looking strangely like Mr. Wright, was passing out gifts to the girls. She allowed her thoughts to ramble on to her last Christmas, the one just before this.

It had been spent in London, in cheap lodgings, although not the cheapest that they finally took. Her father had been ill, and both of them could see the signs of his impending death. It was at this point that she had written, moved by the holiday spirit, to Sir Maurice for his help for her father. She had followed up that letter with a terse announcement of her father's death, and only then did Sir Maurice reply.

But such a year as she had had since!

The ways of Providence were strange indeed, and she was not at all sure she approved of them all. She had escaped from Sir Maurice, but at a price that she wished she had not had to pay.

There was her desperate situation on top of the moor at Penton Crossroads. Providence had promptly furnished a way out of it into a household of great comfort, and she was grateful.

But then she had met Carraford, and she wished that was a meeting she had not had. For he had entwined himself into her thoughts, and her emotions, until she feared she would never be free of him. Yet she knew that only with Carraford had she been truly alive. He had shown her what happiness was, had brought out the woman in her that she could be and shown that woman to her. Now, of course, it all had been for naught.

Carraford wound in and out of her reflections, on Christmases past, and Christmas present, like the Basque stitch that she taught her sewing class. She missed his charm, his sardonic wit, his virility with a longing strong as physical pain.

Father Christmas was now handing out sweetmeats, and she knew the party was drawing to a close. But

Carraford's voice sounded in memory in her ear, the sweetness in it when he told her she could trust him. But she could not reconcile that side of the man with his precipitate departure for the Hollands, a secret trip that he had kept from her. If she herself had not come to Scarborough, she would never have known that the Marquess of Carraford had posted immediately to the Hollands.

She could see him now in her mind's eye, rioting, enjoying himself to the hilt in London, her own problems, his acquaintance with her, completely forgotten. She must forget him, and this time she must really make it final. How lowering it would be to become attached to one who thought so little of her that he could leave without a word of farewell!

With a deliberate effort, she wrenched her attention back to the party. What a dear kind man Mr. Wright was! At that moment he glanced up and caught her eye. She smiled encouragingly at him. He hesitated and then returned to his role as Father Christmas.

The party was over. Narcissa helped Dilly to her room. "It will be good to see the girls when they come back for next term," said Dilly.

Next term! And Narcissa would not be here. In the next two weeks Narcissa must decide what to do for her future. She knew that Miss Dilworth would not set her out on the street, yet she had outlived her usefulness here. It was time to move on. Into a future that she could not even imagine, for there was simply no place to go.

She must begin to look about her for a new situation. She had certainly gained a great deal of experience in the past three months, yet she hesitated to ask Dilly for help in obtaining a new position.

Seeing Dilly settled in her chair, with a rug over her lap, Narcissa went out to speed the departing students. All but one of the carriages had rumbled away over the cobbles, bound for home.

Narcissa saw that the Wrights had not yet left. Probably, since Charlotte would not be coming back, there was packing yet to do.

Unable to sustain the thought of farewells which she knew would be final, she slipped into the office and closed the door. She did not know how long she had sat there, alone, watching the small flame in the grate, before there came a tap on the door and Mr. Wright entered.

He seemed unnaturally solemn. He sat down and looked at his hands. It was a familiar gesture and seemed designed to help him sort out his thoughts.

At length he said, "I want to thank you for your help to my daughter. She thinks the world of you, and I agree. You got her through a hard time. She can't say enough about your kindness to her. I want you to know I appreciate it."

Narcissa said with a smile, "I'm truly fond of Charlotte."

Mr. Wright lifted one hand and sat it back on his knee heavily. "I'm mighty glad to hear you say that, for Charlotte certainly thinks the world of you."

Then, aware that he was repeating himself, he flushed. He tried a new tack. "My girl is anxious to get back to her home, and I can't say I blame her. It's a pleasant, snug little place, with all that we need. There are women to help with the housework, and nobody on the farm ever lacks for food to see them through the winter and wood to keep them warm."

He spoke at length about his farmstead, the number of sheep he owned, the fells of wool he exported. "It's a good life, one any woman would find comfortable. She would have things pretty much her own way."

He looked anxiously at Narcissa. "You know my Charlotte thinks the world and all of you, and I do, too. I've seen enough of how you do here so that I think we could rub along well enough. I know I'm not much, but—I'd be good to you."

Narcissa was stunned. She had a strong affection for the girl, and she respected this man enormously. He was solid and dependable, and she would never want for anything in this world. She had no future anywhere, and the door was opening into a sunny prospect. Providence surely had a hand in this!

She felt a rush of affection toward the man who so awkwardly laid his heart at her feet. She was sorely tempted. Providence had looked out for her so far, and this would be certainly the capstone of her life. She would never have another worry!

Yet there swam before her eyes the wicked glint in the eye of the Marquess of Carraford. And she knew she could not, no matter how kindly meant, no matter how desperate she was for security, accept Mr. Wright.

As though someone else were using her tongue to speak, she said, "How good you are, Mr. Wright! I truly had no idea—I am deeply, deeply honored." She continued, turning down, recklessly, a golden future. "But truly, I cannot."

"Ah, well," he said, after a moment, "I did not let my hopes get up. You are a lady, Miss Bentham, and could wed *anybody!*"

She could not bear to have him think she had refused him because he was a simple farmer, as he put it. "Please, Mr. Wright, it's only that I—I already—" She foundered in her lame excuses.

"A prior attachment." He nodded wisely. "I see. Well, then, that's all right."

Tears stood in her eyes as she rose to say good-bye. "You said it once, sir," she said, gently. "Seems like the good God put us all where we should like it best! And my place is elsewhere."

After Mr. Wright left, closing the door gently behind him, she put her hands to her face, to try to cool her flushing cheeks. The wicked glint in the eye of the Marquess, in her recollection, brought him so vividly to mind that she rocked with pangs of her loss.

She remembered one phrase of Mr. Wright's. His girl, Charlotte, had sorely missed her mother, and Mr. Wright was, according to his best intentions, striving to make it up to her. He would provide Charlotte with another mother and, incidentally, himself with a wife. Having reflected and realizing her place in Mr. Wright's scheme of things, she knew that she had done the right thing in refusing him.

She went to the front door and looked out onto the street. Only Dilly, the cook, and two maids were left in the house. There was nothing more desolate, she thought, than a school, usually full of young voices and laughter and running feet, after the end of term.

She stayed so long that she could feel the chill of the winter wind in her bones. It was late afternoon, and already the sea breeze was quickening. The sky was clouding over, taking on an unpleasant leaden hue. Already flakes of snow were in the air, and a mist rolled in from the sea. It was quite the most unpleasant afternoon she had ever seen.

The mist from the sea turned quickly to heavy fog, and she could not see across the street. The lamps along the walk glowed like faint moons wrapped in rainbows of fog.

She hurried back into the house and sought out the small room where Dilly had first taken her. Nabby had poked up a good fire in the grate and drawn a slipper chair close to the fire. Narcissa sank into it and lifted her wet slippers to the warmth. She fancied she could feel the damp air seeping into the house. Quite soon she heard hard pellets striking against the windows, the first snow of the new storm. It would be an evil night.

Dilly, not quite so strong as she had thought, was napping before supper. Far away there were noises of activity in the kitchen. Otherwise, the school was wrapped in an unearthly silence. She had not realized how much the background of schoolgirls had been a part of her life. Now that they were gone, she felt almost uneasy.

Even the sudden snapping of the coal fire startled her. She realized her nerves were totally on edge. It had been a long, long day. She turned again to the thought that there would be no place for her in the school in the new term. It was time to move on, and she must certainly bend her mind to decide what to do next. She wondered now, left alone, whether she had made the right decision about Mr. Wright. She could have had security and a certain amount of affection. It would have been a comfortable life. She was very low in her mind.

Tomorrow, she vowed, she would pick up her courage and begin to think. Just now, sitting alone for the first time in some months, without responsibilities hovering in the back of her mind, she felt drained of all emotion. She felt as though she were being driven here and there by a wayward wind, and she was content to sit in a state of limbo.

She heard carriage wheels in the street and wondered idly whether some of the students were returning for forgotten items.

The wheels stopped, probably, she thought, before a

neighboring house. She stared into the fire. Tears filled
her eyes and spilled down her cheeks. She detested
weeping, but these silent tears seemed beyond her ability to stop.

Within a few moments, she heard the door behind
her open. Nabby, doubtless, coming in to build up the
fire. She turned her face away and wiped her eyes.
Since Nabby did not move to the fire, Narcissa turned
to look a question and felt her blood drain into her
toes. Her mouth opened as she stared at the elegant figure of the man who had entered. The visitor, stepping
closer, looked with discerning care at her pale, exceedingly thin face. He was startled and more than dismayed. His words came out with force. "Good God,
what's happened to you!" exclaimed Lord Carraford.

29

The Marquess had some explaining to do, she told him. She did not try to hold back her happiness at seeing him, since a part of her mind told her he was only a figment of the fog, conjured up by her desperate wish to see him again, to let him hold her hand tightly, as he was now doing. Surely the grip of his hand should tell her he was real, she thought, but her joyous wits capered without reason—

She begged him, "How did you get here? How did you find me? Tell me—oh, tell me *every*thing!"

Carraford had gone at first to the Hollands. To their surprise he had informed them of the existence of Narcissa Bentham, although he did not know her under that name. Lady Holland and Miss Julia Holland were fully aware of who the woman calling herself Hester Adams must be. They had not received any letter from Narcissa. The letter had gone astray.

Armed with the information that the Hollands had been able to give him, the name Bentham, and the time that her parents had left Scarborough, he was able to take the next step. Now that he knew Narcissa's real name, added to Narcissa's own hints about gambling in Venice, he was able to set in train certain inquiries that at length brought him, piecemeal, the information he was after. He got word from his agents in Heidelberg, in Brussels, Paris, and, of course, news from Venice. Narcissa, almost overcome, managed to say faintly, "But why did you do this?"

The Marquess said, surprised at her question, "Because I feared you were in trouble. I suspected that you would not refuse my offer from any trifling reason, so it seemed to me that my next step should be to discover whatever troubled you and remove it."

"As simple as that?" she said, half laughing. "You had no doubt that you could obliterate it?"

"No," he said. "I found out that your hesitation was because of lack of money and family. And I have taken care of both." He eyed her with anxious concern. "But what has happened to you here?"

She explained, telling him of her months here at Miss Dilworth's school.

He said, "I could have saved you all this if you had trusted me."

"I dared not. You—you are so *rich!*"

She was immensely relieved to have the wicked Marquess sitting close enough for her to touch. She was moving into a state of euphoria in which Carraford would take over all her problems, but she must restrain herself from casting all her troubles on his shoulders.

"But how could you know I was here, at Dilly's school?"

"Your cousin Julia," he said, "saw you on the street one day and recognized you. At least, she was sure you were a Holland, thought you must be the missing Narcissa."

So Julia *had* been the shadow in the coach!

"She sent word to me, and I received it at my London lodging when I returned from the Continent. I had been to Venice. All they knew, however, was that you had gone to London." He took both her hands in his. "You must go to the Hollands, for they wish you to be married from there."

Shakily she answered, "But I still have no fortune and no family."

"Did I not tell you? Lady Holland, your aunt, you know, is beside herself, getting your room ready, telling all her friends that now her niece is coming home. Lord Holland was always very fond of his sister, and you must resemble her very much." He laughed. "As for a fortune, you will have mine, you know."

She let her head drop on his shoulder. He added after a moment, "I think you will be well advised to go. I wish you'd put on a little more weight before I marry you, for I should not like it said that you married me out of desperation. There will be people, you know, who will say you had no way of knowing where your next meal was coming from, and I should not like to hear that."

With returning spirit, she said, "You haven't lost your belief that you know best for everybody. I suppose you have it all arranged that I should leave this very night and go over to the Hollands, to live with strangers."

He looked at her steadily, and the kindling look in his eyes left her unable to breathe.

He said, standing and pulling her to her feet to face him, "Yes, I do know what is best, at least for you. For you must know that your welfare is now and always will be paramount in my life." He proceeded to prove his statement. His method, consisting of certain murmured endearments in her ear and a firm clasp around her waist, convinced her most satisfactorily.